DOVER·THRIFT·EDITIONS

A Bottomless Grave
and Other Victorian Tales of Terror

Edited by
HUGH LAMB

DOVER PUBLICATIONS, INC.
Mineola, New York

Bibliographical Note

This Dover edition, first published in 2001, is a slightly corrected, unabridged republication of the work originally published in 1977 by Taplinger Publishing Company, New York, under the title *Victorian Nightmares*.

Library of Congress Cataloging-in-Publication Data

A bottomless grave and other Victorian tales of terror / edited by Hugh Lamb.
    p. cm.
    Rev. ed. of: Victorian nightmares. 1977.
    ISBN 0-486-41590-2 (pbk.)
    1. Horror tales, English. 2. English fiction—19th century. I. Lamb, Hugh.
II. Victorian nightmares.

PR1309.H6 B68 2001
823'.0873808'09034—dc21

00-047373

Manufactured in the United States of America
Dover Publications, Inc., 31 East 2nd Street, Mineola, N.Y. 11501

*For a good friend, Auntie Liz,
and her magic certificate*

Contents

		Page
EDITOR'S FOREWORD		9
THE DEVIL OF THE MARSH	H. B. Marriott-Watson	13
A TRAGIC HONEYMOON	G. R. Sims	18
THE BATTLE OF THE MONSTERS	Morgan Robertson	31
THE RETURN	R. Murray Gilchrist	43
THE CORPSE LIGHT	Dick Donovan	49
THE SHIP THAT SAW A GHOST	Frank Norris	60
A BOTTOMLESS GRAVE	Ambrose Bierce	74
ONE SUMMER NIGHT	Ambrose Bierce	82
GHOSTS THAT HAVE HAUNTED ME	J. K. Bangs	84
HAUNTED BY SPIRITS	George Manville Fenn	95
A GHOST SLAYER	J. Keighley Snowden	104
THE TOMB	Guy de Maupassant	112
THE MAN WITH THE NOSE	Rhoda Broughton	117
MY NIGHTMARE	Dorothea Gerard	133
A LIFE-WATCH	Georgina C. Clark	142
THE HAUNTED CHAIR	Richard Marsh	155
COOLIES	W. Carlton Dawe	172
THE THREE SOULS	Erckmann-Chatrian	185
A STRANGE GOLDFIELD	Guy Boothby	200
AN ALPINE DIVORCE	Robert Barr	207
THE STORY OF BAELBROW	E. and H. Heron	212

Editor's Foreword

Proving that you can't please everyone, a newspaper reviewer of *Victorian Tales of Terror*, my first volume in what I hope will be a modest series of books, remarked that the Victorian era held many fine ghost and horror stories but anthologies have dredged it almost dry by now. He held in his hands the instant refutation of his own argument, for that first volume contained, as the other two have, fine stories that have been totally ignored since their original Victorian publication.

But that reviewer was merely reciting (and further propagating) an old canard: that the Victorian ghost story and the tale of terror have now been thoroughly researched and the best examples all reprinted. The fact is that nothing could be further from the truth. For far too many years, anthologists have been content to reprint the same old Victorian stories, good though they may be, and not bothering to dig even a fraction deeper to find more unreprinted tales which *can* be found; bear in mind that my three volumes of Victorian tales of terror have only used the *best* of those I found. And I can promise more anthologies along the same lines.

A friendly reader wrote and asked exactly how I manage to find these old rare stories. It would be nice, I suppose, to say that I retire once a year to a darkened room, draw a pentacle, and with the aid of a certain gentleman whose book I had signed in my own blood, conjure up a pile of forgotten stories, covered in dust . . . but alas, nothing so glamorous. To find the tales in this and the first two volumes entailed nothing more or less than hard work. It means continuous reading, of old books of short stories in the hope of finding some nugget, of old journals in the same hope; it means haunting bookshops and junk shops; it means studying old catalogues and digging out likely names; it means long hours in the library looking at such light reading material as the British Museum book catalogue.

But there again, it also means the thrill of discovery, the satisfaction of putting a copy of an old tale in the file and knowing that you are so many more thousand words on the way to the next book's completion. It means the sudden excitement of realising that some dreary old book of short stories actually contains one tale worth reprinting. It means that nice sensation when you find that the tatty book on the dealer's shelf, with the unreadable spine that you almost passed over without bothering to examine, is in fact a volume of Victorian stories that you've been chasing for months.

In short, the preparation of these anthologies means two things: hard work and satisfaction. And I might add that the latter is what will make me produce more volumes in this vein, for the letters I receive from readers make it clear that Victorian tales of terror are still popular and those faithful readers of such works know what they want—and they *don't* want the same old stories again and again.

And so to *Victorian Nightmares*, our third excursion into the realms of the macabre tales of Victoria's reign. The usual criteria apply: these are rare stories, either previously unanthologised or out of print for many years. Of the twenty-one stories, only four have appeared in a similar work before, and one is appearing for the first time in English in this country.

Some famous names make an appearance in these pages, among them Ambrose Bierce, Richard Marsh, Guy de Maupassant and Guy Boothby. From the other side of the Atlantic there are Frank Norris, J. K. Bangs and Morgan Robertson, and from the other side of the Channel, Erckmann-Chatrian with a tale forgotten for over a hundred years.

Some fine English authors are included, fairly well known in other fields, but here contributing rare tales of terror. They include G. R. Sims, H. B. Marriott-Watson, George Manville Fenn, Robert Barr and R. Murray Gilchrist. And to round off this anthology, some forgotten names with forgotten stories, such as Dorothea Gerard, J. Keighley Snowden, W. Carlton Dawe and Georgina C. Clark.

Victorian Nightmares await you—they're strong stuff, for the Victorians liked their thrills in undiluted measures. They also liked an occasional laugh, so you will find herein a trio of their humorous ghost stories. But the accent is on terror, Victorian terror, and in its day, there was nothing better, as you'll find out.

As always, my thanks are due to those who have helped me gather together these assorted Victorian bad dreams. I would like to thank in particular the staff of Sutton Public Library, who still manage an incredible success ratio for finding old books for me. I am indebted to Robert Aickman for his generous help in obtaining the story by Richard Marsh, and for his assistance with information on his grandfather. For their help with the hard work of tracing biographical details of authors, my especial thanks to my friend Mike Ashley, and to Pamela Redknap of the National Book League. And to the readers, who have made it clear that my efforts are indeed appreciated, the sincerest gratitude of all. I hope the result is worthwhile.

HUGH LAMB
Sutton, Surrey

The Devil of the Marsh

by

H. B. MARRIOTT-WATSON

Nightmares I promised you and nightmares you shall have. For a start, try this exceedingly creepy vignette from the end of the Victorian era, by one of the time's most prolific authors.

H. B. Marriott-Watson (1863–1921) was born in New Zealand and made his way to England in 1885. He soon succeeded in his chosen profession, journalism, eventually becoming editor of the Pall Mall Gazette. *In addition to his press work, Watson also wrote over fifty novels and books of short stories. Among his more notable collections were* Alarums and Excursions (1903) *and* The Heart of Miranda (1898). *As with many of his contemporaries, he tried his hand at the occasional ghost story and 'The Devil of the Marsh', from his 1893 collection* Diogenes of London, *shows considerable talent. From the very first sentence we are in the land of the dead, where a master of his craft leads us through a genuine waking nightmare.*

It was nigh upon dusk when I drew close to the Great Marsh, and already the white vapours were about, riding across the sunken levels like ghosts in a churchyard. Though I had set forth in a mood of wild delight, I had sobered in the lonely ride across the moor and was now uneasily alert. As my horse jerked down the grassy slopes that fell away to the jaws of the swamp I could see thin streams of mist rise slowly, hover like wraiths above the long rushes, and then, turning gradually more material, go blowing heavily away across the flat. The appearance of the place at this desolate hour, so remote from human society and so darkly significant of evil presences, struck me with a certain wonder that she should have chosen this spot for our meeting. She was a familiar of the moors, where I had invariably encountered her; but it was like her arrogant caprice to test my devotion by some such dreary assignation. The wide and horrid prospect depressed me beyond reason, but the fact of her neighbourhood drew me on, and my spirits mounted at the thought that at last she was to put me in possession of herself. Tethering my horse upon the verge of the swamp, I soon discovered the path that crossed it, and entering struck out boldly for the heart. The track could have been little used, for the reeds, which stood high above the level of my eyes upon either side, straggled everywhere across in low arches, through which I dodged, and broke my way with some inconvenience and much impatience. A full half-hour I was solitary in that wilderness, and when at last a sound other than my own footsteps broke the silence the dusk had fallen.

I was moving very slowly at the time, with a mind half disposed to turn from the melancholy expedition, which it seemed to me now must surely be a cruel jest she had played upon me. While some such reluctance held me, I was suddenly arrested by a hoarse croaking which broke out upon my left, sounding somewhere from the reeds in the black mire. A little further it came again from close at hand, and when I had passed on a few more steps in wonder and perplexity, I heard it for the third time. I stopped and listened, but the marsh was as a grave, and so taking the noise for the signal of some raucous frog, I resumed my way. But in a little the croaking was repeated, and coming quickly to a stand I pushed the reeds aside and peered into the darkness. I could see nothing, but at the immediate moment of my pause I thought I detected the sound of some body trailing through the rushes. My distaste for the adventure grew with this suspicion, and had it not been for my delirious infatuation I had assuredly turned back and ridden home. The ghastly sound pursued me at intervals along the track, until at last, irritated beyond endurance by the sense of this persistent and invisible company, I broke into a sort of run. This, it seemed, the creature (whatever it was) could not achieve, for I heard no more of it, and continued my way in peace. My path at length ran out from among the reeds upon the smooth flat of which she had spoken, and here my heart quickened, and the gloom of the dreadful place lifted. The flat lay in the very centre of the marsh, and here and there in it a gaunt bush or withered tree rose like a spectre against the white mists. At the further end I fancied some kind of building loomed up; but the fog which had been gathering ever since my entrance upon the passage sailed down upon me at that moment and the prospect went out with suddenness. As I stood waiting for the clouds to pass, a voice cried to me out of its centre, and I saw her next second with bands of mist swirling about her body, come rushing to me from the darkness.

She put her long arms about me, and, drawing her close, I looked into her deep eyes. Far down in them, it seemed to me, I could discern a mystic laughter dancing in the wells of light, and I had that ecstatic sense of nearness to some spirit of fire which was wont to possess me at her contact.

'At last,' she said, 'at last, my beloved!' I caressed her.

'Why,' said I, tingling at the nerves, 'why have you put this dolorous journey between us? And what mad freak is your presence in this swamp?' She uttered her silver laugh, and nestled to me again.

'I am the creature of this place,' she answered. 'This is my home. I have sworn you should behold me in my native sin ere you ravished me away.'

'Come, then,' said I; 'I have seen; let there be an end of this. I know you, what you are. This marsh chokes up my heart. God forbid you should spend more of your days here. Come.'

'You are in haste,' she cried. 'There is yet much to learn. Look, my friend,' she said, 'you who know me, what I am. This is my prison, and I have inherited its properties. Have you no fear?'

For answer I pulled her to me, and her warm lips drove out the horrid humours of the night; but the swift passage of a flickering mockery over her eyes struck me as a flash of lightning, and I grew chill again.

'I have the marsh in my blood,' she whispered: 'the marsh and the fog of it. Think ere you vow to me, for I am the cloud in a starry night.'

A litho and lovely creature, palpable of warm flesh, she lifted her magic face to mine and besought me plaintively with these words. The dews of the nightfall hung on her lashes, and seemed to plead with me for her forlorn and solitary plight.

'Behold!' I cried, 'witch or devil of the marsh, you shall come with me! I have known you on the moors, a roving apparition of beauty; nothing more I know, nothing more I ask. I care not what this dismal haunt means; not what these strange and mystic eyes. You have powers and senses above me; your sphere and habits are as mysterious and incomprehensible as your beauty. But that', I said, 'is mine, and the world that is mine shall be yours also.'

She moved her head nearer to me with an antic gesture, and her gleaming eyes glanced up at me with a sudden flash, the similitude (great heavens!) of a hooded snake. Starting, I fell away, but at that moment she turned her face and set it fast towards the fog that came rolling in thick volumes over the flat. Noiselessly the great cloud crept down upon us, and all dazed and troubled I watched her watching it in silence. It was as if she awaited some omen of horror, and I too trembled in the fear of its coming.

Then suddenly out of the night issued the hoarse and hideous croaking I had heard upon my passage. I reached out my arm to take her hand, but in an instant the mists broke over us, and I was groping in the vacancy. Something like panic took hold of me, and, beating through the blind obscurity, I rushed over the flat, calling upon her. In a little the swirl went by, and I perceived her upon the margin of the swamp, her arm raised as in imperious command. I ran to her, but stopped, amazed and shaken by a fearful sight. Low by the dripping reeds crouched a small squat thing, in the likeness of a monstrous frog, coughing and choking in its throat. As I stared, the creature rose upon its legs and disclosed a horrid human resemblance. Its face was white and thin, with long black hair; its body gnarled and twisted as with the ague of a thousand years. Shaking, it whined in a breathless voice, pointing a skeleton finger at the woman by my side.

'Your eyes were my guide,' it quavered. 'Do you think that after all these years I have no knowledge of your eyes? Lo, is there aught of evil in you I am not instructed in? This is the Hell you designed for me, and now you would leave me to a greater.'

The wretch paused, and panting leaned upon a bush, while she stood silent, mocking him with her eyes, and soothing my terror with her soft touch.

'Hear!' he cried, turning to me, hear the tale of this woman that you may know her as she is. She is the Presence of the marshes. Woman or Devil I know not, but only that the accursed marsh has crept into her soul and she herself is become its Evil Spirit; she herself, that lives and grows young and beautiful by it, has its full power to blight and chill and slay. I, who was once as you are, have this knowledge. What bones lie deep in this black swamp who can say but she? She has drained of health, she has drained of mind and of soul; what is between her and her desire that she should not drain also of life? She has made me a devil in her Hell, and now she would leave me to my solitary pain, and go search for another victim. But she shall not!' he screamed through his chattering teeth; 'she shall not! My Hell is also hers! She shall not!'

Her smiling untroubled eyes left his face and turned to me: she put out her arms, swaying towards me, and so fervid and so great a light glowed in her face that, as one distraught of superhuman means, I took her into my embrace. And then the madness seized me.

'Woman or devil,' I said, 'I will go with you! Of what account this pitiful past? Blight me even as that wretch, so be only you are with me.'

She laughed, and, disengaging herself, leaned, half-clinging to me, towards the coughing creature by the mire.

'Come,' I cried, catching her by the waist. 'Come!' She laughed again a silver-ringing laugh. She moved with me slowly across the flat to where the track started for the portals of the marsh. She laughed and clung to me.

But at the edge of the track I was startled by a shrill, hoarse screaming, and behold, from my very feet, that loathsome creature rose up and wound his long black arms about her shrieking and crying in his pain. Stooping I pushed him from her skirts, and with one sweep of my arm drew her across the pathway; as her face passed mine her eyes were wide and smiling. Then of a sudden the still mist enveloped us once more; but ere it descended I had a glimpse of that contorted figure trembling on the margin, the white face drawn and full of desolate pain. At the sight an icy shiver ran through me. And then through the yellow gloom the shadow of her darted past me, to the further side. I heard the hoarse cough, the dim noise of a struggle, a swishing sound, a thin cry, and then the sucking of the slime over something in the rushes. I leapt forward: and once again the fog thinned, and I beheld her, woman or devil, standing upon the verge, and peering with smiling eyes into the foul and sickly bog. With a sharp cry wrung from my nerveless soul, I turned and fled down the narrow way from that accursed spot; and as I ran the thickening fog closed round me, and I heard far off and lessening still the silver sound of her mocking laughter.

A Tragic Honeymoon

by

G. R. SIMS

'*It was Christmas Day in the workhouse . . .*' *I have not yet met any-body who knows the official next line of that famous verse and even fewer people who know of the author, George R. Sims (1847–1922). Workhouses were something that G. R. Sims knew a lot about, for he was one of Victorian England's greatest reforming spirits on behalf of the poor. It was his letters to the* Daily News *that helped to prompt a Royal Commission to investigate and remedy the appalling conditions of the poor in London.*

George Sims was a poet, playwright and novelist who was born in London and educated at Hanwell College and Bonn University. Under the pseudonym 'Dagonet' he contributed articles to The Referee *from 1877, as well as contributing to such other journals as* Fun. *His best known play was probably* The Lights of London.

As well as his plays and poetry, Sims wrote many short stories, collected into several volumes over the years. One of the best volumes was The Ten Commandments *(1896), ten stories each depicting the breaking of one commandment. Other volumes included* Stories in Black and White *(1885) and* The Ring'o'Bells *(1886). '*A Tragic Honey-moon*' comes from* My Two Wives *(1894) and is a very sombre piece indeed. Typically Victorian, it deals with unrequited love and passion, and has a decidedly gruesome twist.*

My chamber-maid at the —— Hotel, Scarborough, was a nice, motherly, middle-aged woman. I like motherly, middle-aged women for chamber-maids. They know their business better, and they answer the bell quicker than young, flighty chamber-maids. And they are not so fond of reading the letters you leave about you, and prying into your private affairs.

The bump of curiosity is strongly developed in some women, and you find striking examples of the length to which female curiosity will go in hotels, lodging-houses, and places where they let apartments.

I stayed for a fortnight once in private apartments in Broadstairs, and when I left I recommended them to a friend of mine. He took them later on in the season without saying that they had been recommended to him by anyone. The landlady was a gossip—the kind of landlady that comes in herself to clear away the tea-things, and stands at the door for half an hour with the tray in her hand, while she tells you her trials and troubles, and throws in an anecdote or two concerning her former lodger.

I suffered considerably from this kind of landlady in my early days when hotels were beyond my means, and when I had to be content with two rooms in an unfashionable quarter.

It is only fair to say that in after-life I turned my sufferings to good account, and used up a lot of material that had been supplied by lodging-housekeepers.

My friend who took my old apartments at Broadstairs was full of his adventures when he met me again. He assured me that he had learnt more about me in one week than he had learnt in all the ten years he had known me. His informant was the landlady.

She had furnished him with a full, true and particular account of a lodger she had had earlier in the season—a lodger who was always writing and walking up and down the room, and muttering to himself, and she had grave misgivings that he had a crime on his conscience, because one day she picked up a sheet of paper he had left on the table, and it was all about a robbery or something. She fancied her lodger had begun to write a confession of what he had done, and then thought better of it, for she put the paper back, and the next day she found it all torn and 'scrobbled up' in the waste-paper basket. With an utter lack of consideration the landlady gave my real name, and furthermore furnished my friend with choice extracts from some of my private letters, and wound up by saying: 'I wonder what he could have been, sir; I'm sure there was something wrong about him.'

I have a friend, a celebrated novelist, whose housemaid for years read every letter that he left on his table, and a good many that he put away in the pigeon-holes of his desk, and when, in consequence of having stayed out till one o'clock in the morning on a bank holiday, she received notice, her temper got the better of her discretion, and she gave her astonished master a 'bit of her mind', and referred to various matters which she could only have become acquainted with by a very close study of his correspondence.

Hotel servants are not so inquisitive as private servants and lodging-house servants. They have not the same opportunity for minutely investigating; but even in hotels there are chamber-maids who want to know all about the guests, and who chatter among themselves concerning No. 157, No. 63, or No. 215, and speculate as to his profession, his financial position, and his moral qualities. Chamber-maids in large hotels have some curious experiences, and, as the records of the law courts plainly show, they are close observers, and are able months, sometimes years, afterwards to identify parties, and to favour the court with detailed statements worthy of a detective or a paid spy.

Let me hasten to remove the impression that I wish to be 'down' on chamber-maids. As a whole I look upon them as very worthy and decidedly useful members of the community. But I still prefer, when I am staying for any length of time at a hotel, to have a chamber-maid who has passed her first youth and settled down to a staid and matronly sort of person.

Such a chamber-maid was Agnes, who, a few years ago, when for some five days I had to keep my room at the —— Hotel, Scarborough, showed me the greatest kindness and consideration, gave me my medicine, and, like a good, kind-hearted woman, endeavoured to cheer me up and amuse me whenever she came in to tidy up the room, or to see how I was getting on, or to inquire if I wanted anything.

It was one morning while she was dusting my room that she told me the story which I am about to relate. I had been (not entirely without a view to copy) asking her questions as to her experiences as a chamber-maid, and after telling me one or two incidents in her professional career, she informed me that the most curious experience she had ever had in her life was while she was a chamber-maid at one of the big London hotels much frequented by people on their way to the Continent.

'I've seen people arrested there,' said Agnes, 'nice quiet people, that you would never have suspected of anything wrong; and I've seen runaway couples stopped just as they were coming downstairs to go off by the Continental mail. There's always something or other happening in a big hotel, but of all the extraordinary affairs that ever came under my notice the most terrible was one that happened about a year before I left. I was the head-chamber-maid on the third floor then, and had, of course, to look generally after all the rooms, and see that everything was right. One day we received a letter from the country, ordering a suite of rooms to be reserved for a newly-married couple on a certain date.

'The bride and bridegroom were coming up to London on their way to spend their honeymoon abroad, and they would break the journey at our hotel, going on by the Continental train the next day.

'The housekeeper came up to me with the letter, and gave me instructions to get a suite on my floor ready, and to see that everything was in proper order. The bridegroom had been a constant visitor at the hotel in his bachelor days, and the manager was anxious that everything should be made as comfortable for him and the young lady as possible.

'As soon as I had received my orders I began to execute them, and I had the rooms thoroughly turned out, and everything dusted and re-arranged. I put clean curtains at the windows, and womanlike, always feeling interested in bridals and honeymoons, I took extra pains to make the rooms look cheerful and pretty, and I think I succeeded.

'The following evening, about an hour before the young couple were to arrive, I went in and gave a last look round to see that everything was right, and just went over the mantelpiece myself with a duster and gave the furniture a flick here and there where the dust—that no power on earth can keep out of a London room—had settled down again.

'Satisfied that everything was in perfect order, I closed the door and went to give some instructions to one of the girls about lighting a fire in a room at the end of the corridor, which was always a fearful nuisance to us when a fire was wanted in it. But so sure as we were full up, and that room had to be given to a visitor, the visitor would want a fire lit in it. It seemed just as if it was to be. It became a joke all over the hotel by now.

'Whenever a message came up that No. 63 was let, we always used to say, "Of course there's a fire wanted," and, upon my word, it really always was so.

'The girl whose business it was to light the fire passed me in the corridor.

' "Oh," I said to her, "I was coming to see you about No. 63. Be sure to have the window open and the door open when you light the fire.'

' "I've got 'em open," she said, "but the wind's the wrong way or something, and the fire won't light at all."

' "Oh, nonsense!" I said; "I'll come and see to it."

'We went back together and into the room. The gentleman who'd taken it was already there. He was standing with his hands in his pockets looking at the fireplace, and he seemed the picture of misery.

' "Poor young fellow!" I said to myself, "he looks ill and unhappy, and wants cheering up. This is not the sort of room to make him feel at home, any way."

' "If you could do without a fire, sir," I said, "it would be better. We always have a trouble with this fireplace. I am sorry to say it smokes."

' "I must have a fire," said the young gentleman. "If I can't have one here, give me another room."

' "I'm afraid we're full up, sir," I said; "but I'll go and see what can be done if you don't mind waiting a little."

'I really was sorry for the poor young gentleman, he looked so utterly wretched, and I couldn't bear to think of him, ill as he evidently was, shut up in that dreadful No. 63, half suffocated all night. There's nothing I think makes one feel so miserable as a room full of smoke, especially when you're away from home and alone.

'Leaving the girl to struggle with the fire, I went downstairs to the housekeeper's room to see if there was a chance of putting the young gentleman anywhere else, if it was only for the night. As luck would have it, a telegram had just been received from a gentleman who was to have come from Scotland that night. He had missed his train, and wouldn't be in London till the following evening. The room reserved for him was on the fourth floor, immediately over the sitting-room on the third floor which we were keeping for the newly-married pair.

'Having obtained permission, I went back to the young gentleman in No. 63, and told him that if he did not mind we would give him a room on the fourth floor, No. 217, where he could have a fire and be comfortable. I explained to him, however, that he would have to be moved on the following day if he intended staying on.

' "Thank you very much," he said; "that will do very well. I shall not want the room after tomorrow."

'I called one of the porters and told him to take the gentleman's portmanteau up to 217, and then I went to the chamber-maid for the fourth floor, and asked her to get a fire lighted at once.

'When I came downstairs the newly-married couple had just arrived, and were being shown to their rooms.

'I took in the warm water myself, and had an opportunity of seeing the young lady. She was very pretty, I thought, and she looked quite a picture in her lovely travelling dress.

'The bridegroom was a tall, handsome gentleman, but much older than the young lady. I'd seen him several times at the hotel, and so, of course, I knew him. I should say he was about forty-five, and she couldn't have been more than nineteen. It was about seven o'clock when they came, and they ordered dinner for eight o'clock. Of course it was known among all the servants on the floor that they were a newly-married couple. It would have been even if we hadn't been told beforehand.

'You can trust hotel servants for knowing a honeymoon when they see one. Plenty of brides and bridegrooms like to pretend that they've been married ever so long, especially at the very first, but they never deceive *us*. I remember a private sitting-room waiter telling me a story of a newly-married couple once, who, when he went into the sitting-room at breakfast time, began to talk to each other in a way to make him believe they'd been married for years. But when the young lady was pouring out the tea, and said to her husband, "How many lumps of sugar do you take, dear?" he had all his work to prevent himself from grinning. He did smile, and the poor young things went quite scarlet both of them, and he went out of the room and had a good laugh all to himself in the service-room, and, of course, told it to everybody as a good joke. Men have no sympathy with young married people; they're not like women-folk in these matters.

'Of course I had no opportunity of seeing the bride and bridegroom again for some time. But the sitting room waiter told us they seemed nice people, and the young lady was full of spirits.

'I went downstairs to supper at ten o'clock, and was back on duty again soon after ten-thirty. I had one or two things to see to, and when I had finished I sat down to do a little needlework.

'It must have been nearly eleven o'clock, when a bell rang violently. The waiter for the floor had gone downstairs for his supper, so I went into the service-room and saw that it was the sitting-room bell of the bride and bridegroom. While I was looking at the indicator, the bell rang again, this time more violently still. I ran along the corridor to the room and knocked at the door.

' "Come in! come in!" cried a man's voice, and I went in, and there I saw the poor young bride in a chair and her husband bending over her.

' "Some water, quick!" he cried. "She's fainted."

'I ran into the bedroom and brought some water and a towel, and bathed her face.

' "Is anything the matter, sir?" I said.

' "Yes!" he exclaimed, "it's terrible. I wouldn't have had such a thing happen for the world. Look, don't you see?"

'He pointed to her hands, where they lay quite helpless in her lap.

'On one hand—the hand that wore the wedding-ring—was a big, bright drop of blood. It had fallen right on the wedding-ring, and stained her hand as well.

' "Oh dear!" I cried, feeling quite faint myself, "what is it?"

' "I don't know," he said; "I can't understand it. It's the most awful thing I ever knew in my life."

'He seemed quite terrified himself, and certainly it was a dreadful thing, especially to anybody who was at all superstitious or who believed in omens.

'I took the towel, and dipped it in the water and wiped the blood-stain from the poor young lady's hand. Presently she opened her eyes and looked about her.

' "Are you better, my darling?" her husband said, stooping over her, and touching her forehead with his lips.

' "Yes, I'm better, dear," she said; "but it was so dreadful! Oh, what does it mean? what does it mean?"

'She glanced down at her hand with a look of horror in her eyes, and when she saw that the blood had been removed she gave a deep sigh of relief.

'Seeing she was a little better, I got up off my knees—I had been kneeling beside her—and went back into the bedroom with the water.

'I was a little bit dazed myself, for I couldn't understand how that drop of bright red blood could have got on the poor dear's hand.

'I was just putting the tumbler down on the washstand, when I heard a shriek from the bride, followed by a cry from the bridegroom. I ran back into the sitting-room, and there I found them both standing with terrified faces.

'They couldn't speak, but the bridegroom pointed to his wife's hand.

'It was stained with blood again.

' "It has dropped upon her hand—this moment!" cried the gentleman. "I saw it, I saw it—with my own eyes!"

' "Dropped!" I exclaimed; "where—where from?"

'I saw the gentleman look up at the ceiling; my eyes followed his, and then I felt as if I should go through the floor. On the ceiling above was a dark moist patch, and slowly dripping from it were drops of blood.

' "I can't stop here," wailed the poor young bride. "Take me away, take me away!"

' "My dear young lady," I said, trying to soothe her, "don't be frightened; nothing can hurt you here."

'I don't know why I said it, but I felt I must say something.

'The gentleman's face was very pale, and I could see he was trembling. He was terribly upset, and who could wonder at it?

'I think he guessed that something awful had happened up above. I did, and it had come upon me all at once who was in that room. It was the young gentleman who had looked so ill and miserable, and who had wanted a fire in 63.

' "Take her in the next room, sir," I whispered. "She won't see it there, and I'll go and find out what it means."

' "No, no," she cried. "I can't—I won't stay here! Oh, it is too horrible, and on my wedding-day—on my wedding-day!"

'She wrung her hands, and then put them over her face.

'And there on her hand—the hand with the wedding-ring—was still that terrible blood-stain.

'I could not stand it any longer. I felt as if I should go off myself, so I made a desperate effort and got out of the room, and ran downstairs to the manager.

' "Something dreadful's happened, sir, and it's in No. 217. Please go at once. There's blood dripping through the ceiling of No. 13."

' "Good heavens!" exclaimed the manager. "What do you mean?"

'He was at supper when I told him, and he started up quite horrified.

' "Please come at once, sir. The poor young lady's seen it, and she's in a terrible way."

'The manager went up the stairs at once, and I followed him as fast as I could. On the first floor he met one of the porters, and he told him to come with us, and we all three went up on to the fourth floor, and the manager went straight to No. 217 and knocked at the door.

'There was no answer.

'The chamber-maid on the floor had come up, seeing something was the matter, and she gave the manager her master-key.

'He put it in the door and turned it, but the door did not open.

'It was bolted on the inside.

' "Go and get something at once," the manager said to the porter; we must break the door open."

'It seemed an hour while we waited outside that door for the man to fetch his tools.

' "You're sure it's blood?" the manager said to me.

' "Oh yes, sir; I could see it by the stain on the ceiling, and some of it had dropped on to the young lady's hand."

' "What an awful thing!" he exclaimed. "Who's in here—do you know?"

' "Yes, sir. It's a young gentleman who came this afternoon, and we put him into 63 first, and moved him up here because of the smoke. He would have a fire!"

' "I'm afraid it's a case of suicide."

' "It's something dreadful, sir, I'm sure, or the blood couldn't have soaked through like that."

'Presently the porter came back, but it was a long job and a hard job to get that door open, the bolt held so firmly; but at last it went with a terrific crash, and then we all stood outside and peered into the room.

'There was no light, but the fire was still burning brightly, and by the glow it cast over the room we saw something was lying on the floor.

'The chamber-maid brought a light, and the manager went in first and knelt down by the "something".

'He had sent for the doctor directly I'd told him about the blood, and at that moment the doctor came up with the sub-manager.

'The doctor went in and looked at the body while the light was held up for him.

' "He's dead," he said, and the words almost made my heart stand still, though I had expected them.

'The poor young fellow had gashed his throat in a frightful way, and was lying in a pool of blood on the floor.

'I was in the room while they examined the body, but I couldn't look at it. I turned my back and looked at the fireplace. There was a lot of burnt paper on the hearth, and some bits of torn-up letters and envelopes that hadn't fallen into the fire.

'The young fellow had been burning his letters and papers.

'I knew then why he was so particular about having a fire in his room.

'The doctor finished his examination, and then he got up and turned to the manager.

' "It's a case of suicide," he said. "Do you know anything about him?"

' "No; we've never seen him before; he only came this afternoon."

' "Well, you'd better not let anything be touched to-night. Nothing can be done for him. You'll send for the police at once?"

' "Of course."

' "Then, until they come you'd better lock up the room, and leave everything as it is. I'll come down and sit in your room and wait for the police if you like."

' "Yes," said the manager, "that will be best. I've been here ten years, and this is the first case of suicide we've had in the hotel."

'As soon as we were all outside, the manager pulled the door to, but it wouldn't lock. He had forgotten that it had been burst open.

' "I see," said the doctor, "you can't lock it up. You'd better put a man outside, then, to see that nobody goes in. He must remain there till the police come."

'So the porter was put on guard outside, and we all went along the corridor, looking very scared and frightened, as you can imagine, except the doctor, and of course doctors never look scared at anything —they take it all as a matter of business.

'I had been so horrified at seeing the young fellow lying there dead that everything else had gone out of my head; but when we got to the top of the stairs I remembered the young lady, and all at once I thought perhaps it would be only right if the doctor were to see her.

'I spoke to the manager, and he turned to the doctor at once.

' "Doctor," he said, "there are very painful circumstances connected with this unhappy business. It seems, at least so the chambermaid tells me, that blood must have dropped through into the room below."

' "I don't wonder at that," said the doctor; "there's quite a pool on the floor."

' "Unfortunately, the room below is occupied by a newly-married couple, and the blood has fallen on the young lady. The chamber-maid tells me she is terribly upset. I think, perhaps, you had better see her."

' "Certainly I will, but I don't think, under the circumstances, it will be advisable to tell her the truth."

' "No, not if you can help it."

' "I'll see how she is, and try to reassure her, somehow. Where is she?"

' "I'll take you to her," I said. "The poor young lady fainted, and I left her almost beside herself; and no wonder, for the blood was on her hands."

' "Dear me!" said the doctor, his face looking quite grave; "and on her wedding-night, too. Poor thing! why, it's enough to turn her brain."

'I led the way to No. 13 and knocked at the door, and without waiting for an answer, opened it and said: "If you please, sir, here's our doctor, in case the young lady would like to see him."

'Then I pulled the door to again, for I had had enough of horrors, and went to sit in the service-room with two of the waiters.

'I wanted to be with somebody, for I felt too upset and nervous to be alone.

'The waiters were full of it, as anything of that sort soon goes all over a hotel, and they wanted to know all about it, but I said I couldn't talk of it, it had upset me too much; but I told them there was no doubt that the young fellow in No. 217 had killed himself, and that he was quite dead.

'The doctor was with the young lady quite half an hour. He passed me on his way downstairs, and I asked him how she was, and if there was anything I could do.

' "She's a little better now," he said, "but, of course, very much upset. I've persuaded her that it is only someone who has met with an accident and lost a quantity of blood, and although it was a very unpleasant experience, there is nothing for her to take to heart, or to be alarmed at; but I called the husband on one side and told him the truth, and he thinks it better they should go to another hotel."

' "Well, sir," I said, "under the circumstances it will be, perhaps. It would be a dreadful thing for her to know that at the very beginning of her married life there was a suicide's body lying above her."

' "Yes, that's a woman's way of looking at it, no doubt. You can go if you like and see if you can help them to pack and put their things together. I'm going to ask the manager to send out and get them rooms in another hotel, so that they have no bother."

'I could see that the doctor was really sorry for the poor bride and bridegroom, and who could help being, under the circumstances?

'I went in and helped to pack the things they had unpacked, and they were very grateful. I could see they were both awfully shocked and worried, and hardly knew what they were doing.

'Presently the manager came up and said he had got rooms for them at another hotel near, and we got all the luggage down and put it on a cab, and then they came down and drove away.

'It was past midnight when they went, and as I watched them going down the great staircase, the poor girl trembling and holding on to her husband's arm for support, and he as white as a ghost, I couldn't help thinking myself that it was about as unhappy a beginning to a honeymoon as their worst enemy, if they had one, could have wished for them.

'Of course the police were very soon in the hotel, and had taken possession of the room where the suicide lay. I didn't hear anything more that night, for I was tired out and upset, and glad to go to bed when it came to my turn to go off duty; and the next morning when I got up I heard the body had been taken away in the night to the mortuary, and that an inquest was to be held on it.

'Of course I was called at the inquest to give my evidence, and it was then I heard all about the poor young gentleman.

'His friends had been found and communicated with, and it seems that the young gentleman had been disappointed in love, and had been very strange in his manner, and very desponding for some time, but nobody thought he meant to kill himself.

'His brother, who was one of the witnesses, stated that he had been in love with a young lady who had not returned his affection, and this young lady had recently married, and that seemed to have preyed upon his mind very much. "In fact," said the brother, "he killed himself on the very day that the marriage took place."

'A good deal of evidence was given by the doctor and others, and the jury brought in a verdict of temporary insanity.

'After the case was over I saw our manager go away with the brother, and they were talking together. Of course I went back to the hotel, but all day I couldn't help thinking things over, and I thought to myself how strange it was that he should have killed himself right over the room in which there *was* a young lady who had only been married that day.

'That evening when I went downstairs, the manager called me into his office and said he wanted to ask me a question or two.

' "When that poor fellow came to the hotel, did he ask any questions of you?" he said. "Did he mention any names, and ask if they were in the hotel or coming to the hotel?"

' "No, sir," I said; "he only asked for a fire."

' "It was your idea to put him in the room above—217?"

' "Yes, sir. I did it because 63 smoked so badly."

' "Well, it's rather an odd coincidence, then. Do you know that he came to this hotel because the young lady he was in love with was coming to stay here with her husband. He had found out somehow they were coming here after the marriage."

' "Good gracious, sir!" I exclaimed, beginning to see what the manager meant, "you don't mean to say that the young lady in 13 was the one he wanted to marry?"

' "Yes, there is no doubt, from what the brother has told me, that it is so."

'And I had put him, quite by accident, in the room above the bride and bridegroom. Only one thin floor separated him from the girl he had broken his heart over, and on her bridal night, while he lay a corpse above her, his blood had dripped through and had fallen on her hands and stained her wedding-ring.

'He had doubtless timed his suicide. He had intended to take his life upon her wedding-day, and in the building in which she was to pass the first hours of her married life with the husband of her choice.

'But I am sure he did not know when he planned that terrible tragedy that she would be the first to see his life-blood flow—that her cry of horror would be the first thing to lead to the discovery of his terrible fate.

'It was chance that had brought that about—coincidence, as the manager called it—and I had been the innocent means of bringing it to pass.

'I don't know whether the poor bride ever learned the truth. I hope she didn't, for it isn't the sort of thing a woman would ever be able to forget. If she had known the truth that night when she felt a cold, wet splash, and looked at her wedding-ring—but there, it isn't a thing to think about, is it, sir?'

I said that I didn't think it was; but after Agnes had finished her story and left me to myself I thought a good deal about it, and it has remained upon the tablets of my memory until now.

In one thing I cordially agree with Agnes, that it was a strange experience for a chamber-maid. I doubt if many chamber-maids have had one stranger.

The Battle of the Monsters

by

MORGAN ROBERTSON

An enormous liner, considered unsinkable and the most powerful passenger ship in the world, carries insufficient lifeboats. On a voyage across the Atlantic one cold April night, it strikes an iceberg and sinks with appalling loss of life. This was the incredible plot of Futility, or The Wreck of the Titan, *a short novel by Morgan Robertson (1861–1915). Incredible, for he published his work in 1898, fourteen years before the famous sinking of the 'Titanic'. The amazing similarities between Robertson's fiction and the real tragedy go beyond the likeness of names, 'Titan' and 'Titanic'. Both ships relied on watertight compartments to give them their unsinkable reputation; both ships carried the cream of society from both sides of the Atlantic; both ships had almost the same dimensions; both ships so ignored the possibility of disaster that they carried only the legal minimum of lifeboats. Robertson varied his plot somewhat from the later real-life events, in that the 'Titan' was not ripped open by the iceberg like the 'Titanic', but was literally turned* ~~over on her side by it, leaving only a few survivors.~~ *The novel is concerned with one survivor's attempts to obtain justice from the ship's owners for the running down of another vessel by the 'Titan' before the disaster. This incredible literary coincidence stands almost alone in the history of fiction.*

Morgan Robertson was the son of a Great Lakes captain, whose footsteps he followed in becoming a seaman, first on the Lakes then at sea on ocean liners. He spent ten years at sea, rising to become first mate. On leaving the sea, he studied to become a jeweller, but bad eyesight made him turn to writing as a full-time career. He had in fact sketched out the plot of Futility *while still a seaman.*

Not unnaturally, Robertson wrote many sea stories, which appeared in journals on both sides of the Atlantic. A firm believer in reincarnation, he was fond of the occasional creepy story. Not many of his works appeared in book form in Britain, though Futility *is still in print in*

America, thanks to the Titanic Historical Society. Robertson published two books of short stories here, Spun Yarn (1900) and Where Angels Fear To Tread (1899), from which comes ' The Battle of the Monsters'. It is a most unusual tale indeed, fully bearing out the promise of the imagination which conceived of that enormous liner, the 'Titan', striking an iceberg in the Atlantic on a cold April night . . .

Extract from hospital record of the case of John Anderson, patient of Dr Brown, Ward 3, Room 6:

August 3. Arrived at hospital in extreme mental distress, having been bitten on wrist three hours previously by dog known to have been rabid. Large, strong man, full-blooded and well nourished. Sanguine temperament. Pulse and temperature higher than normal, due to excitement. Cauterized wound at once (2 p.m.) and inoculated with antitoxin.

As patient admits having recently escaped, by swimming ashore, from lately arrived cholera ship, now at quarantine, he has been isolated and clothing disinfected. Watch for symptoms of cholera.

August 3, 6 p.m. Microscopic examination of blood corroborative of Metchnikoff's theory of fighting leucocytes. White corpuscles gorged with bacteria.

He was an amphibian, and, as such, undeniably beautiful; for the sunlight, refracted and diffused in the water, gave his translucent, pearl-blue body all the shifting colours of the spectrum. Vigorous and graceful of movement, in shape he resembled a comma of three dimensions, twisted, when at rest, to a slight spiral curve; but in travelling he straightened out with quick successive jerks, each one sending him ahead a couple of lengths. Supplemented by the undulatory movement of a long continuation of his tail, it was his way of swimming, good enough to enable him to escape his enemies; this, and riding at anchor in a current by his cable-like appendage, constituting his main occupation in life. The pleasure of eating was denied him; nature had given him a mouth, but he used it only for purposes of offence and defence, absorbing his food in a most unheard-of manner—through the soft walls of his body.

Yet he enjoyed a few social pleasures. Though the organs of the five senses were missing in his economy, he possessed an inner sixth sense which answered for all and also gave him power of speech. He would converse, swap news and views, with creatures of his own and other species, provided that they were of equal size and prowess; but he wasted no time on any but his social peers. Smaller creatures he pursued when they annoyed him; larger ones pursued him.

The sunlight which made him so beautiful to look at, was distasteful to him; it also made him too visible. He preferred a half-darkness and less fervour to life's battle—time to judge of chances, to figure on an enemy's speed and turning-circle, before beginning flight or pursuit. But his dislike of it really came of a stronger animus—a shuddering recollection of three hours once passed on dry land in a comatose condition, which had followed a particularly long and intense period of bright sunlight. He had never been able to explain the connection, but the awful memory still saddened his life.

And now it seemed, as he swam about, that this experience might be repeated. The light was strong and long-continued, the water uncomfortably warm, and the crowd about him denser—so much so as to prevent him from attending properly to a social inferior who had crossed his bow. But just as his mind grasped the full imminence of the danger, there came a sudden darkness, a crash and vibration of the water, then a terrible, rattling roar of sound. The social inferior slipped from his mouth, and with his crowding neighbours was washed far away, while he felt himself slipping along, bounding and rebounding against the projections of a corrugated wall which showed white in the gloom. There was an unpleasant taste to the water, and he became aware of creatures in his vicinity unlike any he had known—quickly darting little monsters about a tenth as large as himself—thousands of them, black and horrid to see, each with short, fish like body and square head like that of a dog; with wicked mouth that opened and shut nervously; with hooked flippers on the middle part, and a bunch of tentacles on the fore that spread out ahead and around. A dozen of them surrounded him menacingly; but he was young and strong, much larger than they, and a little frightened. A blow of his tail killed two, and the rest drew off.

The current bore them on until the white wall rounded off and was lost to sight beyond the mass of darting creatures. Here was slack water, and with desperate effort he swam back, pushing the small enemies out of his path, meeting some resistance and receiving a few bites, until, in a hollow in the wall, he found temporary refuge and time to think. But he could not solve the problem. He had not the slightest idea where he was or what had happened—who and what were the strange black creatures, or why they had threatened him.

His thoughts were interrupted. Another vibrant roar sounded, and there was pitch-black darkness; then he was pushed and washed away from his shelter, jostled, bumped, and squeezed, until he found himself in a dimly lighted tunnel, which, crowded as it was with swimmers, was narrow enough to enable him to see both sides at once. The walls were dark brown and blue, broken up everywhere into depressions or caves, some of them so deep as to be almost like blind tunnels. The dog-faced creatures were there—as far as he could see; but besides them, now, were others, of stranger shape—of species unknown to him.

A slow current carried them on, and soon they entered a larger tunnel. He swam to the opposite wall, gripped a projection, and watched in wonder and awe the procession gliding by. He soon noticed the source of the dim light. A small creature with barrel-like body and innumerable legs or tentacles, wavering and reaching, floated past. Its body swelled and shrank alternately, with every swelling giving out a phosphorescent glow, with every contraction darkening to a faint red colour. Then came a group of others; then a second living lamp; later another and another: they were evenly distributed, and illumined the tunnel.

They were monstrous shapes, living but inert, barely pulsing with dormant life, as much larger than himself as the dog-headed kind were smaller—huge, unwieldy, disk-shaped masses of tissue, light grey at the margins, dark red in the middle. They were in the majority, and blocked the view. Darting and wriggling between and about them were horrible forms, some larger than himself, others smaller. There were serpents, who swam with a serpent's motion. Some were serpents in form, but were curled rigidly into living corkscrews, and by sculling with their tails screwed their way through the water with surprising rapidity. Others were barrel- or globe-shaped, with swarming tentacles. With these they pulled themselves along, in and out through the crowd, or, bringing their squirming appendages rearward—each an individual snake—used them as propellers, and swam. There were creatures in the form of long cylinders, some with tentacles by which they rolled along like a log in a tideway; others, without appendages, were as inert and helpless as the huge red-and-grey disks. He saw four ball-shaped creatures float by, clinging together; then a group of eight, then one of twelve. All these, to the extent of their volition, seemed to be in a state of extreme agitation and excitement.

The cause was apparent. The tunnel from which he had come was still discharging the dog-faced animals by the thousand, and he knew now the business they were on. It was war—war to the death. They flung themselves with furious energy into the parade, fighting and biting all they could reach. A hundred at a time would pounce on one of the large red-and-grey creatures, almost hiding it from view; then, and before they had passed out of sight, they would fall off and disperse, and the once living victim would come with them, in parts. The smaller, active swimmers fled, but if one was caught, he suffered; a quick dart, a tangle of tentacles, an embrace of the wicked flippers, a bite—and a dead body floated on.

And now into the battle came a ponderous engine of vengeance and defence. A gigantic, lumbering pulsating creature, white and translucent but for the dark, active brain showing through its walls, horrible in the slow, implacable deliberation of its movements, floated down with the current. It was larger than the huge red-and-grey creatures. It was formless, in the full irony of the definition—for it assumed all forms. It was long—barrel-shaped; it shrank to a sphere, then broadened laterally, and again extended above and below. In turn it was a sphere, a disk, a pyramid, a pentahedron, a polyhedron. It possessed neither legs, flippers, nor tentacles; but out from its heaving, shrinking body it would send, now from one spot, now from another, an active arm, or feeler, with which it swam, pulled, or pushed. An unlucky invader which one of them touched made a few more voluntary movements; for instantly the whole side of the whitish mass bristled with arms. They seized, crushed, killed it, and then pushed it bodily through the living walls to the animal's interior to serve for food. And the gaping maws healed at once, like the wounds at Milton's warring angels.

The first white monster floated down, killing as he went; then came another, pushing eagerly into the fray; then came two, then three, then dozens. It seemed that the word had been passed, and the army of defence was mustering.

Sick with horror, he watched the grim spectacle from the shelter of the projection, until roused to an active sense of danger to himself—but not from the fighters. He was anchored by his tail, swinging easily in the eddy, and now felt himself touched from beneath, again from above. A projection downstream was extending outwards and towards him. The cave in which he had taken refuge was closing on him like a great mouth—as though directed by an intelligence behind the wall. With a terrified flirt of his tail he flung himself out, and as he drifted down with the combat the walls of the cave crunched together. It was well for him that he was not there.

The current was clogged with fragments of once living creatures, and everywhere, darting, dodging, and biting, were the fierce black invaders. But they paid no present attention to him or to the small tentacled animals. They killed the large, helpless red-and-grey kind, and were killed by the larger white monsters, each moment marking the death and rending to fragments of a victim, and the horrid interment of fully half his slayers. The tunnel grew larger, as mouth after mouth of tributary tunnels was passed; but as each one discharged its quota of swimming and drifting creatures, there was no thinning of the crowd.

As he drifted on with the inharmonious throng, he noticed what seemed the objective of the war. This was the caves which lined the tunnel. Some were apparently rigid, others were mobile. A large red-and-grey animal was pushed into the mouth of one of the latter, and the walls instantly closed; then they opened, and the creature drifted out, limp and colourless, but alive; and with him came fragments of the wall, broken off by the pressure. This happened again and again, but the large creature was never quite killed—merely squeezed. The tentacled non-combatants and the large white fighters seemed to know the danger of these tunnel mouths, possibly from bitter experiences, for they avoided the walls; but the dog-faced invaders sought this death, and only fought on their way to the caves. Sometimes two, often four or more, would launch themselves together into a hollow, but to no avail; their united strength could not prevent the closing in of the mechanical maw, and they were crushed and flung out, to drift on with other débris.

Soon the walls could not be seen for the pushing, jostling crowd, but everywhere the terrible, silent war went on until there came a time when fighting ceased; for each must look out for himself. They seemed to be in an immense cave, and the tide was broken into cross-currents rushing violently to the accompaniment of rhythmical thunder. They were shaken, jostled, pushed about and pushed together, hundreds of the smaller creatures dying from the pressure. Then there was a moment of comparative quiet, during which fighting was resumed, and there could be seen the swiftly flying walls of a large tunnel. Next they were rushed through a labyrinth of small caves with walls of curious, branching formation, sponge-like and intricate. It required energetic effort to prevent being caught in the meshes, and the large red-and-grey creatures were sadly torn and crushed, while the white ones fought their way through by main strength. Again the flying walls of a tunnel, again a mighty cave, and the cross-currents, and the rhythmical thunder, and now a wild charge down an immense tunnel, the wall of which surged outwards and inwards, in unison with the roaring of the thunder.

The thunder died away in the distance, though the walls still surged —even those of a smaller tunnel which divided the current and received them. Down-stream the tunnel branched again and again, and with the lessening of the diameter was a lessening of the current's velocity, until, in a maze of small, short passages, the invaders, content to fight and kill in the swifter tide, again attacked the caves.

But to the never-changing result: they were crushed, mangled, and cast out, the number of suicides, in this neighbourhood, largely exceeding those killed by the white warriors. And yet, in spite of the large mortality among them, the attacking force was increasing. Where one died two took his place; and the reason was soon made plain— they were reproducing. A black fighter, longer than his fellows, a little sluggish of movement, as though from the restrictive pressure of a large, round protuberance in his middle, which made him resemble a snake which had swallowed an egg, was caught by a white monster and instantly embraced by a multitude of feelers. He struggled, bit, and broke in two; then the two parts escaped the grip of the astonished captor, and wriggled away, the protuberance becoming the head of the rear portion, which immediately joined the fight, snapping and biting with unmistakable jaws. This phenomenon was repeated.

And on went the battle. Illumined by the living lamps, and watched by terrified non-combatants, the horrid carnival continued with never-slacking fury and ever-changing background—past the mouths of tributary tunnels which increased the volume and velocity of the current and added to the fighting strength, on through widening archways to a repetition of the cross-currents, the thunder, and the sponge-like maze, down past the heaving walls of larger tunnels to branched passages, where, in comparative slack water, the siege of the caves was resumed. For hour after hour this went on, the invaders dying by hundreds, but increasing by thousands and ten thousands, as the geometrical progression advanced, until, with swimming-spaces nearly choked by their bodies, living and dead, there came the inevitable turn in the tide of battle. A white monster was killed.

Glutted with victims, exhausted and sluggish, he was pounced upon by hundreds, hidden from view by a living envelope of black, which pulsed and throbbed with his death-throes. A feeler reached out, to be bitten off, then another, to no avail. His strength was gone, and the assailants bit and burrowed until they reached a vital part, when the great mass assumed a spherical form and throbbed no more. They dropped off, and, as the mangled ball floated on, charged on the next enemy with renewed fury and courage born of their victory. This one died as quickly.

And as though it had been foreseen, and a policy arranged to meet it, the white army no longer fought in the open, but lined up along the walls to defend the immovable caves. They avoided the working jaws of the other kind, which certainly needed no garrison, and drifting slowly in the eddies, fought as they could, with decreasing strength and increasing death-rate. And thus it happened that our conservative non-combatant, out in midstream, found himself surrounded by a horde of black enemies who had nothing better to do than attack him.

And they did. As many as could crowd about him closed their wicked jaws in his flesh. Squirming with pain, rendered trebly strong by his terror, he killed them by twos and threes as he could reach them with his tail. He shook them off with nervous contortions, only to make room for more. He plunged, rolled, launched himself forwards and back, up and down, out and in, bending himself nearly double, then with lightning rapidity throwing himself far into the reverse curve. He was fighting for his life, and knew it. When he could, he used his jaws, only once to an enemy. He saw dimly at intervals that the white monsters were watching him; but none offered to help, and he had not time to call.

He thought that he must have become the object of the war; for from all sides they swarmed, crowding about him, seeking a place on which to fasten their jaws. Little by little the large red-and-grey creatures, the non-combatants, and the phosphorescent animals were pushed aside, and he, the centre of an almost solid black mass, fought, in utter darkness, with the fury of extreme fright. He had no appreciation of the passing of time, no knowledge of his distance from the wall, or the destination of this never-pausing current. But finally, after an apparently interminable period, he heard dimly, with failing consciousness, the reverberations of the thunder, and knew momentary respite as the violent cross-currents tore his assailants away. Then, still in darkness, he felt the crashing and tearing of flesh against obstructing walls and sharp corners, the repetition of thunder and the roar of the current which told him he was once more in a large tunnel. An instant of light from a venturesome torch showed him to his enemies, and again he fought, like a whale in his last flurry, slowly dying from exhaustion and pain, but still potential to kill—terrible in his agony. There was no counting of scalps in that day's work; but perhaps no devouring white monster in all the defensive army could have shown a death-list equal to this. From the surging black cloud there was a steady outflow of the dead, pushed back by the living.

Weaker and weaker, while they mangled his flesh, and still in darkness, he fought them down through branching passages to another network of small tunnels, where he caught a momentary view of the walls and the stolid white guard, thence on to what he knew was open space. And here he felt that he could fight no more. They had covered him completely, and try as he might with his failing strength, he could not dislodge them. So he ceased his struggles; and numb with pain, dazed with despair, he awaited the end.

But it did not come. He was too exhausted to feel surprise or joy when they suddenly dropped away from him; but the instinct of self-preservation was still in force, and he swam towards the wall. The small creatures paid him no attention; they scurried this way and that, busy with troubles of their own, while he crept stupidly and painfully between two white sentries floating in the eddies—one of whom considerately made room for him—and anchored to a projection, luckily choosing a harbour that was not hostile.

'Any port in a storm, eh, neighbour?' said the one who had given him room, and who seemed to notice his dazed condition. 'You'll feel better soon. My, but you put up a good fight, that's what you did!'

He could not answer, and the friendly guard resumed his vigil. In a few moments, however, he could take cognizance of what was going on in the stream. There was a new army in the fight, and reinforcements were still coming. A short distance above him was a huge rent in the wall, and the caves around it, crushed and distorted, were grinding fiercely. Protruding through the rent and extending half-way across the tunnel was a huge mass of some strange substance, roughly shaped to a cylindrical form. It was hollow, and out of it, by thousands and hundred thousands, was pouring the auxiliary army, from which the black fighters were now fleeing for dear life.

The newcomers, though resembling in general form the creatures they pursued, were much larger and of two distinct types. Both were light brown in colour; but while one showed huge development of head and jaw, with small flippers, the other kind reversed these attributes, their heads being small, but their flippers long and powerful. They ran their quarry down in the open, and seized them with out-reaching tentacles. No mistakes were made—no feints or false motions; and there was no resistance by the victims. Where one was noticed he was doomed. The tentacles gathered him in—to a murderous bite or a murderous embrace.

At last, when the inflow had ceased—when there must have been millions of the brown killers in the tunnel—the great hollow cylinder turned slowly on its axis and backed out through the rent in the wall, which immediately closed, with a crushing and scattering of fragments. Though the allies were far down-stream now, the war was practically ended; for the white defenders remained near the walls, and the black invaders were in wildest panic, each one, as the resistless current rushed him past, swimming against the stream, to put distance between himself and the destroyer below. But before long an advance-guard of the brown enemy shot out from the tributaries above, and the tide of retreat swung backwards. Then came thousands of them, and the massacre was resumed.

'Hot stuff, eh?' said the friendly neighbour to him.

'Y-y-y-es—I guess so,' he answered, rather vacantly; 'I don't know. I don't know anything about it. I never saw such doings. What is it all for? What does it mean?'

'Oh, this is nothing; it's all in a lifetime. Still, I admit it might ha' been serious for us—and you, too—if we hadn't got help.'

'But who are they, and what? They all seem of a family, and are killing each other.'

'Immortal shade of Darwin!' exclaimed the other sentry, who had not spoken before. 'Where were you brought up? Don't you know that variations from type are the deadliest enemies of the parent stock? These two brown breeds are the hundredth or two-hundredth cousins of the black kind. When they've killed off their common relative, and get to competing for grub, they'll exterminate each other, and we'll be rid of 'em all. Law of nature. Understand?'

'Oh, y-yes, I understand, of course; but what did the black kind attack me for? And what do they want, anyway?'

'To follow out their destiny, I s'pose. They're the kind of folks who have missions. Reformers, we call 'em—who want to enforce their peculiar ideas and habits on other people. Sometimes we call them expansionists—fond of colonising territory that doesn't belong to them. They wanted to get through the cells to the lymph-passages, thence on to the brain and spinal marrow. Know what that means? Hydrophobia.'

'What's that?'

'Oh, say, now! You're too easy.'

'Come, come,' said the other, good-naturedly; 'don't guy him. He never had our advantages. You see, neighbour, we get these points from the subjective brain, which knows all things and gives us our instructions. We're the white corpuscles—phagocytes, the scientists call us—and our work is to police the blood-vessels, and kill off invaders that make trouble. Those red-and-grey chumps can't take care of themselves, and we must protect 'em. Understand? But this invasion was too much for us, and we had to have help from outside. You must have come in with the first crowd—think I saw you—in at the bite. Second crowd came in through an inoculation tube, and just in time to pull you through.'

'I don't know,' answered our bewildered friend. 'In at the bite? What bite? I was swimming round comfortable-like, and there was a big noise, and then I was alongside of a big white wall, and then——'

'Exactly; the dog's tooth. You got into bad company, friend, and you're well out of it. That first gang is the microbe of rabies, not very well known yet, because a little too small to be seen by most microscopes. All the scientists seem to have learned about 'em is that a colony of a few hundred generations old—which they call a culture, or serum —is death on the original bird; and that's what they sent in to help out. Pasteur's dead, worse luck, but sometime old Koch'll find out what we've known all along—that it's only variation from type.'

'Koch!' he answered, eagerly and proudly. 'Oh, I know Koch; I've met him. And I know about microscopes, too. Why, Koch had me under his microscope once. He discovered my family, and named us— the comma bacilli—the Spirilli of Asiatic Cholera.'

In silent horror they drew away from him, and then conversed together. Other white warriors drifting along stopped and joined the conference, and when a hundred or more were massed before him, they spread out to a semi-spherical formation and closed in.

'What's the matter?' he asked, nervously. 'What's wrong? What are you going to do? I haven't done anything, have I?'

'It's not what you've done, stranger,' said his quondam friend, 'or what we're going to do. It's what you're going to do. You're going to die. Don't see how you got past quarantine, anyhow.'

'What—why—I don't want to die. I've done nothing. All I want is peace and quiet, and a place to swim where it isn't too light nor too dark. I mind my own affairs. Let me alone—you hear me—let me alone!'

They answered him not. Slowly and irresistibly the hollow formation contracted—individuals slipping out when necessary—until he was pushed, still protesting, into the nearest movable cave. The walls crashed together and his life went out. When he was cast forth he was in five pieces.

And so our gentle, conservative, non-combative cholera microbe, who only wanted to be left alone to mind his own affairs, met this violent death, a martyr to prejudice and an unsympathetic environment.

Extract from hospital record of the case of John Anderson:

August 18. As period of incubation for both cholera and hydrophobia has passed and no initial symptoms of either disease have been noticed, patient is this day discharged, cured.

The Return

by

R. MURRAY GILCHRIST

'An artist too little known and valued by his own generation, yet no record of the English short story would be complete without a study of his contributions.'

Thus wrote Eden Phillpotts in 1926 about Robert Murray Gilchrist (1868–1917) and what Phillpotts said then holds true to-day. Few people have heard of Gilchrist and I believe I am the first anthologist in the past thirty years to make use of his material. R. Murray Gilchrist began writing early in life and he made what small reputation he acquired from a series of novels and short stories dealing with the people of the High Peak District of Derbyshire. He published several slim volumes of these tales, which were collected posthumously into A Peak-land Faggot (1926).

But early in his writing career, Gilchrist produced The Stone Dragon *(1894), one of the most singular volumes of weird tales in English literature. He never attempted anything like it again which is a pity for it shows him to be a master of this craft. I have used three strange stories from this volume in previous anthologies and here is another, in lighter tone than the rest but still revealing Gilchrist's unique talents. It originally appeared in* The National Observer, *a journal to which the author was a regular contributor.*

Five minutes ago I drew the window curtain aside and let the mellow sunset light contend with the glare from the girandoles. Below lay the orchard of Vernon Garth, rich in heavily flowered fruit-trees—yonder a medlar, here a pear, next a quince. As my eyes, unaccustomed to the day, blinked rapidly, the recollection came of a scene forty-five years past, and once more beneath the oldest tree stood the girl I loved, mischievously plucking yarrow, and, despite its evil omen, twining the snowy clusters in her black hair. Again her coquettish words rang in my ears: 'Make me thy lady! Make me the richest woman in

England, and I promise thee, Brian, we shall be the happiest of God's creatures.' And I remembered how the mad thirst for gold filled me: how I trusted in her fidelity, and without reasoning or even telling her that I would conquer fortune for her sake, I kissed her sadly and passed into the world. Then followed a complete silence until the *Star of Europe*, the greatest diamond discovered in modern times, lay in my hand—a rough unpolished stone not unlike the lumps of spar I had often seen lying on the sandy lanes of my native county. This should be Rose's own, and all the others that clanked so melodiously in their leather bulse should go towards fulfilling her ambition. Rich and happy I should be soon, and should I not marry an untitled gentlewoman, sweet in her prime? The twenty years' interval of work and sleep was like a fading dream, for I was going home. The knowledge thrilled me so that my nerves were strung tight as iron ropes and I laughed like a young boy. And it was all because my home was to be in Rose Pascal's arms.

I crossed the sea and posted straight for Halkton village. The old hostelry was crowded. Jane Hopgarth, whom I remembered a ruddy-faced child, stood on the box-edged terrace, courtesying in matronly fashion to the departing mail-coach. A change in the sign-board drew my eye: the white lilies had been painted over with a mitre, and the name changed from the Pascal Arms to the Lord Bishop. Angrily aghast at this disloyalty, I cross-questioned the ostlers, who hurried to and fro, but failing to obtain any coherent reply I was fain to content myself with a mental denunciation of the times.

At last I saw Bow-Legged Jeffries, now bent double with age, sunning himself at his favourite place, the side of the horse-trough. As of old he was chewing a straw. No sign of recognition came over his face as he gazed at me, and I was shocked, because I wished to impart some of my gladness to a fellow-creature. I went to him, and after trying in vain to make him speak, held forth a gold coin. He rose instantly, grasped it with palsied fingers, and, muttering that the hounds were starting, hurried from my presence. Feeling half sad I crossed to the churchyard and gazed through the grated window of the Pascal burial chapel at the recumbent and undisturbed effigies of Geoffrey Pascal, gentleman, of Bretton Hall; and Margot Maltrevor his wife, with their quaint epitaph about a perfect marriage enduring for ever. Then, after noting the rankness of the docks and nettles, I crossed the worn stile and with footsteps surprising fleet passed towards the stretch of moorland at whose further end stands Bretton Hall.

Twilight had fallen ere I reached the cottage at the entrance of the park. This was in a ruinous condition: here and there sheaves in the thatched roof had parted and formed crevices through which smoke filtered. Some of the tiny windows had been walled up, and even where the glass remained snake-like ivy hindered any light from falling into their thick recesses.

The door stood open, although the evening was chill. As I approached, the heavy autumnal dew shook down from the firs and fell upon my shoulders. A bat, swooping in an undulation, struck between my eyes and fell to the grass, moaning querulously. I entered. A withered woman sat beside the peat fire. She held a pair of steel knitting-needles which she moved without cessation. There was no thread upon them, and when they clicked her lips twitched as if she had counted. Some time passed before I recognised Rose's foster-mother, Elizabeth Carless. The russet colour of her cheeks had faded and left a sickly grey; those sunken, dimmed eyes were utterly unlike the bright black orbs that had danced so mirthfully. Her stature, too, had shrunk. I was struck with wonder. Elizabeth could not be more than fifty-six years old. I had been away twenty years; Rose was fifteen when I left her, and I had heard Elizabeth say that she was only twenty-one at the time of her darling's weaning. But what a change! She had such an air of weary grief that my heart grew sick.

Advancing to her side I touched her arm. She turned, but neither spoke nor seemed aware of my presence. Soon, however, she rose, and helping herself along by grasping the scanty furniture, tottered to a window and peered out. Her right hand crept to her throat; she untied the string of her gown and took from her bosom a pomander set in a battered silver case. I cried out; Rose had loved that toy in her childhood; thousands of times we played ball with it. . . . Elizabeth held it to her mouth and mumbled it, as if it were a baby's hand. Maddened with impatience, I caught her shoulder and roughly bade her say where I should find Rose. But something awoke in her eyes, and she shrank away to the other side of the house-place: I followed; she cowered on the floor, looking at me with a strange horror. Her lips began to move, but they made no sound. Only when I crossed to the threshold did she rise; and then her head moved wildly from side to side, and her hands pressed close to her breast, as if the pain there were too great to endure.

I ran from the place, not daring to look back. In a few minutes I reached the balustraded wall of the Hall garden. The vegetation there was wonderfully luxuriant. As of old, the great blue and white Canterbury bells grew thickly, and those curious flowers to which tradition has given the name of 'Marie's Heart' still spread their creamy tendrils and blood-coloured bloom on every hand. But 'Pascal's Dribble', the tiny spring whose water pulsed so fiercely as it emerged from the earth, had long since burst its bounds, and converted the winter garden into a swamp, where a miniature forest of queen-of-the-meadow filled the air with melancholy sweetness. The house looked as if no careful hand had touched it for years. The elements had played havoc with its oriels, and many of the latticed frames hung on single hinges. The curtain of the blue parlour hung outside, draggled and faded, and half hidden by a thick growth of bindweed.

With an almost savage force I raised my arm high above my head and brought my fist down upon the central panel of the door. There was no need for such violence, for the decayed fastenings made no resistance, and some of the rotten boards fell to the ground. As I entered the hall and saw the ancient furniture, once so fondly kept, now mildewed and crumbling to dust, quick sobs burst from my throat. Rose's spinet stood beside the door of the withdrawing-room. How many carols had we sung to its music! As I passed my foot struck one of the legs and the rickety structure groaned as if it were coming to pieces. I thrust out my hand to steady it, but at my touch the velvet covering of the lid came off and the tiny gilt ornaments rattled downwards. The moon was just rising and only half her disc was visible over the distant edge of the Hell Garden. The light in the room was very uncertain, yet I could see the keys of the instrument were stained brown, and bound together with thick cobwebs.

Whilst I stood beside it I felt an overpowering desire to play a country ballad with an over-word of 'Willow browbound'. The words in strict accordance with the melody are merry and sad by turns: at one time filled with light happiness, at another bitter as the voice of one bereaved for ever of joy. So I cleared off the spiders and began to strike the keys with my forefinger. Many were dumb, and when I struck them gave forth no sound save a peculiar sigh; but still the melody rhythmed as distinctly as if a low voice crooned it out of the darkness. Wearied with the bitterness, I turned away.

By now the full moonlight pierced the window and quivered on the floor. As I gazed on the tremulous pattern it changed into quaint devices of hearts, daggers, rings, and a thousand tokens more. All suddenly another object glided amongst them so quickly that I won-

dered whether my eyes had been at fault—a tiny satin shoe, stained
crimson across the lappets. A revulsion of feeling came to my soul and
drove away all my fear. I had seen that selfsame shoe white and un-
soiled twenty years before, when vain, vain Rose danced amongst her
reapers at the harvest-home. And my voice cried out in ecstasy, 'Rose,
heart of mine! Delight of all the world's delights!'

She stood before me, wondering, amazed. Alas, so changed! The
red-and-yellow silk shawl still covered her shoulders; her hair still
hung in those eldritch curls. But the beautiful face had grown wan and
tired, and across the forehead lines were drawn like silver threads. She
threw her arms round my neck and, pressing her bosom heavily on
mine, sobbed so piteously that I grew afraid for her, and drew back
the long masses of hair which had fallen forward, and kissed again and
again those lips that were too lovely for simile. Never came a word of
chiding from them. 'Love,' she said, when she had regained her breath,
'the past struggle was sharp and torturing—the future struggle will be
crueller still. What a great love yours was, to wait and trust for so long!
Would that mine had been as powerful! Poor, weak heart that could
not endure!'

The tones of a wild fear throbbed through all her speech, strongly,
yet with insufficient power to prevent her feeling the tenderness of
those moments. Often, timorously raising her head from my shoulder,
she looked about and then turned with a soft, inarticulate, and glad
murmur to hide her face on my bosom. I spoke fervently; told of the
years spent away from her; how, when working in the diamond-fields
she had ever been present in my fancy, how at night her name had
fallen from my lips in my only prayer; how I had dreamed of her
amongst the greatest in the land—the richest, and, I dare swear, the
loveliest woman in the world. I grew warmer still: all the gladness
which had been constrained for so long now burst wildly from my lips:
a myriad of rich ideas resolved into words, which, being spoken, wove
one long and delicious fit of passion. As we stood together, the moon
brightened and filled the chamber with a light like the day's. The
ridges of the surrounding moorland stood out in sharp relief.

Rose drank in my declarations thirstily, but soon interrupted me
with a heavy sigh. 'Come away,' she said softly. 'I no longer live in this
house. You must stay with me to-night. This place is so wretched now;
for time, that in you and me has only strengthened love, has wrought
much ruin here.'

Half leaning on me, she led me from the precincts of Bretton Hall.

We walked in silence over the waste that crowns the valley of the Whitelands and, being near the verge of the rocks, saw the great pinewood sloping downwards, lighted near us by the moon, but soon lost in density. Along the mysterious line where the light changed into gloom, intricate shadows of withered summer bracken struck and receded in a mimic battle. Before us lay the Priests' Cliff. The moon was veiled by a grove of elms, whose ever-swaying branches alternately increased and lessened her brightness. This was a place of notoriety—a veritable Golgotha—a haunt fit only for demons. Murder and theft had been punished here; and to this day fireside stories are told of evil women dancing round that Druids' circle, carrying hearts plucked from gibbeted bodies.

'Rose,' I whispered, 'why have you brought me here?'

She made no reply, but pressed her head more closely to my shoulder. Scarce had my lips closed ere a sound like the hiss of a half-strangled snake vibrated amongst the trees. It grew louder and louder. A monstrous shadow hovered above.

Rose from my bosom murmured. 'Love is strong as Death! Love is strong as Death!'

I locked her in my arms, so tightly that she grew breathless. 'Hold me,' she panted. 'You are strong.'

A cold hand touched our foreheads so that, benumbed, we sank together to the ground, to fall instantly into a dreamless slumber.

When I awoke the clear grey light of the early morning had spread over the country. Beyond the Hell Garden the sun was just bursting through the clouds, and had already spread a long golden haze along the horizon. The babbling of the streamlet that runs down to Halkton was so distinct that it seemed almost at my side. How sweetly the wild thyme smelt! Filled with the tender recollections of the night, without turning, I called Rose Pascal from her sleep.

'Sweetheart, sweetheart, waken! waken! waken! See how glad the world looks—see the omens of a happy future.'

No answer came. I sat up, and looking round me saw that I was alone. A square stone lay near. When the sun was high I crept to read the inscription carved thereon:—'*Here, at four cross-paths, lieth, with a stake through the bosom, the body of Rose Pascal, who in her sixteenth year wilfully cast away the life God gave.*'

The Corpse Light

by

DICK DONOVAN

The pen-name Dick Donovan concealed the identity of one of the last century's most prolific authors. J. E. Preston Muddock wrote over 140 books in nearly forty years and to help publish this enormous output he adopted Dick Donovan as his nom de plume. His first book as Muddock, the novel A False Heart, *appeared in 1873, and his first Donovan title,* The Man Hunter, *was published in 1888. Apart from* Stories Weird and Wonderful *(1889) his best work appeared under the name of Dick Donovan, including* Dark Deeds *(1895),* Riddles Read *(1896) and the neglected* Tales of Terror *(1899). 'The Corpse Light' is one of Donovan's tales of terror and is in every way a classic Victorian ghost story.*

What I am about to relate is so marvellous, so weird and startling, that even now, as I dwell upon it all, I wonder why I of all men should have been subjected to the unnatural and unearthly influence. I no longer scoff when somebody reminds me that there is more in heaven and earth than is dreamt of in our philosophy.

It was about twenty years ago that I took up a medical practice in the old-fashioned and picturesque little town of Brinton-on-sea. At that time there was no railway into Brinton, the nearest station being some seven or eight miles away. The result was the town still retained a delightful old-time air, while the people were as primitive and old-fashioned as their town. The nearest village was High Lea, about three miles away. Between the two places was a wide sweep of magnificent rolling down, delightful at all times, but especially so in the summer. Many an ancient farmhouse was dotted about, with here and there a windmill. The down on the seaside terminated in a high headland, from which a splendid lighthouse sent forth its warning beams over the fierce North Sea. Second only in conspicuousness to this lighthouse was an old and half ruined windmill, known all over the countryside as 'The Haunted Mill'.

When I first went to live in Brinton this mill soon attracted my attention, for it was one of the most picturesque old places of its kind I had ever seen; and as I had some artistic instincts, and could sketch, the haunted mill appealed to me. It stood on rising ground, close to the high-road that ran between Brinton and High Lea. I gathered that there had been some dispute about the ownership and for over a quarter of a century that disputed claim had remained unsettled; and during that long period the old mill had been gradually falling into ruin. The foundations had from some cause sunk, throwing the main building out of the perpendicular. Part of the roof had fallen in, and the fierce gales of a quarter of a century had battered the sails pretty well to match-wood. A long flight of wooden steps led up to the principal door, but these steps had rotted away in places, and the door itself had partly fallen inwards. Needless to say, this mill had become the home of bats and owls, and, according to the yokels, of something more fearsome than either. It was a forlorn and mournful-looking place, any way, even in the full blaze of sunshine; but seen in moonlight its appearance was singularly weird, and well calculated to beget in the rustic mind a feeling of horror, and to produce a creepy and uncanny sensation in anyone susceptible to the influence of outre appearances.

To me it did not appeal in any of these aspects. I saw in it only subject matter for an exceedingly effective picture, and yet I am bound to confess that even when transferred to board or canvas there was a certain grim suggestiveness of things uncanny, and I easily understood how the superstitious and unreasoning rustic mind was awed into a belief that this mouldering old mill was haunted by something more creepy and harrowing than bats and owls. Anyway, I heard wonderful tales, at which I laughed, and when I learned that the country people generally gave the mill a wide berth at night, I blamed them for their stupidity. But it was a fact that worthy, and in other respects intelligent, farmers and market folk coming or going between Brinton and High Lea after dark preferred the much longer and dangerous route by the sea cliffs, even in the wildest weather.

I have dwelt thus long on the 'Haunted Mill' because it bulks largely in my story, as will presently be seen, and I came in time to regard it with scarcely less awe than the rustics did.

It was during the second year of my residence in Brinton that a young man named Charles Royce came home after having been absent at sea for three years. Royce's people occupied Gorse Hill Farm, about two miles to the south of Brinton. Young Charley, a fine, handsome, but rather wild youngster, had, it appears, fallen desperately in love with Hannah Trowzell, who was a domestic in the employ of the Rector of the parish. But Charley's people did not approve of his choice, and, thinking to cure him, packed him off to sea, and after an absence of three years and a month the young fellow, bronzed, hearty, more rollicking and handsome than ever, returned to his native village. I had known nothing of Charles Royce or his history up to the day of his return; but it chanced on that very day I had to pay a professional visit to the Rectory, and the Rector pressed me to lunch with him. Greatly interested in all his parishioners, and knowing something of the private history of most of the families in his district, the rev. gentleman very naturally fell to talking about young Royce, and he told me the story, adding, 'Hannah is a good girl, and I think it's rather a pity Charley's people objected to his courting her. I believe she would have made him a capital wife.'

'Has she given him up entirely?' I asked.

'Oh, yes, and is engaged to Silas Hartrop, whose father owns the fishing smack the "North Sea Beauty". I've never had a very high opinion of Silas. I'm afraid he is a little too fond of skittles and beer. However, Hannah seems determined to have him in spite of anything I can say, so she must take her course. But I hope she will be able to reform him, and that the marriage will be a happy one. I really shouldn't be a bit surprised, however, if the girl took up with her old lover again, for I have reason to know she was much attached to him, and I fancy Charley, if he were so minded, could easily influence her to throw Silas overboard.'

This little story of love and disappointment naturally interested me, for in a country town the affairs of one's neighbours are matters of greater moment than is the case in a big city.

So it came to pass that a few weeks after Charley's return it was generally known that, even as the Rector had suggested it might be, young Royce and pretty Hannah Trowzell were spooning again, and Silas had virtually been told to go about his business. It was further known that Silas had taken his dismissal so much to heart that he had been seeking consolation in the beer-pot. Of course, folk talked a good deal, and most of them sympathised with Silas, and blamed Hannah. Very soon it began to be bruited about that Royce's people no longer opposed any objections to the wooing, and that in consequence

Hannah and Charley were to become husband and wife at Christmas, that was in about seven weeks' time.

A month of the time had passed, and the 'askings' were up in the parish church, when one day there went forth a rumour that Charles Royce was missing. Rumour took a more definite shape a few hours later when it was positively stated that two nights previously Charles had left his father's house in high spirits and the best of health to visit Hannah, and walk with her, as she was going into the town to make some purchases. On his way he called at the 'Two Waggoners', a wayside inn, where he had a pint of beer and purchased an ounce of tobacco. From the time he left the inn, all trace of him was lost, and he was seen no more. Hannah waited his coming until long past the appointed hour, and when he failed to put in an appearance, she became angry and went off to the town by herself.

Next day her anger gave place to anxiety when she learnt that he had left his home to visit her, and had not since returned; and anxiety became alarm when two and three days slipped by without bringing any tidings of the truant. On the night that he left his home, the weather was very tempestuous, and it had been wild and stormy since. It was therefore suggested that on leaving the 'Two Waggoners' he might have got confused when he reached the common, which he had to cross to get to the Rectory; and as there were several pools and treacherous hollows on the common, it was thought he had come to grief; but the most diligent search failed to justify the surmise.

Such an event as this was well calculated to cause a sensation, not only in Brinton and its neighbourhood, but throughout the county. Indeed, for many days it was a common topic of conversation, and at the Brinton weekly market the farmers and the rustics dwelt upon it to the exclusion of other things; and, of course, everybody had some wonderful theory of their own to account for the missing man's disappearance. Despite wide publicity and every effort on the part of the rural and county police, to say nothing of a hundred and one amateur detectives, the mystery remained unsolved. Charles Royce had apparently disappeared from off the face of the earth, leaving not a trace behind.

In the process of time the nine days' wonder gave place to something else, and excepting by those directly interested in him, Charles Royce was forgotten. Hannah took the matter very seriously to heart, and for a while lay dangerously ill. Silas Hartrop, who was much affected by his disappointment with regard to Hannah, went to the dogs, as the saying is, and drank so heavily that it ended in an attack of delirium tremens. I was called in to attend him, and had hard work to pull him through. On his recovery his father sent him to an uncle at Yarmouth, who was in the fishing trade, and soon afterwards news came that young Hartrop had been drowned at sea. He was out in the North Sea in his uncle's fishing smack, and, though nobody saw him go, it was supposed that he fell overboard in the night. This set the local tongues wagging again for a time, but even the affairs of Brinton could not stand still because the ne'er-do-weel Silas Hartrop was drowned. So sympathy was expressed with his people, and then the affair was dismissed.

About two years later I received an urgent message late one afternoon to hasten with all speed to High Lea, to attend to the Squire, who had been taken suddenly and seriously ill. I had had rather a heavy day of it, as there had been a good deal of sickness about for some time past, and it had taken me several hours to get through my list of patients. I had just refreshed myself with a cup of tea and was about to enjoy a cigar when the messenger came. Telling him to ride back as quickly as possible and say that I was coming, I busied myself with a few important matters which had to be attended to, as I might be absent for some hours, and then I ordered my favourite mare, Princess, to be saddled.

I set off from Brinton soon after seven. It was a November night, bitterly cold, dark as Erebus, while every now and then violent squalls swept the land from seaward. Princess knew the road well, so I gave the mare her head, and she went splendidly until we reached the ruined mill, when suddenly she wheeled round with such abruptness that, though I was a good horseman, I was nearly pitched from the saddle. At the same moment I was struck in the face by something that seemed cold and clammy. I thought at first it was a bat, but remembered that bats do not fly in November; an owl, but an owl would not have felt cold and clammy. However, I had little time for thought, as my attention had to be given to the mare. She seemed disposed to bolt, and was trembling with fear. Then, to my intense astonishment, I noticed what seemed to be a large luminous body lying on the roadway. It had the appearance of a corpse illuminated in some wonderful and mysterious manner. Had it not been for the fright of my mare I should have thought I was the victim of some optical delusion; but Princess evidently saw the weird object, and refused to pass it. So impressed was I with the idea that a real and substantial body was lying on the road, notwithstanding the strange unearthly light, that I slipped from the saddle, intending to investigate the matter, when suddenly it disappeared, and the cold and clammy *something* again struck me in the face.

I confess that for the first time in my life I felt a strange, nervous, unaccountable fear. Whatever the phenomenon was, there was the hard, stern fact to face that my horse had seen what I had seen, and was terrified. There was something strangely uncanny about the whole business, and when a terrific squall, bringing with it sleet and rain, came howling from the sea, it seemed to emphasise the uncanniness, and the ruined mill, looming gaunt and grim in the darkness, gave me an involuntary shudder. The next moment I was trying to laugh myself out of my nervousness. 'Princess and I', I mentally argued, 'have been the victims of some atmospheric delusion.' That was all very well, but the *something* cold and clammy that struck me in the face, and which *may* have struck the mare in the face also, was no atmospheric delusion. With an alacrity I did not often display, I sprang into the saddle, spoke some encouraging words to the mare, for she was still trembling, and when she bounded forward, and the haunted mill was behind me, I experienced a positive sense of relief.

I found my patient at High Lea in a very bad way. He was suffering from an attack of apoplexy, and though I used all my skill on his behalf he passed away towards midnight. His wife very kindly offered me a bed for the night, but as I had important matters to attend to early in the morning I declined the hospitality. It was half-past twelve when I left the house on my return journey. The incident by the haunted mill had been put out of my head by the case I had been called upon to attend, but as I mounted my mare the groom, who had brought her round from the stable, said, 'It be a bad night, doctor, for riding; the kind o' night when dead things come out o' their graves.'

I laughed, and replied:

'Tom, lad, I am surprised to hear you talk such rubbish. I thought you had more sense than that.'

'Well, I tell 'ee what, doctor; if I had to ride to Brinton to-night I'd go by the cliffs and chance being drowned, rather than pass yon old mill.'

These words for the moment unnerved me, and I honestly confess that I resolved to go by the cliffs, dangerous as the road was in the dark. Nevertheless, I laughed at Tom's fears, and ridiculed him, though when I left the squire's grounds I turned the mare's head towards the cliffs. In a few minutes I was ridiculing myself.

'John Patmore Lindsay,' I mentally exclaimed, 'you are a fool. All your life you have been ridiculing stories of the supernatural, and now, at your time of life, are you going to allow yourself to be frightened by a bogey? Shame on you.'

I bucked up, grew bold, and thereupon altered my course, and got into the high road again.

There had been a slight improvement in the weather. It had ceased to rain, but the wind had settled down into a steady gale, and screeched and screamed over the moorland with a demoniacal fury. The darkness, however, was not so intense as it was, and a star here and there was visible through the torn clouds. But it was an eerie sort of night, and I was strangely impressed with a sense of my loneliness. It was absolutely unusual for me to feel like this, and I suggested to myself that my nerves were a little unstrung by overwork and the anxiety the squire's illness had caused me. And so I rode on, bowing my head to the storm, while the mare stepped out well, and I anticipated that in little more than half an hour I should be snug in bed. As we got abreast of the haunted mill the mare once more gibbed, and all but threw me, and again I was struck in the face by the cold clammy *something*.

I almost think my hair rose on end as I observed that the illuminated corpse was lying in the roadway again; but now it appeared to be surrounded by a lake of blood. It was the most horrible sight that ever human eyes looked upon. I tried to urge Princess forward, but she was stricken with terror, and, wheeling right round, was setting off towards High Lea again. But once more I was struck in the face by the invisible *something*, and its coldness and clamminess made me shudder while there in front of us lay the corpse in the pool of blood. The mare reared and plunged, but I got her head round, determining to make a wild gallop for Brinton and leave the horrors of the haunted mill behind. But the corpse was again in front of us, and I shrank back almost appalled as the *something* once more touched my face.

I cannot hope to describe what my feelings were at this supreme moment. I don't believe anything human could have daunted me; but I was confronted by a supernatural mystery that not only terrified me but the mare I was riding. Whichever way I turned, that awful, ghastly object confronted me, and the blow in the face was repeated again and again.

How long I endured the horrors of the situation I really don't know. Possibly the time was measured by brief minutes. It seemed to me hours. At last my presence of mind returned. I dismounted, and reasoned with myself that, whatever the apparition was, it had some import. I soothed the mare by patting her neck and talking to her, and I determined then to try and find a solution of the mystery. But now a more wonderful thing happened. The corpse, which was still made visible by the unearthly light, rose straight up, and as it did so the blood seemed to flow away from it. The figure glided past me, and a sense of extraordinary coldness made me shiver. Slowly and gracefully the shining corpse glided up the rotting steps of the old mill, and disappeared through the doorway. No sooner had it gone than the mill itself seemed to glow with phosphorescent light, and to become transparent, and I beheld a sight that took my breath away. I am disposed to think that for some moments my brain became so numbed that insensibility ensued, for I am conscious of a blank. When the power of thought returned, I was still holding the bridle of the mare, and she was cropping the grass at her feet. The mill loomed blackly against the night sky. It had resumed its normal appearance again. The wind shrieked about it. The ragged scud raced through the heavens, and the air was filled with the sounds of the raging wind. At first I was inclined to doubt the evidence of my own senses. I tried to reason myself into a belief that my imagination had played me a trick; but I didn't succeed, although the mystery was too profound for my fathoming. So I mounted the mare, urged her to her fastest pace, galloped into Brinton, and entered my house with a feeling of intense relief.

Thoroughly exhausted by the prolonged physical and mental strain I had endured, I speedily sank into a deep though troubled slumber as soon as I got into bed. I was unusually late in rising the next day. I found that I had no appetite for breakfast. Indeed, I felt ill and out of sorts; and, though I busied myself with my professional duties, I was haunted by the strange incidents of the preceding night. Never before in the whole course of my career had I been so impressed, so unnerved, and so dispirited. I wanted to believe that I was still as sceptical as ever, but it was no use. What I had seen might have been unearthly; but I *had seen it*, and it was no use trying to argue myself out of the fact. The result was, in the course of the afternoon I called on my old friend, Mr Goodyear, who was chief of the county constabulary. He was a strong-minded man, and, like myself, a hardened sceptic about all things that smacked of the supernatural.

'Goodyear,' I said, 'I'm out of sorts, and I want you to humour a strange fancy I have. Bring one of your best men, and come with me to the haunted mill. But first let me exact from you a pledge of honour that, if our journey should result in nothing, you will keep the matter secret, as I am very sensitive to ridicule.'

He looked at me in amazement, and then, as he burst into a hearty laugh, exclaimed:

'I say, my friend, you are over-working yourself. It's time you got a *locum tenens*, and took a holiday.'

I told him that I agreed with him; nevertheless, I begged him to humour me, and accompany me to the mill. At last he reluctantly consented to do so, and an hour later we drove out of the town in my dog-cart. There were four of us, as I took Peter, my groom, with me. We had provided ourselves with lanterns, but Goodyear's man and Peter knew nothing of the object of our journey.

When we got abreast of the mill I drew up, and giving the reins to Peter, I alighted, and Goodyear did the same. Taking him on one side, I said, 'I have had a vision, and unless I am the victim of incipient madness we shall find a dead body in the mill.'

The light of the dog-cart was shining full on his face, and I saw the expression of alarm that my words brought.

'Look here, old chap,' he said in a cheery, kindly way, as he put his arm through mine, 'you are not going into that mill, but straight home again. Come, now, get into the cart, and don't let's have any more of this nonsense.'

I felt disposed to yield to him, and had actually placed my foot on the step to mount, when I staggered back and exclaimed:

'My God! am I going mad, or is this a reality?'

Once again I had been struck in the face by the cold clammy some thing; and I saw Goodyear suddenly clap his hand to his face as he cried out—'Hullo, what the deuce is that?'

'Aha,' I exclaimed exultantly, for I no longer thought my brain was giving way, 'you have felt it too?'

'Well, something cold and nasty-like struck me in the face. A bat, I expect. Confound 'em.'

'Bats don't fly at this time of the year,' I replied.

'By Jove, no more they do.'

I approached him, and said in a low tone:

'Goodyear, this is a mystery beyond our solving. I am resolved to go into that mill.'

He was a brave man, though for a moment or two he hesitated; but on my insisting he consented to humour me, and so we lit the lantern, and leaving the groom in charge of the horse and trap, I, Goodyear, and his man made our way with difficulty up the rotting steps, which were slimy and sodden with wet. As we entered the mill an extraordinary scene of desolation and ruin met our gaze as we flashed the light of the lantern about. In places the floor had broken away, leaving yawning chasms of blackness. From the mouldering rafters hung huge festoons of cobwebs. The accumulated dust and dampness of years had given them the appearance of cords. And oh, how the wind moaned eerily through the rifts and crannies and broken windows! We advanced gingerly, for the floor was so rotten we were afraid it would crumble beneath our feet.

My companions were a little bewildered, I think, and were evidently at a loss to know what we had come there for. But some strange feeling impelled me to seek for something; though if I had been asked to define that something, for the life of me I could not have done it. Forward I went, however, taking the lead, and holding the lantern above my head so that its rays might fall afar. But they revealed nothing save the rotting floor and slimy walls. A ladder led to the upper storey, and I expressed my intention of mounting it. Goodyear tried to dissuade me, but I was resolute, and led the way. The ladder was so creaky and fragile that it was not safe for more than one to be on it at a time. When I reachéd the second floor and drew myself up through the trap, I am absolutely certain I heard a sigh. As I turned the lantern round so that its light might sweep every hole and corner of the place, I noticed what seemed to be a sack lying in a corner. I approached and touched it with my foot, and drew back in alarm, for touch and sound told me it contained neither corn nor chaff. I waited until my companions had joined me. Then I said to Goodyear, 'Unless I am mistaken there is something dreadful in that sack.'

He stooped and, whipping out his knife, cut the string which fastened up the mouth of the sack, and revealed a human skull with the hair and shrivelled mummified flesh still adhering to it.

'Great heavens!' he exclaimed, 'here is a human body.'

We held a hurried conversation, and decided to leave the ghastly thing undisturbed until the morrow. So we scuttled down as fast as we could, and went home. I did not return to the mill again myself. My part had been played. Investigation made it absolutely certain that the mouldering remains were those of poor Charley Royce, and it was no less absolutely certain that he had been foully murdered. For not only was there a bullet-hole in the skull but his throat had been cut. It was murder horrible and damnable. The verdict of the coroner's jury pronounced it murder, but there was no evidence to prove who had done the deed. Circumstances, however, pointed to Charley's rival, Silas Hartrop. Was it a guilty conscience that drove him to drink? And did the Furies who avenge such deeds impel him on that dark and stormy night in the North Sea to end the torture of his accursed earthly life? Who can tell?

The Ship that saw a Ghost

by

FRANK NORRIS

The sea, Matthew Arnold's 'unplumb'd, salt, estranging sea', held a fascination for many authors in the Victorian era, both sailors and landsmen. This is hardly surprising, for it symbolised the growth of the Empire, as the British Navy sailed the world and British trade prospered through the sea lanes. One nautical legend beloved by writers was that of the Flying Dutchman, whose blasphemous captain caused the ship to spend eternity trying to round Cape Horn. At least two notable novels were written about the Flying Dutchman, the famous The Phantom Ship *(1839) by Frederick Marryat, and the lesser known but masterly* The Death Ship *(1888) by William Clark Russell.*

Phantom ships formed an enduring fund of sea yarns on both sides of the Atlantic, and I have managed to locate one which seems to have escaped reprinting since its original appearance. It comes from the American author Frank Norris (1870–1902), acclaimed as the great exponent of 'naturalism' in American literature.

Norris was born in Chicago, studied art in Paris and took up journalism as a career. He was a correspondent in South Africa for some time, then covered the American–Spanish war in Cuba in 1898. His first novel, McTeague, *appeared in 1899, and two years later he published what was probably his most famous work,* The Octopus *(1901). This was the first of a projected trilogy,* The Epic of the Wheat, *dealing with the growth of the Californian wheat industry and the resulting struggle between ranchers and railwaymen. Norris managed to complete only two volumes of his trilogy before he died; the second,* The Pit *(1903), appeared posthumously. Another posthumous novel,* Vandover and the Brute *(1914), is acclaimed as a leading work in the macabre vein.*

Frank Norris, from time to time, wrote short stories for American journals, some of which were collected into a forgotten volume, A Deal in Wheat *(1903), from which I have taken 'The Ship that saw a*

Ghost'. It is a fine seafaring tale of the supernatural which has been un-obtainable for many years, and ranks among the best of its kind.

Very much of this story must remain untold, for the reason that if it were definitely known what business I had aboard the tramp steam-freighter *Glarus*, three hundred miles off the South American coast on a certain summer's day, some few years ago, I would very likely be obliged to answer a great many personal and direct questions put by fussy and impertinent experts in maritime law—who are paid to be inquisitive. Also, I would get 'Ally Bazan', Strokher and Hardenberg into trouble.

Suppose on that certain summer's day, you had asked of Lloyds' agency where the *Glarus* was, and what was her destination and cargo. You would have been told that she was twenty days out from Callao, bound north to San Francisco in ballast; that she had been spoken by the bark *Medea* and the steamer *Benevento*; that she was reported to have blown out a cylinder head, but being manageable was proceeding on her way under sail.

That is what Lloyds would have answered.

If you know something of the ways of ships and what is expected of them, you will understand that the *Glarus*, to be some half a dozen hundred miles south of where Lloyds' would have her, and to be still going south, under full steam, was a scandal that would have made her brothers and sisters ostracise her finally and forever.

And that is curious, too. Humans may indulge in vagaries innumerable, and may go far afield in the way of lying; but a ship may not so much as quibble without suspicion. The least lapse of regularity', the least difficulty in squaring performance with intuition, and behold she is on the black list, and her captain, owners, officers, agents and consignors, and even supercargoes, are asked to explain.

And the *Glarus* was already on the black list. From the beginning her stars had been malign. As the *Breda*, she had first lost her reputation, seduced into a filibustering escapade down the South American coast, where in the end a plain-clothes United States detective—that is to say, a revenue cutter—arrested her off Buenos Aires and brought her home, a prodigal daughter, besmirched and disgraced.

After that she was in some dreadful blackbirding business in a far quarter of the South Pacific; and after that—her name changed finally to the *Glarus*—poached seals for a syndicate of Dutchmen who lived in Tacoma, and who afterwards built a club-house out of what she earned.

And after that we got her.

We got her, I say, through Ryder's South Pacific Exploitation Company. The 'President' had picked out a lovely little deal for Hardenberg, Strokher and Ally Bazan (the Three Black Crows), which he swore would make them 'independent rich' the rest of their respective lives. It is a promising deal (B. 300 it is on Ryder's map), and if you want to know more about it you may write to ask Ryder what B. 300 is. If he chooses to tell you, that is his affair.

For B. 300—let us confess it—is, as Hardenberg puts it, as crooked as a dog's hind leg. It is as risky as barratry. If you pull it off you may—after paying Ryder his share—divide sixty-five, or possibly sixty-seven, thousand dollars between you and your associates. If you fail, and you are perilously like to fail, you will be sure to have a man or two of your companions shot, maybe yourself obliged to pistol certain people, and in the end fetch up at Tahiti, prisoner in a French patrolboat.

Observe that B. 300 is spoken of as still open. It is so, for the reason that the Three Black Crows did not pull it off. It still stands marked up in red ink on the map that hangs over Ryder's desk in the San Francisco office; and anyone can have a chance at it who will meet Cyrus Ryder's terms. Only he can't get the *Glarus* for the attempt.

For the trip to the island after B. 300 was the last occasion on which the *Glarus* will smell blue water or taste the trades. She will never clear again. She is lumber.

And yet the *Glarus* on this very blessed day of 1902 is riding to her buoys off Sausalito in San Francisco Bay, complete in every detail (bar a broken propeller shaft), not a rope missing, not a screw loose, not a plank started—a perfectly equipped steam-freighter.

But you may go along the 'Front' in San Francisco from Fisherman's Wharf to the China steamships' docks and shake your dollars under the seamen's noses, and if you so much as whisper *Glarus* they will edge suddenly off and look at you with scared suspicion, and then, as like as not, walk away without another word. No pilot will take the *Glarus* out; no captain will navigate her; no stoker will feed her fires; no sailor will walk her decks. The *Glarus* is suspect. She has seen a ghost.

It happened on our voyage to the island after this same B. 300. We had stood well off from shore for day after day, and Hardenberg had shaped our course so far from the track of navigation that since the *Benevento* had hulled down and vanished over the horizon no stitch of canvas nor smudge of smoke had we seen. We had passed the equator long since, and would fetch a long circuit to the southard, and bear up against the island by a circuitous route. This to avoid being spoken. It was tremendously essential that the *Glarus* should not be spoken.

I suppose, no doubt, that it was the knowledge of our isolation that impressed me with the dreadful remoteness of our position. Certainly the sea in itself looks no different at a thousand than at a hundred miles from shore. But as day after day I came out on deck at noon, after ascertaining our position on the chart (a mere pin-point in a reach of empty paper), the sight of the ocean weighed down upon me with an infinitely great awesomeness—and I was no new hand to the high seas even then.

But at such times the *Glarus* seemed to me to be threading a loneliness beyond all worlds and beyond all conception desolate. Even in more populous waters, when no sail notches the line of the horizon, the propinquity of one's kind is nevertheless a thing understood, and to an unappreciated degree comforting. Here, however, I knew we were out, far out in the desert. Never a keel for years upon years before us had parted these waters; never a sail had bellied to these winds. Perfunctorily, day in and day out we turned our eyes through long habit towards the horizon. But we knew, before the look, that the searching would be bootless. Forever and forever, under the pitiless sun and cold blue sky stretched the indigo of the ocean floor. The ether between the planets can be no less empty, no less void.

I never, till that moment, could have so much as conceived the imagination of such loneliness, such utter stagnant abomination of desolation. In an open boat, bereft of comrades, I should have gone mad in thirty minutes.

I remember to have approximated the impression of such empty immensity only once before, in my younger days, when I lay on my back on a treeless, bushless mountainside and stared up into the sky for the better part of an hour.

You probably know the trick. If you do not, you must understand that if you look up at the blue long enough, the flatness of the thing begins little by little to expand, to give here and there; and the eye travels on and on and up and up, till at length (well for you that it lasts but the fraction of a second), you all at once see space. You generally stop there and cry out, and—your hands over your eyes—are only too glad to grovel close to the good old solid earth again. Just as I, so often on short voyage, was glad to wrench my eyes away from that horrid vacancy, to fasten them upon our sailless masts and stack, or to lay my grip upon the sooty smudged taffrail of the only thing that stood between me and the Outer Dark.

For we had come at last to that region of the Great Seas where no ship goes, the silent sea of Coleridge and the Ancient One, the unplumbed, untracked, uncharted Dreadfulness, primordial, hushed, and we were as much alone as a grain of star-dust whirling in the empty space beyond Uranus and the ken of the greater telescopes.

So the *Glarus* plodded and churned her way onwards. Every day and all day the same pale-blue sky and the unwinking sun bent over that moving speck. Every day and all day the same black-blue water-world, untouched by any known wind, smooth as a slab of syenite, colourful as an opal, stretched out and around and beyond and before and behind us, forever, illimitable, empty. Every day the smoke of our fires veiled the streaked whiteness of our wake. Every day Hardenberg (our skipper) at noon pricked a pin-hole in the chart that hung in the wheel-house, and that showed we were so much farther into the wilderness. Every day the world of men, of civilisation, of newspapers, policemen and street-railways receded, and we steamed on alone, lost and forgotten in that silent sea.

'Jolly lot o' room to turn raound in,' observed Ally Bazan, the colonial, 'withaout steppin' on y'r neighbour's toes.'

'We're clean, clean out o' the track o' navigation,' Hardenberg told him. 'An' a blessed good thing for us, too. Nobody ever comes down into these waters. Ye couldn't pick no course here. Everything leads to nowhere.'

'Might as well be in a bally balloon,' said Strokher.

I shall not tell of the nature of the venture on which the *Glarus* was bound, further than to say it was not legitimate. It had to do with an ill thing done more than two centuries ago. There was money in the venture, but it was not to be gained by a violation of metes and bounds which are better left intact.

The island towards which we were heading is associated in the minds of men with a Horror. A ship had called there once, two hundred years in advance of the *Glarus*—a ship not much unlike the crank high-powered caravel of Hudson, and her company had landed, and having accomplished the evil they had set out to do, made shift to sail away. And then, just after the palms of the island had sunk from sight below the water's edge, the unspeakable had happened. The Death that was not Death had arisen from out the sea and stood before the ship, and over it, and the blight of the thing lay along the decks like mould, and the ship sweated in the terror of that which is yet without a name.

Twenty men died in the first week, all but six in the second. These six, with the shadow of insanity upon them, made out to launch a boat, returned to the island and died there, after leaving a record of what had happened.

The six left the ship exactly as she was, sails all set, lanterns all lit—left her in the shadow of the Death that was not Death.

She stood there, becalmed, and watched them go. She was never heard of again.

Or was she—well, that's as may be.

But the main point of the whole affair, to my notion, has always been this. The ship was the last friend of those six poor wretches who made back for the island with their poor chests of plunder. She was their guardian, as it were, would have defended and befriended them to the last; and also we, the Three Black Crows and myself, had no right under heaven, nor before the law of men, to come prying and peeping into this business—into this affair of the dead and buried past. There was sacrilege in it. We were no better than body-snatchers.

When I heard the others complaining of the loneliness of our surroundings, I said nothing at first. I was no sailor man, and I was on board only by tolerance. But I looked again at the maddening sameness of the horizon—the same vacant, void horizon that we had seen now for sixteen days on end, and felt in my wits and in my nerves that same formless rebellion and protest such as comes when the same note is reiterated over and over again.

It may seem a little thing that the mere fact of meeting with no other ship should have ground down the edge of the spirit. But let the incredulous—bound upon such a hazard as ours—sail straight into nothingness for sixteen days on end, seeing nothing but the sun, hearing nothing but the thresh of his own screw, and then put the question.

And yet, of all things, we desired no company. Stealth was our one great aim. But I think there were moments—towards the last—when the Three Crows would have welcomed even a cruiser.

Besides, there was more cause for depression, after all, than mere isolation.

On the seventh day Hardenberg and I were forward by the cat-head, adjusting the grain with some half-formed intent of spearing the porpoises that of late had begun to appear under our bows, and Hardenberg had been computing the number of days we were yet to run.

'We are some five hundred odd miles off that island by now,' he said, 'and she's doing her thirteen knots handsome. All's well so far—but do you know, I'd just as soon raise that point o' land as soon as convenient.'

'How so?' said I, bending on the line. 'Expect some weather?'

'Mr Dixon,' said he, giving me a curious glance, 'the sea is a queer proposition, put it any ways. I've been a seafarin' man since I was big as a minute, and I know the sea, and what's more, the Feel o' the Sea. Now, look out yonder. Nothin', hey? Nothin' but the same ol' skyline we've watched all the way out. The glass is as steady as a steeple, and this ol' hooker, I reckon, is as sound as the day she went off the ways. But just the same if I were to home now, a-foolin' about Gloucester way in my little dough-dish—d'ye know what? I'd put into port. I sure would. Because why? Because I got the Feel o' the Sea, Mr Dixon. I got the Feel o' the Sea.'

I had heard old skippers say something of this before, and I cited to Hardenberg the experience of a skipper captain I once knew who had turned turtle in a calm sea off Trincomalee. I ask him what this Feel of the Sea was warning him against just now (for on the high sea any premonition is a premonition of evil, not of good). But he was not explicit.

'I don't know,' he answered moodily, and as if in great perplexity, coiling the rope as he spoke. 'I don't know. There's some blame thing or other close to us, I'll bet a hat. I don't know the name of it, but there's a big Bird in the air, just out of sight som'eres, and,' he suddenly exclaimed, smacking his knee and leaning forward, 'I—don't—like—it—one—dam'—bit.'

The same thing came up in our talk in the cabin that night, after the dinner was taken off and we settled down to tobacco. Only, at this time, Hardenberg was on duty on the bridge. It was Ally Bazan who spoke instead.

'Seems to me,' he hazarded, 'as haow they's somethin' or other a-goin' to bump up pretty blyme soon. I shouldn't be surprised, naow, y'know, if we piled her on some bally uncharted reef along o' to-night and went strite daown afore we'd had a bloomin' charnce to s'y "So long, gen'lemen all."'

He laughed as he spoke, but when, just at that moment, a pan clattered in the galley, he jumped suddenly with an oath, and looked hard about the cabin.

Then Strokher confessed to a sense of distress also. He'd been having it since the day before yesterday, it seemed.

'And I put it to you the glass is lovely,' he said, 'so it's no blow. I guess,' he continued, 'we're all a bit seedy and ship-sore.'

And whether or not this talk worked upon my own nerves, or whether in very truth the Feel of the Sea had found me also, I do not know; but I do know that after dinner that night, just before going to bed, a queer sense of apprehension came upon me, and that when I had come to my stateroom, after my turn upon deck, I became furiously angry with nobody in particular, because I could not at once find the matches. But here was a difference. The other man had been merely vaguely uncomfortable.

I could put a name to my uneasiness. I felt that we were being watched.

It was a strange ship's company we made after that. I speak only of the Crows and myself. We carried a scant crew of stokers, and there was also a chief engineer. But we saw so little of him that he did not count. The Crows and I gloomed on the quarterdeck from dawn to dark, silent, irritable, working upon each other's nerves till the creak of a block would make a man jump like cold steel laid to his flesh. We quarrelled over absolute nothings, glowered at each other for half a word, and each one of us, at different times, was at some pains to declare that never in the course of his career had he been associated with such a disagreeable trio of brutes. Yet we were always together, and sought each other's company with painful insistence.

Only once were we all agreed, and that was when the cook, a Chinaman, spoiled a certain batch of biscuits. Unanimously we fell foul of the creature with so much vociferation as fishwives till he fled the cabin in actual fear of mishandling, leaving us suddenly seized with noisy hilarity—for the first time in a week. Hardenberg proposed a round of drinks from our single remaining case of beer. We stood up and formed an Elk's chain and then drained our glasses to each other's health with profound seriousness.

That same evening, I remember, we all sat on the quarterdeck till late and—oddly enough—related each one his life's history up to date; and then went down to the cabin for a game of euchre before turning in.

We had left Strokher on the bridge—it was his watch—and had forgotten all about him in the interest of the game, when—I suppose it was about one in the morning—I heard him whistle long and shrill. I laid down my cards and said:

'Hark!'

In the silence that followed we heard at first only the muffled lope of our engines, the cadenced snorting of the exhaust, and the ticking of Hardenberg's big watch in his waistcoat that he had hung by the arm-hole to the back of his chair. Then from the bridge, above our deck, prolonged, intoned—a wailing cry in the night—came Strokher's voice:

'Sail oh-h-h.'

And the cards fell from our hands, and, like men turned to stone, we sat looking at each other across the soiled red cloth for what seemed an immeasurably long minute.

Then stumbling and swearing, in a hysteria of hurry, we gained the deck.

There was a moon, very low and reddish, but no wind. The sea beyond the taffrail was as smooth as lava, and so still that the swells from the cutwater of the *Glarus* did not break as they rolled away from the bows.

I remember that I stood staring and blinking at the empty ocean— where the moonlight lay like a painted stripe reaching to the horizon —stupid and frowning, till Hardenberg, who had gone on ahead cried:

'Not here—on the bridge!'

We joined Strokher, and as I came up the others were asking:

'Where? Where?'

And there, before he had pointed, I saw—we all of us saw—— And I heard Hardenberg's teeth come together like a spring trap, while Ally Bazan ducked as though to a blow, muttering:

'Gord 'a' mercy, what nyme do ye put to a ship like that?'

And after that no one spoke for a long minute, and we stood there, moveless black shadows, huddled together for the sake of the blessed elbow touch that means so incalculably much, looking off over our port quarter.

For the ship that we saw there—oh, she was not a half-mile distant— was unlike any ship known to present-day construction.

She was short, and high-pooped, and her stern, which was turned a little towards us, we could see, was set with curious windows, not unlike a house. And on either side of this stern were two great iron cressets such as once were used to burn signal-fires in. She had three masts with mighty yards swung 'thwart ship, but bare of all sails save a few rotting streamers. Here and there about her a tangled mass of rigging drooped and sagged.

And there she lay, in the red eye of the setting moon, in that solitary ocean, shadowy, antique, forlorn, a thing the most abandoned, the most sinister I ever remember to have seen.

Then Strokher began to explain volubly and with many repetitions.

'A derelict, of course. I was asleep; yes, I was asleep. Gross neglect of duty. I say I was asleep—on watch. And we worked up to her. When I woke, why—you see, when I woke, there she was,' he gave a weak little laugh, 'and—and now, why, there she is, you see. I turned around and saw her sudden like—when I woke up, that is.'

He laughed again, and as he laughed the engines far below our feet gave a sudden hiccough. Something crashed and struck the ship's sides till we lurched as we stood. There was a shriek of steam, a shout—and then silence.

The noise of the machinery ceased; the *Glarus* slid through the still water, moving only by her own decreasing momentum.

Hardenberg sang, 'Stand by!' and called down the tube to the engine-room.

'What's up?'

I was standing close enough to him to hear the answer in a small, faint voice:

'Shaft gone, sir.'

'Broke?'

'Yes, sir.'

Hardenberg faced about.

'Come below. We must talk.' I do not think any of us cast a glance at the Other Ship again. Certainly I kept my eyes away from her. But as we started down the companionway I laid my hand on Strokher's shoulder. The rest were ahead. I looked him straight between the eyes as I asked:

'Were you asleep? Is that why you saw her so suddenly?'

It is now five years since I asked the question. I am still waiting for Strokher's answer.

Well, our shaft was broken. That was flat. We went down into the engine-room and saw the jagged fracture that was the symbol of our broken hopes. And in the course of the next five minutes' conversation with the chief we found that, as we had not provided against such a contingency, there was to be no mending of it. We said nothing about the mishap coinciding with the appearance of the Other Ship. But I know we did not consider the break with any degree of surprise after a few moments.

We came up from the engine-room and sat down to the cabin table.

'Now what?' said Hardenberg, by way of beginning.

Nobody answered at first.

It was by now three in the morning. I recall it all perfectly. The ports opposite where I sat were open and I could see. The moon was all but full set. The dawn was coming up with a copper murkiness over the edge of the world. All the stars were yet out. The sea, for all the red moon and copper dawn, was grey, and there, less than half a mile away, still lay our consort. I could see her through the portholes with each slow careening of the *Glarus*.

'I vote for the island,' cried Ally Bazan, 'shaft or no shaft. We rigs a bit o' syle, y'know——' and thereat the discussion began.

For upwards of two hours it raged, with loud words and shaken forefingers, and great noisy bangings of the table, and how it would have ended I do not know, but at last—it was then maybe five in the morning—the lookout passed word down to the cabin:

'Will you come on deck, gentlemen?' It was the mate who spoke, and the man was shaken—I could see that—to the very vitals of him. We started and stared at one another, and I watched little Ally Bazan go slowly white to the lips. And even then no word of the ship, except as it might be this from Hardenberg:

'What is it? Good God Almighty, I'm no coward, but this thing is getting one too many for me.'

Then without further speech he went on deck.

The air was cool. The sun was not yet up. It was that strange, queer mid-period between dark and dawn, when the night is over and the day not yet come, just the grey that is neither light nor dark, the dim dead blink as of the refracted light from extinct worlds.

We stood at the rail. We did not speak; we stood watching. It was so still that the drip of steam from some loosened pipe far below was plainly audible, and it sounded in that lifeless, silent greyness like— God knows what—a death tick.

'You see,' said the mate, speaking just above a whisper, 'there's no mistake about it. She is moving—this way.'

'Oh, a current, of course,' Strokher tried to say cheerfully, 'sets her towards us.'

Would the morning never come?

Ally Bazan—his parents were Catholic—began to mutter to himself. Then Hardenberg spoke aloud.

'I particularly don't want—that—out—there—to cross our bows. I don't want it to come to that. We must get some sails on her.'

'And I put it to you as man to man,' said Strokher, 'where might be your wind?'

He was right. The *Glarus* floated in absolute calm. On all that slab of ocean nothing moved but the Dead Ship.

She came on slowly; her bows, the high, clumsy bows pointed towards us, the water turning from her forefoot. She came on; she was near at hand. We saw her plainly—saw the rotted planks, the crumbling rigging, the rust-corroded metal-work, the broken rail, the gaping deck, and I could imagine that the clean water broke away from her sides in refluent wavelets as though in recoil from a thing unclean. She made no sound. No single thing stirred aboard the hulk of her— but she moved.

We were helpless. The *Glarus* could stir no boat in any direction; we were chained to the spot. Nobody had thought to put out our lights, and they still burned on through the dawn, strangely out of place in their red-and-green garishness, like maskers surprised by daylight.

And in the silence of that empty ocean, in that queer half-light between dawn and day, at six o'clock, silent as the settling of the dead to the bottomless bottom of the ocean, grey as fog, lonely, blind, soulless, voiceless, the Dead Ship crossed our bows.

I do not know how long after this the Ship disappeared, or what was the time of day when we at last pulled ourselves together. But we came to some sort of decision at last. This was to go on—under sail. We were too close to the island now to turn back for—for a broken shaft.

The afternoon was spent fitting on the sails to her, and when after nightfall the wind at length came up fresh and favourable, I believe we all felt heartened and a deal more hardy—until the last canvas went aloft, and Hardenberg took the wheel.

We had drifted a good deal since the morning, and the bows of the *Glarus* were pointed homewards, but as soon as the breeze blew strong enough to get steerageway Hardenberg put the wheel over and, as the booms swung across the deck, headed for the island again.

We had not gone on this course half an hour—no, not twenty minutes—before the wind shifted a whole quarter of the compass and took the *Glarus* square in the teeth, so that there was nothing for it but to tack. And then the strangest thing befell.

I will make allowance for the fact that there was no centre-board nor keel to speak of to the *Glarus*. I will admit that the sails upon a nine-hundred-ton freighter are not calculated to speed her, nor steady her. I will even admit the possibility of a current that set from the island towards us. All this may be true, yet the *Glarus* should have advanced. We should have made a wake.

And instead of this, our stolid, steady, trusty old boat was—what shall I say?

I will say that no man may thoroughly understand a ship—after all. I will say that new ships are cranky and unsteady; that old and seasoned ships have their little crochets, their little fussinesses that their skippers must learn and humour if they are to get anything out of them; that even the best ships may sulk at times, shirk their work, grow unstable, perverse, and refuse to answer helm and handling. And I will say that some ships that for years have sailed blue water as soberly and as docilely as a street-car horse has plodded the treadmill of the 'tween-tracks, have been known to balk, as stubbornly and as conclusively as any old Bay Billy that ever wore a bell. I know this has happened, because I have seen it. I saw, for instance, the *Glarus* do it.

Quite literally and truly we could do nothing with her. We will say, if you like, that that great jar and wrench when the shaft gave way shook her and crippled her. It is true, however, that whatever the cause may have been, we could not force her towards the island. Of course, we all said 'current'; but why didn't the log-line trail?

For three days and three nights we tried it. And the *Glarus* heaved and plunged and shook herself just as you have seen a horse plunge and rear when his rider tries to force him at the steam-roller.

I tell you I could feel the fabric of her tremble and shudder from bow to stern-post, as though she were in a storm; I tell you she fell off from the wind, and broad-on drifted back from her course till the sensation of her shrinking was as plain as her own staring lights and a thing pitiful to see.

We rowelled her, and we crowded sail upon her, and we coaxed and bullied and humoured her, till the Three Crows, their fortune only a plain sail two days ahead, raved and swore like insensate brutes, or shall we say like mahouts trying to drive their stricken elephant upon the tiger—and all to no purpose. 'Damn the damned current and the damned luck and the damned shaft and all,' Hardenberg would exclaim, as from the wheel he would catch the *Glarus* falling off. 'Go on, you old hooker—you tub of junk! My God, you'd think she was scared!'

Perhaps the *Glarus* was scared, perhaps not; that point is debatable. But it was beyond doubt of debate that Hardenberg was scared.

A ship that will not obey is only one degree less terrible than a mutinous crew. And we were in a fair way to have both. The stokers, whom we had impressed into duty as A.B.'s, were of course superstitious; and they knew how the *Glarus* was acting, and it was only a question of time before they got out of hand.

That was the end. We held a final conference in the cabin and decided that there was no help for it—we must turn back.

And back we accordingly turned, and at once the wind followed us, and the 'current' helped us, and the water churned under the forefoot of the *Glarus*, and the wake whitened under her stern, and the log-line ran out from the trail and strained back as the ship worked homewards.

We had never a mishap from the time we finally swung her about; and considering the circumstances, the voyage back to San Francisco was propitious.

But an incident happened just after we had started back. We were perhaps some five miles on the homeward track. It was early evening and Strokher had the watch. At about seven o'clock he called me up on the bridge.

'See her?' he said.

And there, far behind us, in the shadow of the twilight, loomed the Other Ship again, desolate, lonely beyond words. We were leaving her rapidly astern. Strokher and I stood looking at her till she dwindled to a dot. Then Strokher said:

'She's on post again.'

And when months afterwards we limped into the Golden Gate and cast anchor off the 'Front' our crew went ashore as soon as discharged, and in half a dozen hours the legend was in every sailors' boarding-house and in every seaman's dive, from Barbary Coast to Black Tom's.

It is still there, and that is why no pilot will take the *Glarus* out, no captain will navigate her, no stoker feed her fires, no sailor walk her decks. The *Glarus* is suspect. She will never smell blue water again, nor taste the trades. She has seen a Ghost.

A Bottomless Grave

and

One Summer Night

by

AMBROSE BIERCE

*If Frank Norris was the great exponent of naturalism in American liter-
ature, then his fellow countryman Ambrose Bierce was undoubtedly the
greatest exponent of cynicism. He was a journalist and writer who
earned himself the nickname of 'Bitter' Bierce, and who specialised in the
most vitriolic articles and stories of his day. In an era when American
journalism was noted for its wholehearted exploitation of the absence of
any laws of libel and journalists sometimes carried guns which they needed
to use, Bierce stands head and shoulders above his fellows as the ultimate
cynic.*

*Ambrose Bierce (1842–1913) was born into an exceedingly strange
family, which could claim a member who had led an unsuccessful expedition in 1838 to liberate Canada from the British. His father was an odd
character who carried out his pet project of naming his children (thirteen
in all) each with a name beginning with the letter 'A'.*

*Bierce left home at the outbreak of the American civil war and dis-
tinguished himself as a soldier in that conflict. His stories of the war are
still among the best written on that subject by a participant and carry even
more conviction than those of Crane or Whitman. Following the war, and
a brief interlude mining gold in the Black Hills of Dakota, Bierce became
a journalist and took to the American style of editorial assassination then
in vogue like a 'hog to the wallow' to quote one critic. In 1887 he was
offered a job by William Randolph Hearst, the beginning of a relationship with the famous publisher that lasted over twenty years.*

*Bierce did not age well; the older he got, the more bitter and cynical he
became, destroying personal friendships with the same cruel perversity
with which he was prone to destroy lesser writers whose works he re-
viewed. In 1913 he went to Mexico, presumably to report on the civil
war, and he disappeared without trace. This sensational disappearance
has done as much to keep his name alive as his writing ever did.*

In the realms of Victorian literature, Bierce stands almost alone in his attitude to life and humanity. In story after story, he revealed his distaste for his fellow man, his impatience with others and his refusal to indulge in any sort of relationship of which he was not the absolute master. His ghost stories are unique; they neither follow any previous author, such as Poe, nor have they been imitated since. Here are two of his stories, rare items both, one of which is in the genuinely shocking humorous vein that Bierce was fond of, and the other a grisly little piece of graveyard antics. Both tell all about their author; in Ambrose Bierce we find the Victorian era's most shockingly cynical and alarming writer.

A BOTTOMLESS GRAVE

My name is John Brenwalter. My father, a drunkard, had a patent for an invention for making coffee-berries out of clay; but he was an honest man and would not himself engage in the manufacture. He was, therefore, only moderately wealthy, his royalties from his really valuable invention bringing him hardly enough to pay his expenses of litigation with rogues guilty of infringement. So I lacked many advantages enjoyed by the children of unscrupulous and dishonourable parents, and had it not been for a noble and devoted mother, who neglected all my brothers and sisters and personally supervised my education, should have grown up in ignorance and been compelled to teach school. To be the favourite child of a good woman is better than gold.

When I was nineteen years of age my father had the misfortune to die. He had always had perfect health, and his death, which occurred at the dinner table without a moment's warning, surprised no one more than himself. He had that very morning been notified that a patent had been granted him for a device to burst open safes by hydraulic pressure, without noise. The Commissioner of Patents had pronounced it the most ingenious, effective and generally meritorious invention that had ever been submitted to him, and my father had naturally looked forward to an old age of prosperity and honour. His sudden death was, therefore, a deep disappointment to him; but my mother, whose piety and resignation to the will of Heaven were conspicuous virtues of her character, was apparently less affected. At the close of the meal, when my poor father's body had been removed from the floor, she called us all into an adjoining room and addressed us as follows:

'My children, the uncommon occurrence that you have just witnessed is one of the most disagreeable incidents in a good man's life, and one in which I take little pleasure, I assure you. I beg you to believe that I had no hand in bringing it about. Of course,' she added, after a pause, during which her eyes were cast down in deep thought, 'of course it is better that he is dead.'

She uttered this with so evident a sense of its obviousness as a self-evident truth that none of us had the courage to brave her surprise by asking an explanation. My mother's air of surprise when any of us went wrong in any way was very terrible to us. One day, when in a fit of peevish temper, I had taken the liberty to cut off the baby's ear, her simple words, 'John, you surprise me!' appeared to me so sharp a reproof that after a sleepless night I went to her in tears, and throwing myself at her feet, exclaimed: 'Mother, forgive me for surprising you.' So now we all—including the one-eared baby—felt that it would keep matters smoother to accept without question the statement that it was better, somehow, for our dear father to be dead. My mother continued:

'I must tell you, my children, that in a case of sudden and mysterious death the law requires the Coroner to come and cut the body into pieces and submit them to a number of men who, having inspected them, pronounce the person dead. For this the Coroner gets a large sum of money. I wish to avoid that painful formality in this instance; it is one which never had the approval of—of the remains. John'—here my mother turned her angel face to me—'you are an educated lad, and very discreet. You have now an opportunity to show your gratitude for all the sacrifices that your education has entailed upon the rest of us. John, go and remove the Coroner.'

Inexpressibly delighted by this proof of my mother's confidence, and by the chance to distinguish myself by an act that squared with my natural disposition, I knelt before her, carried her hand to my lips and bathed it with tears of sensibility. Before five o'clock that afternoon I had removed the Coroner.

I was immediately arrested and thrown into jail, where I passed a most uncomfortable night, being unable to sleep because of the profanity of my fellow-prisoners, two clergymen, whose theological training had given them a fertility of impious ideas and a command of blasphemous language altogether unparalleled. But along towards morning the jailer, who, sleeping in an adjoining room, had been equally disturbed, entered the cell and with a fearful oath warned the reverend gentlemen that if he heard any more swearing their sacred calling would not prevent him from turning them into the street. After that they moderated their objectionable conversation, substituting an accordion, and I slept the peaceful and refreshing sleep of youth and innocence.

The next morning I was taken before the Superior Judge, sitting as a committing magistrate, and put upon my preliminary examination. I pleaded not guilty, adding that the man whom I had murdered was a notorious Democrat. (My good mother was a Republican, and from early childhood I had been carefully instructed by her in the principles of honest government and the necessity of suppressing factional opposition.) The Judge, elected by a Republican ballot-box with a sliding bottom, was visibly impressed by the cogency of my plea and offered me a cigarette.

'May it please your Honour,' began the District Attorney, 'I do not deem it necessary to submit any evidence in this case. Under the law of the land you sit here as a committing magistrate. It is therefore your duty to commit. Testimony and argument alike would imply a doubt that your Honour means to perform your sworn duty. That is my case.'

My counsel, a brother of the deceased Coroner, rose and said: 'May it please the Court, my learned friend on the other side has so well and eloquently stated the law governing in this case that it only remains for me to inquire to what extent it has been already complied with. It is true, your Honour is a committing magistrate, and as such it is your duty to commit—what? That is a matter which the law has wisely and justly left to your own discretion, and wisely you have discharged already every obligation that the law imposes. Since I have known your Honour you have done nothing but commit. You have committed embracery, theft, arson, perjury, adultery, murder—every crime in the calendar and every excess known to the sensual and depraved, including my learned friend, the District Attorney. You have done your whole duty as a comitting magistrate, and as there is no evidence against this worthy young man, my client, I move that he be discharged.'

An impressive silence ensued. The Judge arose, put on the black cap and in a voice trembling with emotion sentenced me to life and liberty. Then turning to my counsel he said, coldly but significantly:

'I will see you later.'

The next morning the lawyer who had so conscientiously defended me against a charge of murdering his own brother—with whom he had a quarrel about some land—had disappeared and his fate is to this day unknown.

In the meantime my poor father's body had been secretly buried at midnight in the back yard of his late residence, with his late boots on and the contents of his late stomach unanalysed. 'He was opposed to display,' said my dear mother, as she finished tamping down the earth above him and assisted the children to litter the place with straw; 'his instincts were all domestic and he loved a quiet life.'

My mother's application for letters of administration stated that she had good reason to believe that the deceased was dead, for he had not come home to his meals for several days; but the Judge of the Crowbait Court—as he ever afterwards contemptuously called it—decided that the proof of death was insufficient, and put the estate into the hands of the Public Administrator, who was his son-in-law. It was found that the liabilities were exactly balanced by the assets; there was left only the patent for the device for bursting open safes without noise, by hydraulic pressure and this had passed into the ownership of the Probate Judge and the Public Administrator—as my dear mother preferred to spell it. Thus, within a few brief months a worthy and respectable family was reduced from prosperity to crime; necessity compelled us to go to work.

In the selection of occupations we were governed by a variety of considerations, such as personal fitness, inclination, and so forth. My mother opened a select private school for instruction in the art of changing the spots upon leopard-skin rugs; my eldest brother, George Henry, who had a turn for music, became a bugler in a neighbouring asylum for deaf mutes; my sister, Mary Maria, took orders for Professor Pumpernickel's Essence of Latchkeys for flavouring mineral springs, and I set up as an adjuster and gilder of crossbeams for gibbets. The other children, too young for labour, continued to steal small articles exposed in front of shops, as they had been taught.

In our intervals of leisure we decoyed travellers into our house and buried the bodies in a cellar.

In one part of this cellar we kept wines, liquors and provisions. From the rapidity of their disappearance we acquired the superstitious belief that the spirits of the persons buried there came at dead of night and held a festival. It was at least certain that frequently of a morning we would discover fragments of pickled meats, canned goods and such débris, littering the place, although it had been securely locked and barred against human intrusion. It was proposed to remove the provisions and store them elsewhere, but our dear mother, always generous and hospitable, said it was better to endure the loss than risk exposure:

if the ghosts were denied this trifling gratification they might set on foot an investigation, which would overthrow our scheme of the division of labour, by diverting the energies of the whole family into the single industry pursued by me—we might all decorate the cross-beams of gibbets. We accepted her decision with filial submission, due to our reverence for her worldly wisdom and the purity of her character.

One night while we are all in the cellar—none dared to enter it alone —engaged in bestowing upon the Mayor of an adjoining town the solemn offices of Christian burial, my mother and the younger children, holding a candle each, while George Henry and I laboured with a spade and pick, my sister Mary Maria uttered a shriek and covered her eyes with her hands. We were all dreadfully startled and the Mayor's obsequies were instantly suspended, while with pale faces and in trembling tones we begged her to say what had alarmed her. The younger children were so agitated that they held their candles un-steadily, and the waving shadows of our figures danced with uncouth and grotesque movements on the walls and flung themselves into the most uncanny attitudes. The face of the dead man, now gleaming ghastly in the light, and now extinguished by some floating shadow, appeared at each emergence to have taken on a new and more for-bidding expression, a maligner menace. Frightened even more than ourselves by the girl's scream, rats raced in multitudes about the place, squeaking shrilly, or starred the black opacity of some distant corner with steadfast eyes, mere points of green light, matching the faint phosphorescence of decay that filled the half-dug grave and seemed the visible manifestation of that faint odour of mortality which tainted the unwholesome air. The children now sobbed and clung about the limbs of their elders, dropping their candles, and we were near being left in total darkness, except for that sinister light, which slowly welled up-wards from the disturbed earth and overflowed the edges of the grave like a fountain.

Meanwhile my sister, crouching in the earth that had been thrown out of the excavation, had removed her hands from her face and was staring with expanded eyes into an obscure space between two wine casks.

'There it is!—there it is!' she shrieked, pointing; 'God in heaven! can't you see it?'

And there indeed it was!—a human figure, dimly discernible in the gloom—a figure that wavered from side to side as if about to fall, clutching at the wine-casks for support, had stepped unsteadily forwards and for one moment stood revealed in the light of our remaining candles; then it surged heavily and fell prone upon the earth. In that moment we had all recognised the figure, the face and bearing of our father—dead these ten months and buried by our own hands!—our father indubitably risen and ghastly drunk!

On the incidents of our precipitate flight from that horrible place— on the extinction of all human sentiment in that tumultuous, mad scramble up the damp and mouldy stairs—slipping, falling, pulling one another down and clambering over one another's back—the lights extinguished, babes trampled beneath the feet of their strong brothers and hurled backwards to death by a mother's arm!—on all this I do not dare to dwell. My mother, my eldest brother and sister and I escaped; the others remained below, to perish of their wounds, or of their terror—some, perhaps, by flame. For within an hour we four, hastily gathering together what money and jewels we had and what clothing we could carry, fired the dwelling and fled by its light into the hills. We did not even pause to collect the insurance, and my dear mother said on her death-bed, years afterwards in a distant land, that this was the only sin of omission that lay upon her conscience. Her confessor, a holy man, assured her that under the circumstances Heaven would pardon the neglect.

About ten years after our removal from the scenes of my childhood I, then a prosperous forger, returned in disguise to the spot with a view to obtaining, if possible, some treasure belonging to us, which had been buried in the cellar. I may say that I was unsuccessful: the dis-covery of many human bones in the ruins had set the authorities digging for more. They had found the treasure and had kept it for their honesty. The house had not been rebuilt; the whole suburb was, in fact, a desolation. So many unearthly sights and sounds had been reported thereabout that nobody would live there. As there was none to question nor molest, I resolved to gratify my filial piety by gazing once more upon the face of my beloved father, if indeed our eyes had deceived us and he was still in his grave. I remembered, too, that he had always worn an enormous diamond ring, and never having seen it nor heard of it since his death, I had reason to think he might have been buried in it. Procuring a spade, I soon located the grave in what had been the backyard and began digging. When I had got down about four feet the whole bottom fell out of the grave and I was precipitated into a large drain, falling through a long hole in its crumbling arch. There was no body, nor any vestige of one.

Unable to get out of the excavation, I crept through the drain, and having with some difficulty removed a mass of charred rubbish and blackened masonry that choked it, emerged into what had been that fateful cellar.

All was clear. My father, whatever had caused him to be 'taken bad' at his meal (and I think my sainted mother could have thrown some light upon that matter) had indubitably been buried alive. The grave having been accidentally dug above the forgotten drain, and down almost to the crown of its arch, and no coffin having been used, his struggles on reviving had broken the rotten masonry and he had fallen through, escaping finally into the cellar. Feeling that he was not welcome in his own house, yet having no other, he had lived in subterranean seclusion, a witness to our thrift and a pensioner on our providence. It was he who had eaten our food; it was he who had drunk our wine—he was no better than a thief! In a moment of intoxication, and feeling, no doubt, that need of companionship which is the one sympathetic link between a drunken man and his race, he had left his place of concealment at a strangely inopportune time, entailing the most deplorable consequences upon those nearest and dearest to him—a blunder that had almost the dignity of crime.

ONE SUMMER NIGHT

The fact that Henry Armstrong was buried did not seem to him to prove that he was dead: he had always been a hard man to convince. That he really was buried, the testimony of his senses compelled him to admit. His posture—flat upon his back, with his hands crossed upon his stomach and tied with something that he easily broke without profitably altering the situation—the strict confinement of his entire person, the black darkness and profound silence, made a body of evidence impossible to controvert and he accepted it without cavil.

But dead—no; he was only very, very ill. He had, withal, the invalid's apathy and did not greatly concern himself about the uncommon fate that had been allotted to him. No philosopher was he—just a plain, commonplace person gifted, for the time being, with a pathological indifference: the organ that he feared consequences with was torpid. So, with no particular apprehension for his immediate future, he fell asleep and all was peace with Henry Armstrong.

But something was going on overhead. It was a dark summer night, shot through with infrequent shimmers of lightning silently firing a cloud lying low in the west and portending a storm. These brief, stammering illuminations brought out with ghastly distinctness the monuments and headstones of the cemetery and seemed to set them dancing. It was not a night in which any credible witness was likely to be straying about a cemetery, so the three men who were there, digging into the grave of Henry Armstrong, felt reasonably secure.

Two of them were young students from a medical college a few miles away; the third was a gigantic negro known as Jess. For many years Jess had been employed about the cemetery as a man-of-all-work and it was his favourite pleasantry that he knew 'every soul in the place'. From the nature of what he was now doing it was inferable that the place was not so populous as its register may have shown it to be.

Outside the wall, at the part of the grounds farthest from the public road, were a horse and a light wagon, waiting.

The work of excavation was not difficult: the earth with which the grave had been loosely filled a few hours before offered little resistance and was soon thrown out. Removal of the casket from its box was less easy, but it was taken out, for it was a perquisite of Jess, who carefully unscrewed the cover and laid it aside, exposing the body in black

trousers and white shirt. At that instant the air sprang to flame, a crack-
ing shock of thunder shook the stunned world and Henry Armstrong
tranquilly sat up. With inarticulate cries the men fled in terror, each in
a different direction. For nothing on earth could two of them have
been persuaded to return. But Jess was of another breed.

In the grey of the morning the two students, pallid and haggard from
anxiety and with the terror of their adventure still beating tumul-
tuously in their blood, met at the medical college.

'You saw it?' cried one.

'God! yes—what are we to do?'

They went around to the rear of the building, where they saw a
horse, attached to a light wagon, hitched to a gatepost near the door of
the dissecting-room. Mechanically they entered the room. On a bench
in the obscurity sat the negro Jess. He rose, grinning, all eyes and teeth.

'I'm waiting for my pay,' he said.

Stretched naked on a long table lay the body of Henry Armstrong,
the head defiled with blood and clay from a blow with a spade.

Ghosts that have Haunted Me

by

J. K. BANGS

We come now to the light relief—three ghost stories in a humorous vein. I've put them all together so that those in quest of thrills alone may bypass them should they so wish. But if you do, I rather think you'll be missing something special.

In the course of researching material for this third Victorian volume, I came across a host of stories which confirmed an opinion I formed when compiling the previous two: many Victorian authors could only write about ghosts in humorous style. Whether or not this was through a disinclination to admit their own belief in ghosts or through genuine disbelief and a desire to ridicule the subject, I cannot say with certainty, though some hints may be found in the next three works. What is certain is that time and again I have unearthed comic ghost stories and rather than let so much material go to waste (and suffer many more years of neglect) I have included three of the best.

Our first humorous author, John Kendrick Bangs (1862–1922), was in fact renowned for his amusing ghost stories. This American humorist, lecturer and editor, started his writing career on Harper's Magazine *in 1888. After eleven years he moved on to edit* Munsey's Weekly, *then the new* Harper's Weekly. *From then until he went freelance in 1907, he occupied the editorial chair of such publications as* Puck *and* New Metropolitan. *As well as writing, Bangs took more than a passing interest in politics, unsuccessfully standing as a candidate for the office of mayor of Yonkers, New York, in 1894. In later life he was a close friend of Teddy Roosevelt.*

Bang's most famous work was probably The Houseboat On The Styx *(1896) which consisted of imaginary conversations with dead historical figures. Another humorous Bangs work dealing with spirits was* Ghosts I Have Met *(1898) from which is taken 'Ghosts that have Haunted Me'. No doubt any shaking you may experience while reading this and the next two tales will be from laughter—but you never know . . .*

If we could only get used to the idea that ghosts are perfectly harmless creatures, who are powerless to affect our well-being unless we assist them by giving way to our fears, we should enjoy the supernatural exceedingly, it seems to me. Coleridge, I think it was, was once asked by a lady if he believed in ghosts, and he replied, 'No, madame; I have seen too many of them.' Which is my case exactly. I have seen so many horrid visitants from other worlds that they hardly affect me at all, so far as the mere inspiration of terror is concerned. On the other hand, they interest me hugely; and while I must admit that I do experience all the purely physical sensations that come from horrific encounters of this nature, I can truly add on my own behalf that mentally I can rise above the physical impulse to run away, and, invariably standing my ground, I have gained much useful information concerning them. I am prepared to assert that if a thing with flashing green eyes, and clammy hands, and long, dripping strips of sea-weed in place of hair, should rise up out of the floor before me at this moment, 2 a.m., and nobody in the house but myself, with a fearful, nerve-destroying storm raging outside, I should without hesitation ask it to sit down and light a cigar and state its business—or, if it were of the female persuasion, to join me in a bottle of sarsaparilla—although every physical manifestation of fear of which my poor body is capable would be present. I have had experiences in this line, which if I could get you to believe them, would convince you that I speak the truth. Knowing weak, suspicious human nature as I do, however, I do not hope ever to convince you—though it is none the less true—that on one occasion, in the spring of 1895, there was a spiritual manifestation in my library which nearly prostrated me physically, but which mentally I hugely enjoyed, because I was mentally strong enough to subdue my physical repugnance for the thing which suddenly and without any apparent reason materialised in my arm-chair.

I'm going to tell you about it briefly, though I warn you in advance that you will find it a great strain upon your confidence in my veracity. It may even shatter that confidence beyond repair; but I cannot help that. I hold that it is a man's duty in this life to give to the world the benefit of his experience. All that he sees he should set down exactly as he sees it, and so simply, withal, that to the dullest comprehension the moral involved shall be perfectly obvious. If he is a painter, and an auburn-haired maiden appears to him to have blue hair, he should paint her hair blue, and just so long as he sticks by his principles and is true to himself, he need not bother about what you may think of him. So it is with me. My scheme of living is based upon being true to myself. You may class me with Baron Munchausen if you choose; I shall not mind so long as I have the consolation of feeling, deep down in my heart, that I am a true realist, and diverge not from the paths of truth as truth manifests itself to me.

This intruder of whom I was just speaking, the one that took posession of my arm-chair in the spring of 1895, was about as horrible a spectre as I have ever had the pleasure to have haunt me. It was grotesque beyond description. Alongside of it the ordinary poster of the present day would seem to be as accurate in drawing as a bicycle map, and in its colouring it simply shrieked with discord.

If colour had tones which struck the ear, instead of appealing to the eye, the thing would have deafened me. It was about midnight when the manifestation first took shape. My family had long before retired, and I had just finished smoking a cigar—which was one of a thousand which my wife had bought for me at a Monday sale at one of the big department stores in New York. I don't remember the brand, but that is just as well—it was not a cigar to be advertised in a civilised piece of literature—but I do remember that they came in bundles of fifty, tied about with blue ribbon. The one I had been smoking tasted and burned as if it had been rolled by a Cuban insurrectionist while fleeing from a Spanish regiment through a morass, gathering its component parts as he ran. It had two distinct merits, however. No man could possibly smoke too many of them, and they were economical, which is how the ever-helpful little madame came to get them for me, and I have no doubt they will some day prove very useful in removing insects from the rose-bushes. They cost $3.99 a thousand on five days a week, but at the Monday sale they were marked down to $1.75, which is where my wife, to whom I had recently read a little lecture on economy, purchased them for me. Upon the evening in question I had been at work on this cigar for about two hours, and had smoked one side of it three-quarters of the way down to the end, when I concluded that I had smoked enough—for one day—so I rose up to cast the other side into the fire, which was flickering fitfully in my spacious fireplace. This done, I turned about, and there, fearful to see, sat this thing grinning at me from the depths of my chair. My hair not only stood on end, but tugged madly in an effort to get away. Four hairs—I can prove the statement if it be desired—did pull themselves loose from my scalp in their insane desire to rise above the terrors of the situation, and flying upwards, stuck like nails into the oak ceiling

directly over my head, whence they had to be pulled the next morning
with nippers by our hired man, who would no doubt testify to the
truth of the occurrence as I have asserted it if he were still living,
which, unfortunately, he is not. Like most hired men, he was subject
to attacks of lethargy, from one of which he died last summer. He
sank into a rest about weed-time, last June, and lingered quietly along
for two months, and after several futile efforts to wake him up, we
finally disposed of him to our town crematory for experimental purposes. I am told he burned very actively, and I believe it, for to my
certain knowledge he was very dry, and not so green as some persons
who had previously employed him affected to think. A cold chill came
over me as my eye rested upon the horrid visitor and noted the
greenish depths of his eyes and the claw-like formation of his fingers,
and my flesh began to creep like an inch-worm. At one time I was
conscious of eight separate corrugations on my back, and my arms
goose-fleshed until they looked like one of those miniature plaster
casts of the Alps which are so popular in Swiss summer resorts; but
mentally I was not disturbed at all. My repugnance was entirely
physical, and, to come to the point at once, I calmly offered the spectre
a cigar, which it accepted, and demanded a light. I gave it, nonchalantly lighting the match upon the goose-fleshing of my wrist.

Now I admit that this was extraordinary and hardly credible, yet it
happened exactly as I have set it down, and, furthermore, I enjoyed
the experience. For three hours the thing and I conversed, and not once
during that time did my hair stop pulling away at my scalp, or the
repugnance cease to run in great rolling waves up and down my back.
If I wished to deceive you, I might add that pin feathers began to grow
from the goose-flesh, but that would be a lie, and lying and I are not
friends, and, furthermore, this paper is not written to amaze, but to
instruct.

Except for its personal appearance, this particular ghost was not
very remarkable, and I do not at this time recall any of the details of
our conversation beyond the point that my share of it was not particularly coherent, because of the discomfort attendant upon the fearful
hair-pulling process I was going through. I merely cite its coming to
prove that, with all the outward visible signs of fear manifesting themselves in no uncertain manner, mentally I was cool enough to cope
with the visitant, and sufficiently calm and at ease to light the match
upon my wrist, perceiving for the first time, with an Edison-like
ingenuity, one of the uses to which goose-flesh might be put, and

knowing full well that if I tried to light it on the sole of my shoe I should have fallen to the ground, my knees being too shaky to admit of my standing on one leg even for an instant. Had I been mentally overcome, I should have tried to light the match on my foot, and fallen ignominiously to the floor then and there.

There was another ghost that I recall to prove my point, who was of very great use to me in the summer immediately following the spring of which I have just told you. You will possibly remember how that the summer of 1895 had rather more than its fair share of heat, and that the lovely Hudson River town in which I have the happiness to dwell appeared to be the headquarters of the temperature. The thermometers of the nation really seemed to take orders fron Bronxdale, and properly enough, for our town is a born leader in respect to heat. Having no property to sell, I candidly admit that Bronxdale is not of an arctic nature in summer, except socially, perhaps. Socially, it is the coolest town on the Hudson; but we are at this moment not discussing cordiality, fraternal love, or the question raised by the Declaration of Independence as to whether all men are born equal. The warmth we have in hand is what the old lady called 'Fahrenheat', and, from a thermometric point of view, Bronxdale, if I may be a trifle slangy, as I sometimes am, had heat to burn. There are mitigations of this heat, it is true, but they generally come along in winter.

I must claim, in behalf of my town, that never in all my experience have I known a summer so hot that it was not, sooner or later—by January, anyhow—followed by a cool spell. But in the summer of 1895 even the real-estate agents confessed that the cold wave announced by the weather bureau at Washington summered elsewhere—in the tropics, perhaps, but not at Bronxdale. One hardly dared take a bath in the morning for fear of being scalded by the fluid that flowed from the cold-water faucet—our reservoir is entirely unprotected by shade-trees, and in summer a favourite spot for young Waltons who like to catch bass already boiled—my neighbours and myself lived on cracked ice, ice-cream, and destructive cold drinks. I do not myself mind hot weather in the daytime, but hot nights are killing. I can't sleep. I toss about for hours, and then, for the sake of variety, I flop, but sleep cometh not. My debts double, and my income seems to sizzle away under the influence of a hot, sleepless night; and it was just here that a certain awful thing saved me from the insanity which is a certain result of parboiled insomnia.

It was about the 16th of July, which, as I remember reading in an extra edition of the *Evening Bun*, got out to mention the fact, was the hottest 16th of July known in thirty-eight years. I had retired at half-past seven, after dining lightly upon a cold salmon and a gallon of iced tea—not because I was tired, but because I wanted to get down to first principles at once, and remove my clothing, and sort of spread myself over all the territory I could, which is a thing you can't do in a library, or even in a white-and-gold parlour. If man were constructed like a machine, as he really ought to be, to be strictly comfortable—a machine that could be taken apart like an eight-day clock—I should have taken myself apart, putting one section of myself on the roof, another part in the spare room, hanging a third on the clothes-line in the yard, and so on, leaving my head in the ice-box; but unfortunately we have to keep ourselves together in this life, hence I did the only thing one can do, and retired, and incidentally spread myself over some freshly baked bedclothing. There was some relief from the heat, but not much. I had been roasting, and while my sensations were some-what like those which I imagine come to a planked shad when he first finds himself spread out over the plank, there was a mitigation. My temperature fell off from 167 to about 163, which is not quite enough to make a man absolutely content. Suddenly, however, I began to shiver. There was no breeze, but I began to shiver.

'It is getting cooler,' I thought, as the chill came on, and I rose and looked at the thermometer. It still registered the highest possible point, and the mercury was rebelliously trying to break through the top of the glass tube and take a stroll on the roof.

'That's queer,' I said to myself. 'It's as hot as ever, and yet I'm shiver-ing. I wonder if my goose is cooked? I've certainly got a chill.'

I jumped back into bed and pulled the sheet up over me; but still I shivered. Then I pulled the blanket up, but the chill continued. I couldn't seem to get warm again. Then came the counterpane, and finally I had to put on my bath-robe—a fuzzy woollen affair, which in midwinter I had sometimes found too warm for comfort. Even then I was not sufficiently bundled up, so I called for an extra blanket, two afghans, and the hot-water bag.

Everybody in the house thought I had gone mad, and I wondered myself if perhaps I hadn't, when all of a sudden I perceived, off in the corner, the Awful Thing, and perceiving it, I knew all.

I was being haunted, and the physical repugnance of which I have spoken was on. The cold shiver, the invariable accompaniment of the ghostly visitant, had come, and I assure you I never was so glad of anything in my life. It has always been said of me by my critics that I am raw; I was afraid that after that night they would say I was half baked, and I would far rather be the one than the other; and it was the Awful Thing that saved me. Realising this, I spoke to it gratefully.

'You are a heaven-born gift on a night like this,' said I, rising up and walking to its side.

'I am glad to be of service to you,' the Awful Thing replied, smiling at me so yellowly that I almost wished the author of the *Blue-Button of Cowardice* could have seen it.

'It's very good of you,' I put in.

'Not at all,' replied the Thing; 'you are the only man I know who doesn't think it necessary to prevaricate about ghosts every time he gets an order for a Christmas story. There have been more lies told about us than about any other class of things in existence, and we are getting a trifle tired of it. We may have lost our corporeal existence, but some of our sensitiveness still remains.'

'Well,' said I, rising and lighting the gas-logs—for I was on the very verge of congealment—'I am sure I am pleased if you like my stories.'

'Oh, as for that, I don't think much of them,' said the Awful Thing, with a purple display of candour which amused me, although I cannot say that I relished it; 'but you never lie about us. You are not at all interesting, but you are truthful, and we spooks hate libellers. Just because one happens to be a thing is no reason why writers should libel it, and that's why I have always respected you. We regard you as a sort of spook Boswell. You may be dull and stupid, but you tell the truth, and when I saw you in imminent danger of becoming a mere grease spot, owing to the fearful heat, I decided to help you through. That's why I'm here. Go to sleep now. I'll stay here and keep you shivering until daylight anyhow. I'd stay longer, but we are always laid at sunrise.'

'Like an egg,' I said, sleepily.

'Tutt!' said the ghost. 'Go to sleep. If you talk I'll have to go.'

And so I dropped off to sleep as softly and as sweetly as a tired child. In the morning I awoke refreshed. The rest of my family were prostrated, but I was fresh. The Awful Thing was gone, and the room was warming up again; and if it had not been for the tinkling ice in my water-pitcher, I should have suspected it was all a dream. And so throughout the whole sizzling summer the friendly spectre stood by me and kept me cool, and I haven't a doubt that it was because of his good offices in keeping me shivering on those fearful August nights

that I survived the season, and came to my work in the autumn as fit
as a fiddle—so fit, indeed, that I have not written a poem since that
has not struck me as being the very best of its kind, and if I can find a
publisher who will take the risk of putting those poems out, I shall
unequivocally and without hesitation acknowledge, as I do here, my
debt of gratitude to my friends in the spirit world.

Manifestations of this nature, then, are harmful, as I have already
observed, only when the person who is haunted yields to his physical
impulses. Fought stubbornly inch by inch with the will, they can be
subdued, and often they are a boon. I think I have proved both these
points. It took me a long time to discover the facts, however, and my
discovery came about in this way. It may perhaps interest you to know
how I made it. I encountered at the English home of a wealthy friend
at one time a 'presence' of an insulting turn of mind. It was at my
friend Jarley's little baronial hall, which he had rented from the Earl of
Brokedale the year Mrs Jarley was presented at court. The Countess of
Brokedale's social influence went with the château for a slightly increased rental, which was why the Jarleys took it. I was invited to
spend a month with them, not so much because Jarley is fond of me as
because Mrs Jarley had a sort of an idea that, as a writer, I might say
something about their newly acquired glory in some American
Sunday newspaper; and Jarley laughingly assigned to me the 'haunted
chamber', without at least one of which no baronial hall in the old
country is considered worthy of the name.

'It will interest you more than any other,' Jarley said; 'and if it has a
ghost, I imagine you will be able to subdue him.'

I gladly accepted the hospitality of my friend, and was delighted
at his consideration in giving me the haunted chamber, where I might
pursue my investigations into the subject of phantoms undisturbed.
Deserting London, then, for a time, I ran down to Brokedale Hall, and
took up my abode there with a half-dozen other guests. Jarley, as usual
since his sudden 'gold-fall', as Wilkins called it, did everything with a
lavish hand. I believe a man could have got diamonds on toast if he had
chosen to ask for them. However, this is apart from my story.

I had occupied the haunted chamber about two weeks before anything of importance occurred, and then it came—and a more unpleasant
ill-mannered spook never floated in the ether. He materialised about
3 a.m. and was unpleasantly sulphurous to one's perceptions. He sat
upon the divan in my room, holding his knees in his hands, leering
and scowling upon me as though I were the intruder, and not he.

'Who are you?' I asked, excitedly, as in the dying light of the log fire he loomed grimly up before me.

'None of your business,' he replied, insolently, showing his teeth as he spoke. 'On the other hand, who are you? This is my room, and not yours, and it is I who have the right to question. If you have any business here, well and good. If not, you will oblige me by removing yourself, for your presence is offensive to me.'

'I am a guest in the house,' I answered, restraining my impulse to throw the ink-stand at him for his impudence. 'And this room has been set apart for my use by my host.'

'One of the servant's guests, I presume?' he said, insultingly, his lividly lavender-like lip upcurling into a haughty sneer, which was maddening to a self-respecting worm like myself.

I rose up from my bed, and picked up the poker to bat him over the head, but again I restrained myself. It will not do to quarrel, I thought. I will be courteous if he is not, thus giving a dead Englishman a lesson which wouldn't hurt some of the living.

'No,' I said, my voice tremulous with wrath—'no; I am the guest of my friend Mr Jarley, an American, who——'

'Same thing,' observed the intruder, with a yellow sneer. 'Race of low-class animals, those Americans—only fit for gentlemen's stables, you know.'

This was too much. A ghost may insult me with impunity, but when he tackles my people he must look out for himself. I sprang forward with an ejaculation of wrath, and with all my strength struck at him with the poker which I still held in my hand. If he had been anything but a ghost, he would have been split vertically from top to toe; but as it was, the poker passed harmlessly through his misty make-up, and rent a great gash two feet long in Jarley's divan. The yellow sneer faded from his lips, and a maddening blue smile took its place.

'Humph!' he observed, nonchalantly. 'What a useless ebullition, and what a vulgar display of temper! Really you are the most humorous insect I have yet encountered. From what part of the States do you come? I am truly interested to know in what kind of soil exotics of your particular kind are cultivated. Are you part of the fauna or the flora of your tropical States—or what?'

And then I realised the truth. There is no physical method of combating a ghost which can result in his discomfiture, so I resolved to try the intellectual. It was a mind-to-mind contest, and he was easy prey after I got going. I joined him in his blue smile, and began to talk about the English aristocracy; for I doubted not, from the spectre's manner, that he was or had been one of that class. He had about him that haughty lack of manners which bespoke the aristocrat I waxed very eloquent when, as I say, I got my mind really going. I spoke of kings and queens and their uses in no uncertain phrases, of divine right, of dukes, earls, marquises—of all the pompous establishments of British royalty and nobility—with that contemptuously humorous tolerance of a necessary and somewhat amusing evil which we find in American comic papers. We had a battle royal for about one hour, and I must confess he was a foeman worthy of any man's steel, so long as I was reasonable in my arguments; but when I finally observed that it wouldn't be ten years before Barnum and Bailey's Greatest Show on Earth had the whole lot engaged for the New York circus season, stalking about the Madison Square Garden arena, with the Prince of Wales at the head beating a tomtom, he grew iridescent with wrath, and fled madly through the wainscoting of the room. It was purely a mental victory. All the physical possibilities of my being would have exhausted themselves futilely before him; but when I turned upon him the resources of my fancy, my imagination unrestrained, and held back by no sense of responsibility, he was as a child in my hands, obstreperous, but certain to be subdued. If it were not for Mrs Jarley's wrath— which, I admit, she tried to conceal—over the damage; to her divan, I should now look back upon that visitation as the most agreeable haunting experience of my life; at any rate, it was at that time that I first learned how to handle ghosts, and since that time I have been able to overcome them without trouble save in one instance, with which I shall close this chapter of my reminiscences, and which I give only to prove the necessity of observing strictly one point in dealing with spectres.

It happened last Christmas, in my own home. I had provided as a little surprise for my wife a complete new solid silver service marked with her initials. The tree had been prepared for the children, and all had retired save myself. I had lingered later than the others to put the silver service under the tree, where its happy recipient would find it when she went to the tree with the little ones the next morning. It made a magnificent display: the two dozen of each kind of spoon, the forks, the knives, the coffee-pot, water-urn, and all; the salvers, the vegetable-dishes, olive-forks, cheese-scoops, and other dazzling attributes of a complete service, not to go into details, presented a fairly scintillating picture which would have made me gasp if I had not, at the moment when my own breath began to catch, heard another gasp in the corner immediately behind me. Turning about quickly to see whence it came, I observed a dark figure in the pale light of the moon which streamed in through the window.

'Who are you?' I cried, starting back, the physical symptoms of a ghostly presence manifesting themselves as usual.

'I am the ghost of one long gone before,' was the reply, in sepulchral tones.

I breathed a sigh of relief, for I had for a moment feared it was a burglar.

'Oh!' I said. 'You gave me a start at first. I was afraid you were a material thing come to rob me.' Then turning towards the tree, I observed, with a wave of the hand, 'Fine layout, eh?'

'Beautiful,' he said, hollowly. 'Yet not so beautiful as things I've seen in realms beyond your ken.'

And then he set about telling me of the beautiful gold and silver ware they used in the Elysian Fields, and I must confess Monte Cristo would have had a hard time, with Sinbad the Sailor to help, to surpass the picture of royal magnificence the spectre drew. I stood enthralled until, even as he was talking, the clock struck three, when he rose up, and moving slowly across the floor, barely visible, murmured regretfully that he must be off, with which he faded away down the back stairs. I pulled my nerves, which were getting rather strained, together again, and went to bed.

Next morning every bit of that silverware was gone; and, what is more, three weeks later I found the ghost's picture in the Rogue's Gallery in New York as that of the cleverest sneak-thief in the country.

All of which, let me say to you, dear reader, in conclusion, proves that when you are dealing with ghosts you mustn't give up all your physical resources until you have definitely ascertained that the thing by which you are confronted, horrid or otherwise, is a ghost, and not an all too material rogue with a light step, and a commodious jute bag for plunder concealed beneath his coat.

'How to tell a ghost?' you ask.

Well, as an eminent master of fiction frequently observes in his writings, 'that is another story', which I shall hope some day to tell for your instruction and my own aggrandisement.

Haunted by Spirits

by

GEORGE MANVILLE FENN

Our second humorous tale, a piece with its tongue very firmly in its cheek, comes from an early work of one of the last century's most prolific writers. George Manville Fenn (1831–1909) wrote over 170 books, sketches, novels and children's stories. and contributed to most of the leading magazines of his day. Born in London, Fenn's early career included work as a teacher and private tutor; then came a complete change when he became a printer, setting up his own press in Lincolnshire and publishing his own magazine, Modern Metre. *His first opportunity of a wider circulation occurred when Charles Dickens bought one of his stories for the famous* All The Year Round.*

As well as his writing, Fenn took an interest in the theatre, becoming drama critic of the Echo *and even producing his own farce in 1888. Comedy was one of his stronger talents and he produced many amusing short stories and articles. One of his first short story collections,* Christmas Penny Readings *(1867), contained quite a few humorous pieces and, as one might expect with such a seasonal publication, some ghost stories. 'Haunted by Spirits' is one of Fenn's Christmas stories that combines both ghosts and comedy, though in what proportions I leave you to find out.*

'But what an out-of-the-way place to get to,' I said, after being most cordially received by my old school fellow and his wife, one bitter night after a long ride. 'But you really are glad to see me, eh?'

'Now, hold your tongue, do,' cried Ned and his wife in a breath. 'You won't get away again under a month, so don't think of it. But where we are going to put you I don't know,' said Ned.

'Oh I can sleep anywhere, chairs, table, anything you like; only make me welcome. Fine old house this seems, but however came you to take it?'

'Got it cheap, my boy. Been shut up for twenty years. It's haunted, and no one will live in it. But I have it full for this Christmas, at all events, and what's more I have some potent spirits in the place too, but they are all corked down tightly, so there is no fear at present. But I say, Lilly,' cried Ned, addressing his wife, 'why, we shall have to go into the haunted room and give him our place.'

'That you won't,' I said. 'I came down here on purpose to take you by surprise, and to beg for a snack of dinner on Christmas-day; and now you are going to give me about the greatest treat possible, a bed in a haunted room. What kind of a ghost is it?'

'You mustn't laugh,' said Ned, trying to appear very serious; 'for there is not a soul living within ten miles of this place, that would not give you a long account of the horrors of the Red Chamber: of spots of blood upon the bedclothes coming down in a regular rain; noises; clashing of swords; shrieks and groans; skeletons or transparent bodies. Oh, my dear fellow, you needn't grin, for it's all gospel truth about here, and if we did not keep that room screwed up, not a servant would stay in the house.'

'Wish I could buy it and take it away,' I said.

'I wish you could, indeed,' cried Ned, cordially.

Half an hour after, Ned and I were busy with screwdriver and candle, down in the large corridors, turning the rusty screws which held a large door at the extreme end of the house. First one and then another was twirled out till nothing held the door but the lock; the key for which Ned Harrington now produced from his pocket—an old, many-warded, rusty key, at least a couple of hundred years old.

'Hold the candle a little lower,' said Ned, 'here's something in the keyhole,' when pulling out his knife, he picked out a quantity of paper, evidently very recently stuffed in. He then inserted the key, and after a good deal of effort it turned, and the lock shot back with a harsh, grating noise. Ned then tried the handle, but the door remained fast; and though he tugged and tugged, it still stuck, till I put one hand to help him, when our united efforts made it come open with a rush, knocking over the candle, and there we were standing upon the portals of the haunted room in the dark.

'I'll fetch a light in a moment out of the hall,' said Ned, and he slipped off, while I must confess to a certain feeling of trepidation on being left alone, listening to a moaning, whistling noise, which I knew to be the wind, but which had all the same a most dismal effect upon my nerves, which, in spite of my eagerness to be the inmate of the closed room, began to whisper very strongly that they did not like it at all. But the next minute Ned was beside me with the light, and we entered the gloomy dusty old chamber—a bed-chamber furnished after the fashion of the past century. The great four-poster bedstead looked heavy and gloomy, and when we drew back the curtains, I half expected to see a body lying in state, but no, all was very dusty, very gloomy, and soul-chilling, but nothing more.

'Come, there's plenty of room for a roaring fire,' said Ned, 'and I think after all we had better come here ourselves, and let you have our room.'

'That you will not,' I said, determinedly. 'Order them to light a fire, and have some well-aired things put upon that bed, and it will be a clever ghost that wakes me to-night, for I'm as tired as a dog.'

'Here, Mary,' shouted Ned to one of the maids, 'coals and wood here, and a broom.'

We waited about, peering here and there at the old toilet-ware and stands, the old chest of drawers and armoire, old chairs and paintings, for all seemed as if the room had been suddenly quitted; while inside a huge cupboard beside the fireplace hung a dusty horseman's cloak, and in the corner were a long thin rapier and a quaint old-fashioned firelock.

'Strikes chilly and damp,' said I, snuffing the smell of old boots and fine dust.

'Ah, but we'll soon drive that out,' said Ned. 'But you'd better give in, my boy. 'Pon my word, I'm ashamed to let you come in here.'

'Pooh! nonsense!' I said. 'Give me a roaring fire, and that's all I want.'

'Ah!' cried Ned. 'But what a while that girl is'; and then he stepped out into the passage. 'Why, what are you standing there for?' he cried. 'Come and light this fire.'

'Plee', sir, I dussen't,' said the maid.

'Here, give me hold,' cried Ned, in a pet; 'and send your mistress here'; and then he made his appearance with a coal-scuttle, paper, and wood; when between us we soon had a fire alight and roaring up the huge chimney, while the bright flames flickered and danced, and gave quite a cheerful aspect to the place.

'Well,' cried Mrs Harrington, who now appeared, 'how are you getting on?' but neither Ned's wife nor her sister stood looking, for, in spite of all protestations, dressed as they were, they set to sweeping, dusting, airing linen, bed, mattress, etcetera, we helping to the best of our ability—for no maid, either by threats or persuasion, would enter the place—and at last we made the place look, if not comfortable, at all events less dismal than before we entered. The old blinds came down like so much tinder when touched, while, as to the curtains, the first attempt to draw them brought down such a cloud of dust, that they were left alone, though Mrs Harrington promised that the place should be thoroughly seen to in the morning.

Returning to the drawing-room, the remainder of the evening was most agreeably spent; while the cause of my host and hostess's prolonged absence produced endless comments and anecdotes respecting the Red Chamber—some of them being so encouraging in their nature that Ned Harrington, out of sheer compassion, changed the conversation.

'Well, my boy,' said Ned, when the ladies had all retired for the night, 'you shan't go to bed till the witching hour is past'; so he kept me chatting over old times, till the clock had gone one—the big old turret-clock, whose notes flew booming away upon the frosty air. 'Christmas-eve to-morrow, so we'll have a tramp on the moors after the wild ducks—plenty out here. I say, my boy, I believe this is the original Moated Grange, so don't be alarmed if you hear the mice.'

'There's only one thing I care for,' I said, 'and that is anything in the shape of a practical joke.'

'Honour bright! my boy,' said Ned; 'you need fear nothing of that kind'; and then I was alone in the Haunted Chamber, having locked myself in.

My first proceeding was to give the large fire an extra poke, which sent a flood of light across the room, and the flames gushing up the chimney; my next, to take one of the candles and make a tour of my bedroom, during which I looked under the bed, behind the curtains, and into armoire and cupboard, but discovered nothing. Next thing I tried the windows, through which I could just dimly see the snow-white country, but they were fast and blackened with dirt. The chimney-glass, too, was so injured by damp, that the dim reflection given back was something startling, being more like a bad photograph of life-size than anything else; and at length, having fully made up my mind that I was alone, and that, as far as I could make out, there were neither trap-doors nor secret passages in the wall, I undressed, put out the candles, and plunged into bed.

But I was wrong in what I had said to my host about sleeping, for I never felt more wakeful in my life. I watched the blaze of the fire sink down to a ruddy glow, the glow turn blacker and blacker till at last the fire was all but extinct, while the room was dark as could be. But my eyesight was painfully acute, while my hearing seemed strained to catch the slightest passing sound. The wind roared and rumbled in the great chimney, and swept sighing past the windows; and, though it had a strange, wild sound with it, yet I had heard the wind before, and therefore paid but little heed to its moans.

All at once the fire seemed to fall together with a tinkling sound, a bright flame leaped up, illumining the room for a moment, then becoming extinct, and leaving all in darkness; but there was light for a long enough interval for me to see, or fancy I saw, the cupboard door open and the great horseman's cloak stand out in a weird-like manner before me, as though covering the shoulders of some invisible figure.

I felt warm—then hot—then in a profuse perspiration, but I told myself it was fancy, punched my pillow, and turned over upon the other side to sleep. Now came a long, low, dreary moan, hollow and heartrending, for it seemed like a cry of some one in distress; when I raised myself upon one elbow and listened.

'Old cowl on a chimney,' I muttered, letting myself fall back again, now thoroughly determined to sleep, but the moaning continued, the wind whistled and howled, while now came a gentle tap, tap, tapping at my window, as if someone was signalling to be admitted.

'Tap, tap, tap'; still it kept on, as though whoever tapped was fearful of making too much noise; and at length, nerving myself, I slipped out of bed, crossed the room, and found that the closet door was open; but a vigorous poke inside produced nothing but dust and two or three very sharp sneezes. So I fastened the door, and listened. All silent: but the next moment began the tapping upon the dirty window-pane again; and, impelled by a mingled sensation of fear and attraction, I crept closer to the sash, and at length made out the shadow of something tapping at the glass.

'Bah! Bah!' I exclaimed the next moment as I shuffled across the room and back to my bed, 'strand of ivy and the wind.' But I was not to be at peace yet, for now there came a most unmistakable noise behind the wainscot—louder and louder, as if some one were trying to tear a piece of the woodwork down. The place chosen seemed to be the corner beside the cupboard; and at last, having made up my mind that it was the rats, I dropped off to sleep, and slept soundly till morning, when I heard the cheery voice of my host at the door.

'Oh, all right,' he said as I answered; 'I only came because the girl knocked, and said that something must be the matter, for she could not make you hear.'

On descending to breakfast, I found that I was to undergo a rigorous cross-examination as to what I had seen and heard; but one elderly lady present shook her head ominously, freely giving it as her opinion that it was little better than sacrilege to open the haunted chamber, and finishing a very solemn peroration with the words—

'Stop a bit; they don't walk every night.'

This was encouraging, certainly; but in the course of the afternoon I went up to my room, and found that it had been well cleaned out, while many little modern appliances had been added to the dingy furniture, so that it wore quite a brightened appearance. The insides of the windows had been cleaned, and a man was then upon a ladder polishing away at the exterior, when I drew his attention to a number of loose ivy strands, which he cut off.

In the cupboard I found plenty of traces of rats in the shape of long-gnawed-off fragments of wood pushed beneath the skirting-board; while, upon holding my head against the chimney, the groaning of the cowl was plainly to be heard, as it swung round dolefully upon some neighbouring chimney.

A pleasant day was spent, and then, after a cosy evening, I was once more ushered into the chamber of horrors, this time being escorted by the whole of the visitors, the gentlemen affectionately bidding me farewell, but not one seeming disposed to accept my offer of changing rooms. However, Ned and Mrs Harrington both wished me to go to their room, when I of course refused; and once more I was alone.

It was now about half-past twelve and Christmas morning, a regular storm was hurrying round the house, and a strange feeling of trepidation came upon me when I had extinguished the light; and then on climbing into bed I sat and listened for a while, laid my head upon my pillow, and the next moment, or what seemed the next moment, I was startled by a strange beating sound, and as I became aware of a dim, peculiar light, penetrating the room, I heard a low, muffled voice cry appealingly—

'Your hot water, sir—quarter to eight!' while I could hardly believe my eyes had been closed.

Christmas-day passed as it generally does in the country, that is to say, in a most jovial, sociable way; and after fun, frolic, sport, pastime, forfeit, dance, and cards, I stood once more within the haunted chamber with the strange sensation upon me, that though I had met with nothing so far to alarm me—this night, a night when, of all nights in the year, spirits might be expected to break loose, I was to suffer for my temerity.

As soon as I entered and secured the door, I felt that something was wrong, but I roused up the fire, lit the wax candles upon the dressing-table, and then looked round the room.

Apparently I was alone, but upon opening the big closet door, the great cloak fell down with a ghostly rustle, while a peculiar odour seemed to rise from the heap. The long, thin sword too, fell, with a strange clanging noise as I hastily closed the door, and then setting down the candle tried to compose myself to look at matters in a calm, philosophical manner. But things would not be looked at in that way, and now I began to feel that I was being punished for all, since the next moment I could see the eyes of the large portrait between the windows gleam and roll, now showing the whites, now seeming to pierce me, so intense was their gaze. Then the figure seemed to be slowly coming down from the frame nearer and nearer, till it was close to me, when it slowly receded, and a shade passed over the canvas, so that it was gone.

But for shame and the fear of ridicule, I should have opened the door and cried for aid; in fact, I believe I did rise from the chair and try to reach the door, but some invisible power drew me into a corner of the room, where I leaned panting against the wall to gaze upon a fresh phenomenon. I had brought a chamber candlestick into the room, and after igniting the pair of candles upon the toilet table, placed the flat candlestick between them, and left it alight, but now—no—yes—I rubbed my eyes—there was no mistake.

There were six candles burning.

I started, shook myself, muttering that it was deception; but no, there burned six candles, while their flames were big and blurred with a large, ghastly, blue halo round each, that had a strange weird light; and now I tried to recall what I had read in old ghost stories about corpse candles, for I felt that these three must be of that character.

In an agony of fear I tried to run up to the dressing-table to dash the weird lights over, but again the same strange influence guided my steps, so that I curved off to the bed, where I sat down, trembling in every limb—limbs that refused their office—while I gazed upon the candles which now began to float backwards and forwards before me, till I could bear the strange sight no more, and throwing myself back, I buried my face in the bed.

But there was no relief here, for as I threw myself down at full length, the great bedstead gave a crack, a rattle, and a bound, and then in an agony of dread I was clinging to the bedding, for the huge structure began to rise slowly higher—higher—higher—sailing away apparently upon the wings of the wind, and then again sinking lower and lower and lower to interminable depths, so that I involuntarily groaned and closed my eyes. But that was of no avail, for I could feel the great bedstead career, now on one side, now on the other, and ever going onward through space like some vessel upon a vast aerial sea.

The rapid gliding upward, in spite of the dread, seemed attended with somewhat of an exhilarating effect; but the falling was hideous in the extreme—for now it was slowly and gently, but the next moment the speed was fearful, and I lay trembling in expectation of feeling the structure dash upon the ground, while every time I unclosed my eyes I could see the gyrating candles, and turned giddy with confusion.

And now with one tremendously-swift gliding swoop, away we went, faster and faster, more rapidly than swallows upon the wing. Space seemed obliterated; and, by the rushing noise and singing in my ears, I could feel that the bedstead was careering on where the atmosphere was growing more and more attenuated, while soon, from the catching of my breath, I felt sure that we should soon be beyond air altogether. The candles were gone, but there were stars innumerable, past which we sped with inconceivable rapidity, so that their light seemed continued in one long luminous streak, while ever more and more the speed was increasing, till it seemed that we were attached to some mighty cord, and being whirled round and round with frightful velocity, as if at the end of the string; and now I trembled for the moment when the cord should be loosed, and we should fly off into illimitable space, to go on—on—on for ever!

At last it came, and away I went; but now separated from the bedstead, to which I had clung to the last. On—on—on, with something large and undefined in front of me, which I felt that I should strike, though I was powerless to prevent the collision. Nearer—nearer—nearer, but ever darting along like a shooting-star in its course, I was swept on, till, with a fearful crash, I struck what I now found to be the lost bed, and tried to cling to it once more; but, no! I rolled off, and fell slowly and gradually lower—lower, and evidently out of the sphere of the former attraction, so that at last I fell, with only a moderate bump, upon the floor, when, hastily rising, I found all totally dark, and that the bedpost was beside me; when, shudderingly dragging off some of the clothes on to the carpet, I rolled myself in them, and went off into a heavy sleep.

The next morning several of my friends made remarks upon my pale and anxious looks; and soon after breakfast, Ned beckoned me into his study, and begged of me to tell him whether I had been disturbed.

For a few minutes I felt that I could not tell of the horrors of the past night, even though I had vowed to sleep in the haunted room still; but at last I began my recital, and had arrived at the point where the bedstead set sail, when Ned jumped up, crying:

'Why, I thought from your looks that you really had been disturbed. But I say, old boy, I suppose we must look over it, as it's Christmas; but, do you know, judging by my own feelings, I think I'd better make the punch rather less potent to-night.'

'Well, really,' I said, 'I think so too.'

'Do you?' said Ned.

'Oh, yes,' I said, 'for my head aches awfully'; and no wonder, seeing how it has been Haunted by Spirits!

A Ghost Slayer

by

J. KEIGHLEY SNOWDEN

To round off this trio of humorous stories, a very unusual item indeed from a forgotten author. Described by the St James's Gazette as a 'new instance for those to quote who maintain that journalism is a good school for fiction', J. Keighley Snowden was born in Preston in 1860 and started a long reporting career on the Keighley News, spent ten years in Birmingham and then joined the Yorkshire Post in 1893 as assistant leader-writer. Keighley Snowden had already sold several of his short stories set in Yorkshire to such journals as Black and White and Pall Mall Magazine, and the same year that he joined the Yorkshire Post he also published his first collection of short stories, Tales of the Yorkshire Wolds.

Snowden described himself as a Yorkshireman 'no longer privileged to dwell amongst his kinfolk' and made his book 'a tribute of affection'. In his tales he sketched scenes of life in the North West Riding, depicting memories and places he knew from his youth, acquired from his father and grandfather, both Yorkshiremen. Many of the stories were comical and in 'A Ghost Slayer' he describes the hilarious downfall of a dubious hunter of ghosts.

A word of warning: Snowden utilised in all his stories broad York-shire dialect. To have brought it into plain English would have been a pointless and rather mean exercise, so I have left it as it stands. After nearly eighty years, it's still quite comprehensible and we can take comfort from Snowden himself who says: 'The author begs Yorkshire-men to believe that set down with phonetic precision their simple mother tongue might have been unintelligible'. So it's not as bad as it could have been!

There is no printer's error in the title of this story. The word, I wish to say indubitably, is 'slayer', from to slay—to put to death by violence. The story relates to that barbarous age, hardly reckoned yet as part of the past, when the march of scientific invention had not reached the spirit world. At times, by a happy blunder of empirical research, some dilettante ghost would succeed in banging a door, imitating with some fidelity the clanking of chains, emptying a plate-rack, altering the colour of a candle, or even effecting a momentary and imperfect materialisation. To the same extent that these little accidents gave delight to their authors, they came upon people still in the flesh as a surprise. The weak thing about them was that they conveyed so little. Since then, of course, keeping pace with the times, the dim investigators of the underworld have in turn perfected a rudimentary sign-language of knocks, a very perfect and ingenious method of manipulating a bit of slate pencil, and several other processes the nature of which, in the absence of patent rights, they prefer to keep secret—lest unauthorised imitators should make money out of them. We miss the old, sweet flavour of romance; but henceforth the function of the 'medium' is not less easy and simple than it is honourable.

Not so in the times of which I write. It required a special talent to prophesy with facility and precision on the spontaneous howling of a dog in the dark. Anyone can see a spirit hand nowadays; some have even been privileged to grasp one, and to recognise its smooth and waxy texture: but the seer who, in those days, could sometimes discern a poor formless, impalpable ghost where other men saw nothing, possessed a rare and precious gift.

Such a gift had Weasel. And nobody respected him much for any other characteristic. He had his faults, like the greatest men. He was very worldly, or, as they say in Cragside, leet gi'en'; he took more whiskey than is good for any man; and his love of practical joking was a thing to be regretted. But the mantle worn long ago by the fearsome Witch of Endor had come down to him in a direct line of apostolic succession. There was not a boggart in all the country side, from the Coach and Six with the headless coachman and postillions to the Lonesome Babby, that wailed in a leafless wood before the first snow fell, with which he was not on nodding terms. And when the spirit of prophecy came upon him, and he spake of the things which he had heard and seen, a bleak and mournful sense of awe—a consciousness of wintry desolation with thirty degrees of frost—stole over the festivities in Molly's alehouse kitchen.

He had a pretty gift of descriptive story-telling. His dramatic effects were rapid and staggering, and the sincerity of his own fright was convincing. Nevertheless he always managed to convey, by some unobtrusive fragment of innocent detail, that he had acted more bravely than his listeners knew that they would have done in the same unusual circumstances.

It even appeared that he had carried irreverent boldness to the rash pitch of airy jocularity. He had spoken flippantly to the sheeted dead about the weather, and lightly reminded certain of them of a tarnished past, or which, being a kind of legendary historian, he knew rather more than was pleasant. Indeed there was one unquiet spirit towards whom he was guilty of a piece of wanton brutality so shocking, that, as I heard of it by his own confession, I shall take the liberty of recording it, in justice to the poor thing's memory.

When he got married—which happened to him late in life and after a scandalous bachelorhood—he did so under the persuasion of Binney Driver, who refused to look upon his concubinage with any tolerance, and who overcame his last objection by offering him a house and home rent free. It is true that the house was haunted (by a disagreeable old woman in spectacles and a red shawl, who, though bent on no conceivable errand, carried an eternal marketing basket), that the windows had been stoned out, and that the roof let the weather in through a gap made by the fallen chimney. But Binney Driver was ready to put the place in repair, and Weasel held in derision the doddering, grandmotherly spectre.

'Shoo'll quit,' he said, 'when shoo sees ahr Susannah.'

So he got in a few sticks of furniture, made himself hilariously drunk before bed-time, and bade the neighbourhood good night several times from the bedroom window, before he tumbled in between the blankets.

From the statement he made to a gaping crowd next morning, it would appear that his rest was not undisturbed. 'Owd Betty Rathera' awoke him on the stroke of midnight by a sly attempt to filch the bedclothes. She had little green shining eyes, that peered at you viciously, and a shrivelled mouth that was continually in motion, and long fingers with rheumatic knobs on the knuckles. Well, he sprang out of bed and routed her at the first onset; and then he awoke Susannah to tell her of his cheap and glorious victory. However, at Susannah's urgent entreaty, they pulled the bed-clothes over their heads as if they were afraid, and tucked them well in, so that they would be sure to 'feel her if shoo melled (interfered) agean'; and no sooner had they done so than they were holding on with all their might against a vivacious and irresistible tugging. But when Weasel made to spring after her again, she slipped away out of the room 'wi' a scutter like a rat runnin' '.

'Aw'll fix tha!' said Weasel, as he leaned a weaver's heavy beam against the door; and after that they got off to sleep.

He awoke suddenly, and found himself sitting bolt upright. The bed-clothes were clean gone this time, and there in the doorway stood Owd Betty Rathera, grinning at him with a mocking gleam in her green eyes, and pointing to the beam laid on one side and the bed-clothes trailing from her basket. It was too much: the thing would presently develop into a persecution. Weasel reached the door at a bound, seized the beam, and, in a frenzy of terror, dashed it down the stone stairs in her wake.

'Hit her? Aye, for seur it hit her,' he added, in reply to a question which his calculated silence had provoked. 'Wha, ther' a blue rick (smoke) come up an' filled t' cham'er, an' Aw hed to oppen t' window to let aht a strang smell o' sulphur 'at ommost choaked ahr Susannah! We saw nowt no moor of Owd Betty efter that, an' willn't, Aw'se wager.' Then, after a reflective pause, he spoke in a low uneasy voice these fearful words: 'Bud some way, we nivver gate warm agean all t' neet. T'air smelled o' moulds—clammy-like.' Nor did they get warm on subsequent nights, as it would seem—till Binney Driver said a prayer in the room, and gave them another pair of blankets.

Alas, poor ghost! In this way a grievous felony was piously condoned.

Weasel was more of a hero than ever after that. It is not every man who has killed his ghost. For a while, it may be, there were wiseacres who cast doubts upon the story, on the ground that it was well known that you couldn't harm a ghost, any more than you could damage your own shadow. Dave Berry, a disrespectful man, went so far as to scoff at it quietly. 'He'll be tellin' next,' said the humorist, "at he's puzzened one wi' henbane.' But as, according to Susannah's testimony, the phantom no longer troubled the house, and as Owd Betty Rathera had been known to 'walk' any time these ten years, the voice of envy was gradually silenced. Weasel sat in the chimney nook at Molly's, and drank out of every man's pot. He was led to discourse so often of the Cornshaw Screamer, of Dick Swash with the halter, of Cheepie and of all the accredited ghosts for miles around, that he began to find it needful, with the view of some day varying the monotony, to darkly hint at the possibility of there being others.

His prestige was still at its height when, one wild night in autumn, he and a company of stout carousers came roaring home from Glusburn. They might have kept to the high road, but Dave Berry had 'dared' them to walk through the ancient park where the apparition of the Coach and Six was wont to ride; and in spite of the vivid picture of its gruesome terrors which Weasel had offered as if by way of encouragement, they had felt pot-valiant enough to brave the danger. One of them said flatly that there was no such thing: nobody but Weasel had ever seen it.

'Bud tha's seen it, Weasel,' said Dave Berry.

'Say nowt,' responded the seer. 'Say nowt. Wait till we git by th' owd mistal wheer t'—hic!—t' mooin cannot shine through. Aw knaw. See 'at it doesn't—hic!—ride ower ye, that's all. Them 'at it rides ower 'll dee afore they're a—hic! Damn that sour ale!—dee afore they're a year owder. It rade ower my father t' week afore he henged hissen—Aw mind him t—tellin' on 't.'

'Bud tha'd nut dee, wo'd ta?' asked Dave Berry.

Weasel lurched up alongside to dig him in the ribs. 'Say nowt!' he hiccoughed again.

'Wha, freeze me if he bean't flaid!' cried another, with a great laugh; and they nearly came to blows over that mortal insult—for Weasel, though now past the prime of his strength, was afraid, at all events, of nothing that was made of flesh and blood.

The night was black, and full of clamour. The sun had set among driving clouds, and the wind had gathered fury as 'the dead of the night's high noon' drew near. Blast upon blast came hurtling down from the hills. The fallen leaves went scurrying by them along the gravel path, or, caught up in eddies, flicked sharply against the strollers' faces. Somewhere in the deep and gloomy park an iron gate kept clanking. Between the gusts the big trees moaned unceasingly, and they heard the bleating of frightened sheep, and the swish and rattle of a swollen beck, coursing down its perilous channel close by. Occasionally the harvest lightning gleamed faintly for a moment, and when it flickered out a wall of darkness rose up before them, barring the way. A bat, wheeling blindly at one of these times, struck Weasel's calumniator pat on the neck, and clinging for an instant, administered a shock to his bravado.

A sober man, with a cheerful heart in his bosom, might have admired the storm. I have known men, blessed with strong animal spirits and clear consciences, who would shout for sheer joy when they heard the elements brawl so. But upon these tipsy revellers the effect was different. Once within the park, they had not been beaten about for ten minutes before their fiery courage was miraculously tamed. Without being conscious of it, they had ceased to sing, or shout, or blaspheme. Weasel had given himself up to a bitter melancholy, and another man, having fallen over a tree-root, refused to be helped up again, and maintained that it was bed-time. But by the patient efforts of Dave Berry, his slothfulness was at last overcome, and they resumed the expedition arm in arm.

The tempest rose towards its height. A black squall charged down the valley with a slogan in its throat, and when it burst among the old beech-trees their lustiest branches snapped off. The men could hear it give yell upon yell as it raced away triumphant. 'By Gow!' shouted Dave Berry, dragged backwards by the swaying line of his companions, 'next time one o' them comes we'se do better to tak' it liggin'!' Just then a feeble moonbeam shone out from a rift in the clouds, and revealed, within a dozen paces, the mouth of that tortuous and gloomy avenue where the old mistal is, and as they drew back; hesitating, the fiercest blast of all swept them asunder. A giant beech was rent from its roots with a long and strident detonation, and fell crashing behind them.

While they stood shaking with terror, Weasel uttered something between a scream and a sob, and sank to the ground with one arm across his face. They were sober enough by this time, but perfectly unable to move a step.

'Ho'd thi din,' cried Dave Berry, thickly. 'Ther's noise enew baht they blether.' But the others were glancing fearfully round, and Weasel, grovelling and fairly whimpering, had seized the nearest round his knees.

'Theer!' he gasped, with a rapid and tremulous gesture directed towards the gloomy place ahead.

They gazed with straining eye-balls, but saw nothing more than the waving branches and the blackness. 'Ther's nowt theer,' bawled Dave Berry. 'It's behind tha. Ther's a tree fa'en.'

'Aw tell yo' Aw seed it,' whined the exorcist in a shrill and palpitating falsetto. 'Aw've seed t' Coach an' Six, an' Aw'm a deead man!' An inhuman, melancholy cry—that of an owl shaken from her roost, perhaps—made itself heard above their heads, and simultaneously the moonlight vanished.

They were scared past the shame of confessing it. They huddled together in the dark, clutching one another's garments and uttering incoherent lamentations. But Weasel's palsied gibbering rose loudest.

'A gurt yoller coach, an' men wi' bleedin' necks—Oh! dear; Oh! dear. Reight ower t' bank it drave, an dahn t' beck-hoil. Their heeads rollin' abaht inside it—all starin' an' laughin', starin' an' laughin' at *me*! Eh, Aw'm a deead man. It's a judgment on me. Oh, dear, oh, dear!'

A chorus of pious response went up after each phrase.

'Does—does ony on yo' knaw a prayer-piece?' asked one man, and his teeth chattered as he spoke.

'Weasel knaws one, likely,' said Dave Berry.

'Nay, nay—Aw knaw noan, Aw knaw noan. Lewk sharp an' say one, for God's mercy sake, some on yo'! It'll be back agean, Aw knaw it will. It com' aht o' t' mistal.'

There was an embarrassed silence. This sudden and unexpected examination in religious knowledge was altogether too severe. Then, in a lull of the wind, Weasel's voice was heard again, fervently muttering, 'Our Father—Father which art i' heaven. Our Father which art i' heaven—i' heaven——'

'Nay, Weasel,' laughed Dave Berry; and then they all laughed.

It did them good. They got up from their knees and made the park echo with peal after peal of hysterical laughter. Weasel, after gazing at them sullenly for a time, took the infection of their merriment.

'Ye—ye're just as flaid as a pack o' childer,' he said when they had done laughing.

'Wha, didn't ta see nowt, then?' asked one simpleton, tricked by his sudden change of tone.

'Did *tha* see nowt?'

'Nay.'

'What browt tha dahn o' thi knees then?'

'Well, ye said——'

'Aw said ye'd be flaid, an' ye're as white as a sheet this minute.'

Which sundry others felt to be true of themselves also, for the conversation was bringing back a twinge of their banished fear. Only Dave Berry stood a step or two apart, with a queer smile on his big face.

The storm was already abating. It had satisfied its rage; and by one of those surprising changes that often attend the cessation of high winds, the full moon rode smoothly out from behind the last cloud and lighted them home.

'Aw say, Weasel,' said Dave Berry, as they came out upon the highway: and he had so much the air of having a discovery to impart that they all stopped to hear it.

'Well?'

'Well, tha mud ha' thrawn that tree at it if we'd nobbud thowt on 't!'

But the version which survives in Cragside of that awful experience, on which a scoffer could so lightly jest, is not Dave Berry's.

The Tomb

by

GUY DE MAUPASSANT

The brief life and even briefer writing career of Guy de Maupassant (1850–1893) make his eminence in French literature all the more remarkable. The widely acclaimed master of the short story was born near Dieppe, brought up in Normandy and studied law in Paris. After military service in the Franco-Prussian war, he worked as a civil servant until his writing brought him a good income. And a good income it was—Maupassant was a bestseller in his own lifetime, not just in France but on both sides of the Atlantic.

Maupassant's life was marred by his discovery, in his early twenties, that he suffered from syphilis, probably hereditary. As the disease increased its hold on him, he suffered from bouts of mental disturbance, and his more powerful works of the macabre stemmed from this period of his life. The most famous is undoubtedly 'The Horla', his fevered story of the emergence of an invisible super-being, set to supplant man from his mastery of the earth, which has more than once been noted for its possibly subconscious depiction of paranoia.

Maupassant's mental condition deteriorated until, in January 1892, he cut his throat in an unsuccessful attempt at suicide. He was committed to an asylum where he died eighteen months later.

There is an alarming hint of paranoia in the following grim little tale by Guy de Maupassant, which seems to have escaped the wide circulation of some of his more well known tales of terror. As with many of his other stories, it can be read as the author's view of his own condition: mental stability and emotion being powerless in the face of physical corruption.

On the seventeenth of July, eighteen hundred and eighty-three, at half-past two o'clock in the morning, the caretaker of Béziers cemetery, who lived in a little house at the end of the burying-ground, was awakened by the yelping of his dog, which was locked in the kitchen.

He immediately went downstairs, and saw that the animal was scenting something under the door and barking furiously, as though some tramp had been prowling about the house. Vincent, the caretaker, took up his gun and went out cautiously.

His dog ran off in the direction of General Bonnet's Avenue and stopped short in front of Madame Tomoiseau's monument.

The caretaker, advancing cautiously, soon noticed a dim light in the direction of Malenvers Avenue. He slipped in amongst the tombstones and witnessed a most horrible deed of desecration.

A young man had disinterred the corpse of a young woman, buried the day before, and he was dragging it out of the grave.

A small dark lantern, placed on a pile of earth, lit up this hideous scene.

Vincent, the caretaker, pounced upon the criminal, felled him to the ground, bound his hands and took him to the police station.

He was a young lawyer from the city, rich and well thought of. His name was Courbataille.

He was tried. The public prosecutor recalled the monstrous deeds committed by Sergeant Bertrand and aroused the audience.

The crowd was thrilled with indignation. As soon as the magistrate sat down the cry arose: 'Put him to death! Put him to death!' The president had great difficulty in restoring silence.

Then he said, in a serious tone of voice:

'Accused, what have you to say in your defence?'

Courbataille, who had refused counsel, arose. He was a handsome youth, large, dark, with an open countenance, strong features, and a fearless eye.

The crowd began to hiss.

He was not disconcerted, but commenced speaking with a slightly husky voice, a little low in the beginning, but gradually gaining in strength:

'Your Honour,

'Gentlemen of the Jury,

'I have very little to say. The woman whose tomb I violated was my mistress. I loved her.

'I loved her, not with a sensual love, not simply from kindness of soul and heart, but with an absolute, perfect love, with mad passion.

'Listen to what I have to say:

'When I first met her, I felt a strange sensation on seeing her. It was not astonishment, nor admiration, for it was not what is called love at first sight, but it was a delightful sensation, as though I had been plunged in a tepid bath. Her movements captivated me, her voice enchanted me, it gave me infinite pleasure to watch everything about her. It also seemed to me that I had known her for a long time, that I had seen her before. She seemed to have some of my spirit within her.

'She seemed to me like an answer to an appeal from my soul, to this vague and continuous appeal which forces us towards Hope throughout the whole course of our lives.

'When I became a little better acquainted with her, the mere thought of seeing her again filled me with a deep and exquisite agitation; the touch of her hand in mine was such a joy to me that I had never imagined the like before; her smile made my eyes shine with joy, and made me feel like running about, dancing, rolling on the ground.

'Then she became my mistress.

'She was more than that to me, she was my life itself. I hoped for nothing more on earth, I wished for nothing more, I longed for nothing more.

'Well, one evening, as we were taking a rather long walk by the bank of the stream, we were caught by the rain. She felt cold.

'The next day she had inflammation of the lungs. Eight days later she died.

'During those dying hours, astonishment and fear prevented me from understanding or thinking.

'When she was dead, I was so stunned by brutal despair that I was unable to think. I wept.

'During all the horrible phases of interment my wild, excessive grief was the sorrow of a man beside himself, a sort of sensual physical grief.

'Then when she was gone, when she was under the ground, my mind suddenly became clear, and I passed through a train of mental suffering so terrible that even the love she had given me was dear at such a price.

'Then I was seized with an obsession.

'I shall never see her again.

'After reflecting on that for a whole day, it maddens you.

'Think of it! A being is there, one whom you adore, a unique being, for in the whole wide world there is no one who resembles her. This being has given herself to you, with you she creates this mysterious union called love. Her glance seems to you vaster than space, more charming than the world, her bright glance full of tender smiles. This being loves you. When she speaks to you her voice overwhelms you with happiness.

'And suddenly she disappears! Think of it! She disappears not only from your sight, but from everybody's. She is dead. Do you understand what that word means? Never, never, never more, nowhere, will this being exist. Those eyes will never see again. Never will this voice, never will any voice like this, among human voices, pronounce one word in the same way that she pronounced it.

'There will never be another face born like hers. Never, never! The cast of statues is kept; the stamp that reproduces objects with the same outlines and the same colours is preserved. But this body and this face will never be seen again on this earth. And still there will be born thousands of beings, millions, thousands of millions, and even more, and among all these women there will never be found one like her. Can that be possible? It makes one mad to think of it!

'She lived twenty years, no more, and she has disappeared forever, forever, forever! She thought, she smiled, she loved me. Now there is nothing more. The flies which die in the autumn are of as much importance as we in creation. Nothing more! And I thought how her body, her fresh, warm body, so soft, so white, so beautiful, was rotting away in the depths of a box under the ground. And her soul, her mind, her love—where were they?

'Never to see her again! Never again! My mind was haunted by the thought of that decomposing body, which I, however, might still recognise!

'I set out with a shovel, a lantern and a hammer. I climbed over the cemetery wall. I found the hole where her grave was. It had not yet been entirely filled up. I uncovered the coffin, and raised one of the planks. An awful odour, the abominable breath of putrefaction, arose in my face. Oh, her bed, perfumed with iris!

'However, I opened the coffin and thrust in my lighted lantern, and saw her. Her face was blue, swollen, horrible! Black liquid had flowed from her mouth.

'She! It was she! I was seized with horror. But I put out my arm and caught her hair to pull this monstrous face towards me! It was at that moment I was arrested.

'All night I carried with me, as one retains the perfume of a woman after a sexual embrace, the filthy smell of this putrefaction, the odour of my beloved!

'Do what you like with me.'

A strange silence seemed to hang over the hall. People appeared to be awaiting something more. The Jury withdrew to deliberate. When they returned after a few minutes, the accused did not seem to have any fears, nor even any thoughts. In the traditional formula the Judge informed him that his peers had found him not guilty.

He did not make a movement, but the public applauded.

The Man with the Nose

by

RHODA BROUGHTON

If there was one thing that Victorian authoresses loved, it was a ghost story. Both the famous and the not so famous, they all tried their hand at tales of terror, with varying degrees of success. Those who succeeded included Elizabeth Braddon, Mrs Oliphant, Mary Molesworth, Mrs J. H. Riddell, Mrs Gaskell and Rhoda Broughton.

It was on the cards that Rhoda Broughton (1840–1920) would succeed at this type of writing, for she was the niece of the famous J. Sheridan le Fanu. Born in Denbigh, North Wales, Rhoda Broughton never married and lived with her parents until they died, when she moved to Headington, Oxford.

Her novels were extremely successful in the late 1880s (le Fanu himself bought her first novel, Not Wisely But Too Well, *as a serial in his* Dublin University Magazine) *and her success enabled her to turn to short story writing for her own convenience.*

In 1879 she published Twilight Stories, *her only volume of ghostly tales, from which comes* 'The Man with the Nose'. *It is a chilling story and the first to utilise a theme later taken up by E. F. Benson in his famous tale* 'The Face'.

(The details of this story are, of course, imaginary, but the main incidents are, to the best of my belief, fact.)

I

'Do you like the seaside?' asks Elizabeth, lifting her little brown head and her small happy face from the map of English sea-coast along which her forefinger is slowly travelling.

'Since you ask me, distinctly *no*,' reply I, for once venturing to have a decided opinion of my own, which during the last few weeks of imbecility I can be hardly said to have had. 'I broke my last wooden spade five and twenty years ago. I have but a poor opinion of cockles—sandy red-nosed things, are not they? and the air always makes me bilious.'

'Then we certainly will not go there,' says Elizabeth, laughing. 'A bilious bridegroom! alliterative but horrible! None of our friends show the least eagerness to lend us their country house. It is evident, therefore, that we must go somewhere,' she says, making her forefinger resume its employment, and reaching Torquay.

'I suppose so,' say I, with a sort of sigh; 'for once in our lives we must resign ourselves to having the finger of derision pointed at us by waiters and landlords.

'You shall leave your new portmanteau at home, and I will leave all my best clothes, and nobody will guess that we are bride and bridebroom; they will think that we have been married—oh, ever since the world began' (opening her eyes very wide).

I shake my head. 'With an old portmanteau and in rags we shall still have the mark of the beast upon us.'

'Do you mind much? do you hate being ridiculous?' asks Elizabeth, meekly, rather depressed by my view of the case; 'because if so, let us go somewhere out of the way, where there will be very few people to laugh at us.'

'On the contrary,' return I, stoutly, 'we will betake ourselves to some spot where such as we do chiefly congregate—where we shall be swallowed up and lost in the multitude of our fellow-sinners.' A pause devoted to reflection. 'What do you say to the Lakes?' My arm is round her, and I feel her supple body shiver though it is mid July and the bees are booming about in the still and sleepy noon garden outside.

'Oh—no—no—not *there*!'

'Why such emphasis?' I ask gaily.

'Something dreadful happened to me there,' she says, with another shudder. 'But indeed I did not think there was any harm in it—I never thought anything would come of it.'

'What the devil was it? cry I, in a jealous heat and hurry; 'what the mischief *did* you do, and why have not you told me about it before?'

'I did not *do* much,' she answers meekly, seeking for my hand, 'but I was ill—very ill—there; I had a nervous fever. I was in a bed hung with a chintz with a red and green fern-leaf pattern on it. I have always hated red and green fern-leaf chintzes ever since.'

'It would be possible to avoid the obnoxious bed, would not it?' say I, laughing a little. 'Where does it lie? Windermere? Ulleswater? Wastwater? Where?'

'We were at Ulleswater,' she says, speaking rapidly, while a hot colour grows on her small white cheeks—'Papa, mamma, and I; and there came a mesmeriser to Penrith, and we went to see him—everybody did—and he asked leave to mesmerise me—he said I should be such a good medium—and—and—I did not know what it was like. I thought it would be quite good fun—and—and—I let him.'

She is trembling exceedingly; even the loving pressure of my arms cannot abate her shivering.

'Well?'

'And after that I do not remember anything—I believe I did all sorts of extraordinary things that he told me—sang and danced, and made a fool of myself—but when I came home I was very ill, very—I lay in bed for five whole weeks, and—and was off my head, and said odd and wicked things that you would not have expected me to say—that dreadful bed! shall I ever forget it?'

'We will *not* go to the Lakes,' I say, decisively, 'and we will not talk any more about mesmerism.'

'That is right,' she says, with a sigh of relief, 'I try to think about it as little as possible; but sometimes, in the dead black of the night, when God seems a long way off, and the devil near, it comes back to me so strongly—I feel, do not you know, as if he were *there* somewhere in the room, and I *must* get up and follow him.'

'Why should not we go abroad?' suggest I, abruptly turning the conversation.

'Do you fancy the Rhine?' says Elizabeth, with a rather timid suggestion; 'I know it is the fashion to run it down nowadays, and call it a cocktail river; but—but—after all it cannot be so *very* contemptible, or Byron could not have said such noble things about it.'

 ' "The castled crag of Drachenfels
  Frowns o'er the wide and winding Rhine,
  Whose breast of waters broadly swells
   Between the banks which bear the vine," '

say I, spouting. 'After all, that proves nothing, for Byron could have made a silk purse out of a sow's ear.'

'The Rhine will not do then?' says she resignedly, suppressing a sigh.

'On the contrary, it will do admirably: it *is* a cocktail river, and I do not care who says it is not,' reply I, with illiberal positiveness; 'but everybody should be able to say so from their own experience, and not from hearsay: the Rhine let it be, by all means.'

So the Rhine it is.

II

I have got over it; we have both got over it, tolerably, creditably; but after all, it is a much severer ordeal for a man than a woman, who, with a bouquet to occupy her hands, and a veil to gently shroud her features, need merely be prettily passive. I am alluding, I need hardly say, to the religious ceremony of marriage, which I flatter myself I have gone through with a stiff sheepishness not unworthy of my country. It is a three-days-old event now, and we are getting used to belonging to one another, though Elizabeth still takes off her ring twenty times a day to admire its bright thickness; still laughs when she hears herself called 'Madame.'

Now we are at Brussels, she and I, feeling oddly, joyfully free from any chaperone. We had been mildly sight-seeing—very mildly most people would say, but we have resolved not to take our pleasure with the railway speed of Americans, or the hasty sadness of our fellow Britons. Slowly and gaily we have been taking ours. To-day we have been to visit Wiertz's pictures. Have you ever seen them, oh reader? They are known to comparatively few people, but if you have a taste for the unearthly terrible—if you wish to sup full of horrors, hasten thither. We have been peering through the appointed peep-hole at the horrible cholera picture—the man buried alive by mistake, pushing up the lid of his coffin, and stretching a ghastly face and livid hands out of his winding sheet towards you, while awful grey-blue coffins are piled around, and noisome toads and giant spiders crawl damply about. On first seeing it, I have reproached myself for bringing one of so nervous a temperament as Elizabeth to see so haunting and hideous a spectacle; but she is less impressed than I expected—less impressed than I myself am.

'He is very lucky to be able to get his lid up,' she says, with a half-laugh; 'we should find it hard work to burst our brass nails, should not we? When you bury me, dear, fasten me down very slightly, in case there may be some mistake.'

And now all the long and quiet July evening we have been prowling together about the streets, flattening our noses against the shop windows, and making each other imaginary presents. Elizabeth has not confined herself to imagination, however; she has made me buy her a little bonnet with feathers—'in order to look married,' as she says, and the result is such a delicious picture of a child playing at being grown up, having practised a theft on its mother's wardrobe, that for the last two hours I have been in a foolish ecstacy of love and laughter over her and it. We are at the 'Bellevue', and have a fine suite of rooms, *au premier*, evidently specially devoted to the English, to the gratification of whose well-known loyalty the Prince and Princess of Wales are simpering from the walls. Is there any one in the three kingdoms who knows his own face as well as he knows the faces of Albert Victor and Alexandra?

The long evening has at last slidden into night—night far advanced —night melting into earliest day. All Brussels is asleep. One moment ago I also was asleep, soundly as any log. What is it that has made me take this sudden, headlong plunge out of sleep into wakefulness? Who is it that is clutching at and calling upon me? What is it that is making me struggle mistily up into a sitting posture, and try to revive my sleep-numbed senses? A summer night is never wholly dark; by the half light that steals through the closed *persiennes* and open windows I see my wife standing beside my bed; the extremity of terror on her face, and her fingers digging themselves with painful tenacity into my arm.

'Tighter, tighter!' she is crying wildly. 'What are you thinking of? You are letting me go!'

'Good heavens!' say I, rubbing my eyes, while my muddy brain grows a trifle clearer. 'What is it? What has happened? Have you had a nightmare?'

'You saw him,' she says, with a sort of sobbing breathlessness; 'you know you did! You saw him as well as I.'

'I!' cry I, incredulously—'not I! Till this second I have been fast asleep. *I* saw nothing.'

'You did!' she cries, passionately. 'You know you did. Why do you deny it? You were as frightened as I.'

'As I live,' I answer, solemnly, 'I know no more than the dead what you are talking about; till you woke me by calling and catching hold of me, I was as sound asleep as the seven sleepers.'

'Is it possible that it can have been a *dream*?' she says, with a long sigh, for a moment loosing my arm, and covering her face with her hands. 'But no—in a dream I should have been somewhere else, but I was here—*here*—on that bed, and he stood *there*,' pointing with her forefinger, 'just *there*, between the foot of it and the window!'

She stops panting.

'It is all that brute Wiertz,' say I, in a fury. 'I wish I had been buried alive myself before I had been fool enough to take you to see his beastly daubs.'

'Light a candle,' she says, in the same breathless way, her teeth chattering with fright. 'Let us make sure he is not hidden somewhere in the room.'

'How could he be?' say I, striking a match; 'the door is locked.'

'He might have got in by the balcony,' she answers, still trembling violently.

'He would have had to have cut a very large hole in the *persiennes*,' say I, half mockingly. 'See, they are intact, and well fastened on the inside.'

She sinks into an arm-chair, and pushes her loose soft hair from her white face.

'It *was* a dream then, I suppose?'

She is silent for a moment or two, while I bring her a glass of water, and throw a dressing-gown round her cold and shrinking form.

'Now tell me, my little one,' I say coaxingly, sitting down at her feet, 'what it was—what you thought you saw?'

'*Thought* I saw!' echoes she, with indignant emphasis, sitting up-right, while her eyes sparkle feverishly. 'I am as certain that I saw him standing there as I am that I see that candle burning—that I see this chair—that I see you.'

'*Him*! but who is *him*?'

She falls forward on my neck, and buries her face in my shoulder.

'That—dreadful—man!' she says, while her whole body is one tremor.

'*What* dreadful man?' cry I impatiently.

She is silent.

'Who was he?'

'I do not know.'

'Did you ever see him before?'

'Oh, no—no, never! I hope to God I may never see him again!'

'What was he like?'

'Come closer to me,' she says, laying hold of my hand with her small and chilly fingers; 'stay *quite* near me, and I will tell you,'—after a pause—'he had a *nose*!'

'My dear soul,' cry I, bursting out into a loud laugh in the silence of the night, 'do not most people have noses? Would not he have been much more dreadful if he had had *none*?'

'But it was *such* a nose!' she says, with perfect trembling gravity.

'A bottle nose?' suggest I, still cackling.

'For heaven's sake, don't laugh!' she says nervously; 'if you had seen his face, you would have been as little disposed to laugh as I.'

'But his nose?' return I, suppressing my merriment, 'what kind of nose was it? See, I am as grave as a judge.'

'It was very prominent,' she answers, in a sort of awe-struck half-whisper, 'and very sharply chiselled; the nostrils very much cut out.' A little pause. 'His eyebrows were one straight black line across his face, and under them his eyes burnt like dull coals of fire, that shone and yet did not shine; they looked like dead eyes, sunken, half extinguished, and yet sinister.'

'And what did he do?' asked I, impressed, despite myself, by her passionate earnestness; 'when did you first see him?'

'I was asleep,' she said—'at least, I thought so—and suddenly I opened my eyes, and he was *there—there*—pointing again with trembling finger—'between the window and the bed.'

'What was he doing? Was he walking about?'

'He was standing as still as stone—I never saw any live thing so still—*looking* at me; he never called or beckoned, or moved a finger, but his eyes *commanded* me to come to him, as the eyes of the mesmeriser at Penrith did.' She stops, breathing heavily. I can hear her heart's loud and rapid beats.

'And you?' I say, pressing her more closely to my side, and smoothing her troubled hair.

'I hated it,' she cries, excitedly, 'I loathed it—abhorred it. I was ice cold with fear and horror, but—I *felt* myself going to him.

'Yes?'

'And then I shrieked out to you, and you came running, and caught fast hold of me, and held me tight at first—quite tight—but presently I felt your hold slacken—slacken—and though I *longed* to stay with you, though I was *mad* with fright, yet I felt myself pulling strongly away from you—going to him; and he—he stood there always looking—looking—and then I gave one last loud shriek, and I suppose I awoke—and it was a dream!'

'I never heard of a clearer case of nightmare,' say I, stoutly; 'that vile Wiertz! I should like to see his whole *Musée* burnt by the hands of the hangman to-morrow.'

She shakes her head. 'It had nothing to say to Wiertz; what it meant I do not know, but——'

'It meant nothing,' I answer, reassuringly, 'except that for the future we will go and see none but good and pleasant sights, and steer clear of charnel-house fancies.'

III

Elizabeth is now in a position to decide whether the Rhine is a cocktail river or not, for she is on it, and so am I. We are sitting, with an awning over our heads, and little wooden stools under our feet. Elizabeth has a small sailor's hat and blue ribbon on her head. The river breeze has blown it rather awry; has tangled her plenteous hair; has made a faint pink stain on her pale cheeks. It is some fête day, and the boat is crowded. Tables, countless camp stools, volumes of black smoke pouring from the funnel, as we steam along. 'Nothing to the Caledonian Canal!' cries a burly Scotsman in leggings, speaking with loud authority, and surveying with an air of contempt the eternal vine-clad slopes, that sound so well, and look so *sticky* in reality. 'Cannot hold a candle to it!' A rival bride and bridegroom opposite, sitting together like love-birds under an umbrella, looking into each other's eyes instead of at the Rhine scenery.

'They might as well have stayed at home, might not they?' says my wife, with a little air of superiority. 'Come, we are not so bad as that, are we?'

A storm comes on: hailstones beat slantwise and reach us—stone and sting us right under our awning. Everybody rushes down below, and takes the opportunity to feed ravenously. There are few actions more disgusting than eating *can* be made. A handsome girl close to us—her immaturity evidenced by the two long tails of black hair down her back—is thrusting her knife halfway down her throat.

'Come on deck again,' says Elizabeth, disgusted and frightened at this last sight. 'The hail was much better than this!'

Se we return to our camp stools, and sit alone under one mackintosh in the lashing storm, with happy hearts and empty stomachs.

'Is not this better than any luncheon?' asks Elizabeth, triumphantly, while the rain-drops hang on her long and curled lashes.

'Infinitely better,' reply I, madly struggling with the umbrella to prevent its being blown inside out, and gallantly ignoring a species of gnawing sensation at my entrails.

The squall clears off by-and-by, and we go steaming, steaming on past the unnumbered little villages by the water's edge with church spires and pointed roofs, past the countless rocks with their little pert castles perched on the top of them, past the tall, stiff poplar rows. The church bells are ringing gaily as we go by. A nightingale is singing from a wood. The black eagle of Prussia droops on the stream behind us, swish-swish through the dull green water.

The day steals on; at every stopping place more people come on. There is hardly elbow room; and, what is worse, almost everybody is drunk. Rocks, castles, villages, poplars, slide by, while the paddles churn always the water, and the evening draws greyly on. At Bingen a party of big blue Prussian soldiers, very drunk, 'glorious' as Tam o' Shanter, come and establish themselves close to us. They call for Lager Beer; talk at the tip-top of their strong voices; two of them begin to spar; all seem inclined to sing. Elizabeth is frightened. We are two hours late in arriving at Biebrich. It is half an hour more before we can get ourselves and our luggage into a carriage and set off along the winding road to Wiesbaden. 'The night is chilly, but not dark.' There is only a little shabby bit of a moon, but it shines as hard as it can. Elizabeth is quite worn out, her tired head droops in uneasy sleep on my shoulder. Once she wakes up with a start.

'Are you sure that it meant nothing?' she asks, looking me eagerly in my face; 'do people often have such dreams?'

'Often, often,' I answer, reassuringly.

'I am always afraid of falling asleep now,' she says, trying to sit up-right and keep her heavy eyes open, 'for fear of seeing him standing there again. Tell me, do you think I shall? Is there any chance, any probability of it?'

'None, none!'

We reach Wiesbaden at last, and drive up to the Hôtel des Quatre Saisons. By this time it is full midnight. Two or three men are standing about the door. Morris, the maid, has got out—so have I, and I am holding out my hand to Elizabeth when I hear her give one piercing scream, and see her with ash-white face and starting eyes point with her fore-finger——

'There he is!—there!—there!'

I look in the direction indicated, and just catch a glimpse of a tall figure standing half in the shadow of the night, half in the gas-light from the hotel. I have not time for more than one cursory glance, as I am interrupted by a cry from the bystanders, and turning quickly round, am just in time to catch my wife, who falls in utter insensibility into my arms. We carry her into a room on the ground floor; it is small, noisy, and hot, but it is the nearest at hand. In about an hour she re-opens her eyes. A strong shudder makes her quiver from head to foot.

'Where is he? she says, in a terrified whisper, as her senses come slowly back. 'He is somewhere about—somewhere near. I feel that he is!'

'My dearest child, there is no one here but Morris and me,' I answer soothingly. 'Look for yourself. See.'

I take one of the candles and light up each corner of the room in succession.

'You saw him!' she says, in trembling hurry, sitting up and clenching her hands together. 'I know you did—I pointed him out to you—you cannot say that it was a dream this time.'

'I saw two or three ordinary-looking men as we drove up,' I answer, in a commonplace, matter-of-fact tone. 'I did not notice anything remarkable about any of them; you know, the fact is, darling, that you have had nothing to eat all day, nothing but a biscuit, and you are over-wrought, and fancy things.'

'Fancy!' echoes she, with strong irritation. 'How you talk! Was I ever one to fancy things? I tell you that as sure as I sit here—as sure as you stand there—I saw him—him—the man I saw in my dream, if it was a dream. There was not a hair's breadth of difference between them—and he was looking at me—looking——'

She breaks off into hysterical sobbing.

'My dear child!' say I, thoroughly alarmed, and yet half angry, 'for God's sake do not work yourself up into a fever: wait till to-morrow, and we will find out who he is, and all about him; you yourself will laugh when we discover that he is some harmless bagman.'

'Why not now?' she says, nervously; 'why cannot you find out now —this minute?'

'Impossible! Everybody is in bed! Wait till to-morrow, and all will be cleared up.'

The morrow comes, and I go about the hotel, inquiring. The house is so full, and the data I have to go upon are so small, that for some time I have great difficulty in making it understood to whom I am alluding. At length one waiter seems to comprehend.

'A tall and dark gentleman, with a pronounced and very peculiar nose? Yes; there has been such a one, certainly, in the hotel, but he left at "grand matin" this morning; he remained only one night.'

'And his name?'

The garçon shakes his head. 'That is unknown, monsieur; he did not inscribe it in the visitors' book.'

'What countryman was he?'

Another shake of the head. 'He spoke German, but it was with a foreign accent.'

'Whither did he go?'

That also is unknown. Nor can I arrive at any more facts about him.

IV

A fortnight has passed; we have been hither and thither; now we are at Lucerne. Peopled with better inhabitants, Lucerne might well do for Heaven. It is drawing towards eventide, and Elizabeth and I are sitting hand in hand on a quiet bench, under the shady linden trees, on a high hill up above the lake. There is nobody to see us, so we sit peaceably hand in hand. Up by the still and solemn monastery we came, with its small and narrow windows, calculated to hinder the holy fathers from promenading curious eyes on the world, the flesh, and the devil, tripping past them in blue gauze veils: below us grass and green trees, houses with high-pitched roofs, little dormer-windows, and shutters yet greener than the grass; below us the lake in its ripple-less peace, calm, quiet, motionless as Bethesda's pool before the coming of the troubling angel.

'I said it was too good to last,' say I, doggedly, 'did not I only yesterday? Perfect peace, perfect sympathy, perfect freedom from nagging worries—when did such a state of things last more than two days?'

Elizabeth's eyes are idly fixed on a little steamer, with a stripe of red along its side, and a tiny puff of smoke from its funnel, gliding along and cutting a narrow white track on Lucerne's sleepy surface.

'This is the fifth false alarm of the gout having gone to his stomach within the last two years,' continue I resentfully. 'I declare to Heaven, that if it has not really gone there this time, I'll cut the whole concern.'

Let no one cast up their eyes in horror, imagining that it is my father to whom I am thus alluding; it is only a great-uncle by marriage, in consideration of whose wealth and vague promises I have dawdled professionless through twenty-eight years of my life.

'You *must* not go,' says Elizabeth, giving my hand an imploring squeeze. 'The man in the Bible said, "I have married a wife, and therefore I cannot come"; why should it be a less valid excuse nowadays?'

'If I recollect rightly, it was considered rather a poor one even then,' reply I, dryly.

Elizabeth is unable to contradict this; she therefore only lifts two pouted lips (Monsieur Taine objects to the redness of English women's mouths, but I do not) to be kissed, and says, 'Stay.' I am good enough to comply with her unspoken request, though I remain firm with regard to her spoken one.

'My dearest child,' I say, with an air of worldly experience and superior wisdom, 'kisses are very good things—in fact, there are few better—but one cannot live upon them.'

'Let us try,' she says coaxingly.

'I wonder which would get tired first?' I say, laughing. But she only goes on pleading, 'Stay, stay.'

'How *can* I stay?' I cry impatiently; you talk as if I *wanted* to go! Do you think it is any pleasanter to me to leave you than to you to be left? But you know his disposition, his rancorous resentment of fancied neglects. For the sake of two days' indulgence, must I throw away what will keep us in ease and plenty to the end of our days?'

'I do not care for plenty,' she says, with a little petulant gesture. I do not see that rich people are any happier than poor ones. Look at the St Clairs; they have £40,000 a year, and she is a miserable woman, perfectly miserable, because her face gets red after dinner.'

'There will be no fear of *our* faces getting red after dinner,' say I, grimly, 'for we shall have no dinner for them to get red after.'

A pause. My eyes stray away to the mountains. Pilatus on the right, with his jagged peak and slender snow-chains about his harsh neck; hill after hill rising silent, eternal, like guardian spirits standing hand in hand around their child, the lake. As I look, suddenly they have all flushed, as at some noblest thought, and over all their sullen faces streams an ineffable rosy joy—a solemn and wonderful effulgence, such as Israel saw reflected from the features of the Eternal in their prophet's transfigured eyes. The unutterable peace and stainless beauty of earth and sky seem to lie softly on my soul. 'Would God I could stay! Would God all life could be like this!' I say, devoutly, and the aspiration has the reverent earnestness of a prayer.

'Why do you say, "*Would God*!"' she cries passionately, 'when it lies with yourself? Oh my dear love,' gently sliding her hand through my arm, and lifting wetly-beseeching eyes to my face, 'I do not know why I insist upon it so much—I cannot tell you myself—I dare say I seem selfish and unreasonable—but I feel as if your going now would be the end of all things—as if——' She breaks off suddenly.

'My child,' say I, thoroughly distressed, but still determined to have my own way, 'you talk as if I were going for ever and a day; in a week, at the outside, I shall be back, and then you will thank me for the very thing for which you now think me so hard and disobliging.'

'Shall I?' she answers, mournfully. 'Well, I hope so.'

'You will not be alone, either; you will have Morris.'

'Yes.'

'And every day you will write me a long letter, telling me every single thing that you do, say, and think.'

'Yes.'

She answers me gently and obediently; but I can see that she is still utterly unreconciled to the idea of my absence.

'What is it that you are afraid of?' I ask, becoming rather irritated. 'What do you suppose will happen to you?'

She does not answer; only a large tear falls on my hand, which she hastily wipes away with her pocket handkerchief, as if afraid of exciting my wrath.

'Can you give me any good reason why I *should* stay?' I ask, dictatorially.

'None—none—only—stay—stay!'

But I am resolved *not* to stay. Early the next morning I set off.

V

This time it is not a false alarm; this time it really has gone to his stomach, and, declining to be dislodged thence, kills him. My return is therefore retarded until after the funeral and the reading of the will. The latter is so satisfactory, and my time is so fully occupied with a multiplicity of attendant business, that I have no leisure to regret the delay. I write to Elizabeth, but receive no letters from her. This surprises and makes me rather angry, but does not alarm me. 'If she had been ill, if anything had happened, Morris would have written. She never was great at writing, poor little soul. What dear little babyish notes she used to send me during our engagement! Perhaps she wishes to punish me for my disobedience to her wishes. Well, *now* she will see who was in the right.' I am drawing near her now; I am walking up from the railway station at Lucerne. I am very joyful as I march along under an umbrella, in the grand broad shining of the summer afternoon. I think with pensive passion of the last glimpse I had of my beloved—her small and wistful face looking out from among the thick fair fleece of her long hair—winking away her tears and blowing kisses to me. It is a new sensation to me to have anyone looking tearfully wistful over my departure. I draw near the great glaring Schweizerhof, with its colonnaded tourist-crowded porch; here are all the pomegranates as I left them, in their green tubs, with their scarlet blossoms, and the dusty oleanders in a row. I look up at our windows; nobody is looking out from them; they are open, and the curtains are alternately swelled out and drawn in by the softly-playful wind. I run quickly upstairs and burst noisily into the sitting-room. Empty, perfectly empty! I open the adjoining door into the bedroom, crying 'Elizabeth! Elizabeth!' but I receive no answer. Empty too. A feeling of indignation creeps over me as I think, 'Knowing the time of my return, she might have managed to be indoors.' I have returned to the silent sitting-room, where the only noise is the wind still playing hide-and-seek with the curtains. As I look vacantly round my eye catches sight of a letter lying on the table. I pick it up mechanically and look at the address. Good heavens! what can this mean? It is my own, that I sent her two days ago, unopened, with the seal unbroken. Does she carry her resentment so far as not even to open my letters? I spring at the bell and violently ring it. It is answered by the waiter who has always specially attended us.

'Is madame gone out?'

The man opens his mouth and stares at me.

'Madame! Is monsieur then not aware that madame is no longer at the hotel?'

'*What?*'

'On the same day as monsieur, madame departed.'

'*Departed!* Good God! what are you talking about?'

'A few hours after monsieur's departure—I will not be positive as to the exact time, but it must have been between one and two o'clock as the midday *table d'hôte* was in progress—a gentleman came and asked for madame——'

'Yes—be quick.'

'I demanded whether I should take up his card, but he said "No," that was unnecessary, as he was perfectly well known to madame; and, in fact, a short time afterwards, without saying anything to anyone, she departed with him.'

'And did not return in the evening?'

'No, monsieur; madame has not returned since that day.'

I clench my hands in an agony of rage and grief. 'So this is it! With that pure child-face, with that divine ignorance—only three weeks married—this is the trick she has played me!' I am recalled to myself by a compassionate suggestion from the garçon.

'Perhaps it was the brother of madame.'

Elizabeth has no brother, but the remark brings back to me the necessity of self-command. 'Very probably,' I answer, speaking with infinite difficulty. 'What sort of looking gentleman was he?'

'He was a very tall and dark gentleman with a most peculiar nose—not quite like any nose that I ever saw before—and most singular eyes. Never have I seen a gentleman who at all resembled him.'

I sink into a chair, while a cold shudder creeps over me as I think of my poor child's dream—of her fainting fit at Wiesbaden—of her unconquerable dread of and aversion from my departure. And this happened twelve days ago! I catch up my hat, and prepare to rush like a madman in pursuit.

'How did they go?' I ask incoherently; 'by train?—driving?—walking?'

'They went in a carriage.'

'What direction did they take? Whither did they go?'

He shakes his head. 'It is not known.'

'It *must* be known,' I cry, driven to frenzy by every second's delay. 'Of course the driver could tell; where is he?—where can I find him?'

'He did not belong to Lucerne, neither did the carriage; the gentleman brought them with him.'

'But madame's maid,' say I, a gleam of hope flashing across my mind; 'did she go with her?'

'No, monsieur, she is still here; she was as much surprised as monsieur at madame's departure.'

'Send her at once,' I cry eagerly; but when she comes I find that she can throw no light on the matter. She weeps noisily and says many irrelevant things, but I can obtain no information from her beyond the fact that she was unaware of her mistress's departure until long after it had taken place, when, surprised at not being rung for at the usual time, she had gone to her room and found it empty, and on inquiring in the hotel, had heard of her sudden departure; that, expecting her to return at night, she had sat up waiting for her till two o'clock in the morning, but that, as I knew, she had not returned, neither had anything since been heard of her.

Not all my inquiries, not all my cross-questionings of the whole staff of the hotel, of the visitors, of the railway officials, of nearly all the inhabitants of Lucerne and its environs, procure me a jot more knowledge. On the next few weeks I look back as on a hellish and insane dream. I can neither eat nor sleep; I am unable to remain one moment quiet; my whole existence, my nights and my days, are spent in seeking, seeking. Everything that human despair and frenzied love can do is done by me. I advertise, I communicate with the police, I employ detectives; but that fatal twelve days' start for ever baffles me. Only on one occasion do I obtain one tittle of information. In a village a few miles from Lucerne the peasants, on the day in question, saw a carriage driving rapidly through their little street. It was closed, but through the windows they could see the occupants—a dark gentleman, with the peculiar physiognomy which has been so often described, and on the opposite seat a lady lying apparently in a state of utter insensibility. But even this leads to nothing.

Oh, reader, these things happened twenty years ago; since then I have searched sea and land, but never have I seen my little Elizabeth again.

My Nightmare

by

DOROTHEA GERARD

Those Victorian ladies who wrote their splendid ghost stories very often performed this task to much better effect than their male rivals. However, thanks to the era's lingering prejudice against female writers, many of them were forced to adopt male pseudonyms. The more famous, as I listed in my introduction to Rhoda Broughton's story, did not need to make such a concession to Victorian male chauvinism.

But as well as the more famous female writers in this vein during the last century, there were a host of others who did not achieve the same degree of fame or who are now remembered for just one macabre story. They include Amelia Edwards (noted for her fine tale 'The Phantom Coach'), Helen Zimmern, Rosa Mulholland, Vernon Lee (the pen-name of Violet Paget), Emma Dawson (a protégée of Ambrose Bierce), Katharine Macquoid, Gertrude Atherton, Florence Marryat (daughter of the famous Captain Frederick Marryat), Mrs Baillie Reynolds, Jessie L. Weston, Lucas Malet (the pen-name of Mary Harrison who produced in 1900 a splendid supernatural novel The Gateless Barrier), *Violet Tweedale (herself a psychic researcher), Sarah Tytler and our next two contributors.*

Our first lesser known female writer of macabre tales is Dorothea Gerard (1855–1915), who wrote several novels and books of short stories in the 1890s, including Things That Have Happened (1899) *and* On The Way Through (1892). *'My Nightmare' comes from the latter and is a grim tragedy set in an unusual location. The story's colourful setting would have been familiar to the author; in 1887, she married Captain Julius Longard of the 7th Austrian Lancers.*

Most people have a pet nightmare. Mine consists of a single human figure, sitting immovable, in an attitude which is stamped so deeply on my memory that, although almost twenty years have passed since the day on which I saw it, I could draw it to-day—supposing I could draw at all—down to the most trivial details of its appearance, down to the last touch of its immediate surroundings.

How it happened that I came to look upon this haunting figure I propose to make the subject of this reminiscence.

In the year 1867 the Lancer regiment in which I was then serving and which for eleven years had lain in Eastern Galicia, received marching orders for Silberstadt, a large town in one of the German speaking provinces of the Empire. The officers were all delighted with the change, the men, on the contrary, were deeply dejected. Recruited, as they all were, in the neighbourhood, the hardships of service had for them been hitherto much lightened by the familiarity of their surroundings. The roads they now marched on were the same they had played on as children; the mountain-chain which they saw on the horizon was the same they had looked on all their lives, and though they were no longer free men yet they remained in contact with their own people.

Our men appeared, as it were, stunned by the noise and bustle of the town. The size of the barrack-building, the huge rooms, the heavily grated windows, the long vaulted passages where every step echoed back from the stone floor, all was strange and bewildering. Originally the building had been a convent.

At the time we reached Silberstadt I belonged to the squadron of Captain Stigler. The Captain had in his service a lancer by the name of Jan Baryuk, whom he had selected as valet, principally I believe from a species of instinctive fellow-feeling. Captain Stigler was a pedant of the first water. From the quantity of beer which he drank at dinner to the number of pieces of glycerine soap which he used in a year, everything was done systematically, by rules which were to him as immovable as the laws which guide the universe. Of the servant it will be sufficient to say that in point of pedantry he was an aggravated copy of his master. Baryuk accomplished all his duties with a certain conscientious, immovable and ponderous thoroughness which I have never seen equalled. He was capable of cleaning away at one boot of his parade pair for a whole morning and of filling up the afternoon of that same day with his operations upon the second boot. He was a tall, good-looking young fellow, with somewhat mournful brown eyes; the sort of man who never shows emotion of any sort, and never speaks unless he is addressed.

We had been in Silberstadt for a little more than three weeks, when one morning my servant entered the room with a message from Captain Stigler, whose lodging adjoined mine. Would I oblige him by the loan of my bottle of spirits of wine for his coffee-machine? He could not find his own.

The idea of Captain Stigler not being able to find anything that belonged to him was so startling and unnatural that I immediately supposed he must be ill. Accordingly I betook myself to his rooms with the intention of inquiring after his health. I found the Captain in his shirt sleeves, struggling with a coffee-machine, his face half-shaved.

'Where is Baryuk?' I asked in surprise.

'If I knew where Baryuk was,' answered the Captain with some irritation, 'I should certainly not be burning my fingers with this intolerable machine. First time since he entered my service that he has not called me at the proper time.'

'Was he at home last night?'

'I can't say. Everything was laid out as usual for the night. His bed is made. Whether he slept in it or not I can't possibly say. It's a great nuisance; it puts out one's arrangements so.' The poor Captain looked thoroughly wretched. A long course of Baryuk had evidently had an enervating effect upon him.

'The chances are,' I remarked, 'that he has begun to appreciate town life at last, and has been at some nocturnal jollification where he has failed to observe the appearance of daylight.'

'Nonsense,' said the Captain, 'such a man as Baryuk would feel about as comfortable at a jollification as a herring would feel in a meal-tub.'

I then suggested the possibility of Baryuk having ventured out of the barracks and lost his way. 'We all know how the rattle of an omnibus or the jingle of a tram-car upsets the composure of these men, and deprives them of all sense of locality. I argued, 'but he is pretty sure to turn up before midday.'

The Captain grunted out a hope to the same effect, and thereupon I withdrew.

I did not happen to see Captain Stigler again till next day, when we met in the riding-school.

'Well,' I asked him, 'what explanation does Baryuk give?'

'None,' said the Captain, whose face still bore the same expression of angry perplexity which I had seen on it yesterday. 'It's becoming more mysterious every moment, and I hate mysteries, they put out one's calculations.'

'Do you mean to say that you have not seen him since yesterday?'

'Not so much as the lobe of his ear.'

My attention began to be aroused, for there is a distinct touch of the detective in my nature.

'Do you believe in a desertion?' I asked. 'Somehow that doesn't seem to me very probable.'

'Of course not; it's all a mixture of improbabilities. Still there's no denying that we have had desertions, and there's no denying either that the corners of Baryuk's mouth have been going down lower ever since we got into barracks;—homesick, I suppose.'

Several days passed during which I scarcely exchanged a word with Captain Stigler. I was enjoying town-life immensely and thought no more of Baryuk. When at last it did occur to me to ask a question I was told that he had not reappeared. Notice had been given to the Colonel and inquiries had been made, which, however, had produced a purely negative result. Nothing had been seen of Baryuk at his home.

'The desertion theory must then be thrown overboard,' I remarked. 'How about a theft? Have you missed nothing?'

Instead of answering me at once Captain Stigler stood with his hands deep in his pockets, gazing into my face with a perplexed air.

'I have missed *one* thing,' he said at last, somewhat reluctantly, 'but it isn't a thing that any man in his senses would steal. Come along, I will show you.'

We had been standing in the passage, and I now followed him into his bedroom. On the wall at the head of his bed there was, hanging upon brass hooks, a row of weapons in carefully graduated order, according to their size. One of the nails was unoccupied.

'There used to be a revolver upon that nail,' said the Captain.

A revolver? The detective in me immediately pricked up his ears. 'Do you believe in the possibility of a suicide?'

Captain Stigler burst out laughing rather loudly.

'Suicide with *that* revolver! Why, it would be a much simpler process to chop oneself to pieces with a blunt pen-knife.'

He then explained to me that the missing weapon dated from the time when the idea of the modern revolver was still struggling into existence, being, in fact, a species of cross-bred production, no longer quite a pistol and not yet quite a revolver. It was solely as a curiosity that Captain Stigler had preserved it so long.

'Besides,' said the Captain, following his own train of thought, 'even though he might have shot himself he couldn't well have buried himself at the same time, and he can't have got so very far, either; something would have been heard of him by this time.'

I could not do otherwise than assent to this, and yet the idea of that missing revolver remained obstinately fixed in my head.

There passed another few days. It was in the end of September that we had come to Silberstadt, and we were now getting on towards the end of October. The weather was getting cold. 'Where are we to store our fuel?' the soldiers' ladies asked of their husbands, and the much-worried husbands passed the question on to the yet more worried Colonel and asked: 'Where are we to store our fuel?'

It was ascertained that the cellars, which were very extensive and not of much use owing to the distance at which they lay from the different lodgings, had, for years past, been assigned to the officers as store-places for wood and coal. Presently there came out an order which decreed that on a given day the cellars should be visited by a commission. The officer who had the day's inspection received orders to accompany the commission, and as on the 29th of October the inspection happened to fall to my lot, I thus came to be of the party. There existed an old tattered plan of the cellars, showing the various cross-passages, which document was to guide us in our expedition. Two lancers carrying lanterns accompanied us.

The key of the cellar region, somewhat rusty with disuse, hung in the guard-room. It was a certain old Sergeant Baum who first tried and failed to unlock the heavy iron door. Captain Wertel, who was the commander of the expedition, had the next try with the same result. Then I took my turn, and in doing so my sword, which I had tucked under my arm, happened to run against the door, upon which it immediately swung back upon its hinges. No wonder we had failed to unlock it since it was unlocked already. There was nothing wrong with the lock, however, as an examination proved. We supposed therefore that it could only have been from an oversight that the last person who had descended to the cellars—now months ago, presumably—had omitted to turn the key.

From the door a stone staircase led us straight down to the lower regions. Arrived at the bottom we ascertained that we were in a long and tolerably broad vaulted stone passage, sparely lighted at intervals by grated openings from above, probably from the yard. The expedition we had embarked on was by no means a trifling one, as we soon recognised, but on the contrary a true voyage of discovery. We were in the midst of a network of passages, branching off in all directions from our first point of departure. Some of these ended abruptly and forced us to turn back again, others took unexpected twists which we had considerable difficulty in following up on the old map, so as not to lose all idea of locality.

We had not taken very many turns round the various corners, when I made a halt and declared that I could not go a step further without the assistance of a lighted cigar. I likewise offered one to Captain Wertel, who declined it with a laugh, adding jocularly, that it was a pity I had not brought my scent-bottle with me, as I might have known, that cellars, especially when they have been shut up for months, don't generally smell as sweet as a lady's *boudoir*. Here was probably damp wood lying about, possibly also a few stray dead rats, not to speak of the want of ventilation.

We went on for a hundred yards or so, and presently Captain Wertel, who had quite dropped the jocular tone, remarked that, after all, he wouldn't mind taking that cigar, in case I thought of repeating the offer. There certainly could be no doubt that these lower regions were shockingly ill ventilated.

I gave him the cigar, and for a few minutes longer we moved onwards, Lieutenant Meyer, of the Engineers, meanwhile doing his best to decipher the numbers over the cellar entrances, and to compare them by the dim lantern light with the figures on the old plan.

Looking at Captain Wertel after a little time it struck me that he was strangely white.

'Captain,' I said, making a halt, 'I don't think this atmosphere is agreeing with you. Hadn't we better go back for a doctor and disinfectants? The air down here has been shut up for so long that it is scarcely fit for human breathing.'

The Captain began by demurring, but ended by acquiescing, and, with great alacrity on the part of all the members of the party, we retraced our steps.

The doctor on inspection was fetched, and two more lancers with lanterns were put into requisition, and presently the reinforced expedition started once more on its quest. What idea Captain Wertel had in his mind when he called for the two extra lancers, or whether he had any distinct idea at all, I am not able to say. Though we avoided exchanging words on the subject, I cannot help fancying that we both had a presentiment of an unpleasant discovery in store.

Probably it was for this reason that the numbering of the doors was now somewhat slurred over, and that we instinctively pushed on, bent upon reaching the extreme limits of this underground region. One of the lancers with a lantern walked at the head; I trod close upon his heels, feeling more and more like a detective on some burning quest. Each door as we passed it, was pushed open and a lantern held into the entrance. There was nothing to be seen but now and then a few scattered pieces of wood, once an old tub, rotten and burst, once again the handle of an axe. Some of the cellars were still black with coal-dust. We had walked for fully ten minutes when the man in front of me pushed open another door in one of the narrow cross-passages and again held the lantern forward. At the same instant there was a crash; he had dropped the lantern to the ground and started back so suddenly that he all but knocked me over. I could hear his teeth chattering.

'There is something sitting there,' he whispered.

The lantern had been shivered to atoms in the fall, and, as we were standing single file behind each other on account of the narrowness of the passage, it took a minute or two before one of the lights in the rear could be got to the front. The cellar itself, being lighted only by a small opening above the door, was practically pitch-dark. I thought that second lantern was never coming. When it came at last this is what I saw.

Against the wall, opposite the door, was piled a layer of firewood, which the former possessor of the cellar must have left behind him; blotches of mildew and clumps of tiny yellow fungus had formed themselves upon the wood. In the middle of the cellar stood the block on which the firewood is split—a shapeless black lump. Upon this lump, there sat a human figure, sunk, as it were, into itself, the head low on the breast, the left hand—the one towards the doorway—resting on the knee, the right arm hanging straight down. The figure was in shirt-sleeves. I tore the lantern out of the hand of the soldier who was holding it and went a few steps nearer. The man sitting on the block had high boots on and grey trousers, of the sort worn by officers' servants. On the floor beside him lay his blue coat, carefully folded up and neatly smoothed out, lining uppermost; the cap lay on the top. A thick, white spot was sticking to the block, close beside the figure—a patch of melted tallow in which the last remnant of the burnt-down wick lay all aslant. As I stepped up quite close a small dark object dropped from the block to the floor and slipped away noise-lessly among the piled up firewood—a rat. I now perceived that the dead man's right hand, which hung straight down, was grasping some object. Holding the lantern a little nearer I saw that it was a revolver, an awkward-looking old-fashioned revolver. The shirt was wide-open; and the left side of the chest half-shot to pieces. The features of the man's face were not clearly recognisable, owing to the lowered position of the head, but the clothes and the revolver were proofs enough for me that the man sitting here was none other than the lost Baryuk.

It was Captain Wertel who spoke first:—'Don't touch him,' he said quickly. 'Don't touch a thing about him: we have done all that we have to do here, the rest must be left to a new commission.'

It scarcely required the Captain's appeal to make us all gladly beat our retreat from the cellar. Two lancers were posted on guard at the door, where they stood pale as death staring into each other's horror-stricken faces; the rest of us hurried up to daylight, and I went straight to the Colonel with my report.

That same afternoon the facts of the case were put on paper. In my character of officer on inspection, I again accompanied the commission appointed for this purpose, and for the third time that day descended to the cellar-region. The inquiry brought to light the following circumstances; the revolver had originally been loaded with seven bullets, six of which had been fired, while the seventh was still in its place.

I took the weapon from the dead man's hand in the presence of the commission and examined it minutely. Then I lifted the dead man's head and counted the bullet-wounds on his chest, and found they tallied exactly; five shots were planted round about the heart, it was the sixth one only that had gone clean through it. The man had sat himself down there with the deliberate intention of shooting himself through the heart, but his anatomical knowledge not being such as to enable him to hit the right mark at once, he had failed five times; the sixth time at last, his perseverance had been crowned with success. He must have watched for some favourable moment to abduct the key of the cellar-entrance from the guard-room, must then have unlocked the door and conscientiously returned the key to its place, after which he methodically set about carrying his plan into effect. The thickness of the old walls had completely deadened all echo of the shots.

There followed the formal identification of Baryuk, at which Captain Stigler had to be present, and with a verdict of 'Suicide from unknown motives', the commission finally dispersed.

To me, a compatriot of Baryuk's, these motives are, however, not 'unknown', but, on the contrary, perfectly clear. I have called attention to them at the opening of this narrative. It was neither remorse for a crime committed, nor the fear of its consequences, nor was it a love sorrow which had played any part here it was nothing but the big town which had killed this honest, slow-thinking, narrow-minded man. He had not had enough spirit of enterprise for desertion, but he had had the horribly stubborn energy to shoot himself gradually to death with Captain Stigler's ridiculous old revolver.

It is this bent figure on the wood-block that returns to haunt me in my nightmares.

A Life-Watch

by

GEORGINA C. CLARK

Regrettably, I can find out nothing at all about our next female con-
tributor, which is unfortunate, for her story should have perpetuated the
name of Georgina C. Clark. First published in the Belgravia
Annual, *1867, this is a very odd piece indeed with extremely sinis-*
ter undertones running below the florid Victorian style. I imagine it
must have made a bit of a stir when it first appeared, for people just
didn't do things like this in those days (or now, thank goodness).

We do many foolish things in early life. I did what the world esteems
a very foolish thing—married for love. Harry and I were equally poor,
and the affronted world turned its back upon us. The wealthy heads
of both houses, determining to give us leisure to repent after having
married in haste, left us to ourselves. Harry obtained, through an old
friend of the family, a situation as clerk in a mercantile house in the
City. The salary was a small one, and many a shift and contrivance was
endured by us in those days. And yet we were very happy. Like an
obstinate fond young couple, we refused to learn the lesson our
offended elders set us, and we would not repent, but struggled on
through the battle of life in the ranks with the rest. Yes, I am proud to
say that we fought and conquered. Now that our mansion is built in
the favoured locality of the West; now that I rumble along streets in
my carriage that I have trodden once burdened with goloshes and
umbrella when the weather would not smile, however much we smiled
at Fate; now that, amongst not a few good and true and tried friends,
many throng to our gay parties who would not then have condes-
cended to cross our threshold—now I can look back and call to mind
many an incident of our early life with pleasure. There is one story,
however, mixed up with those days that is fraught with inexplicable
horror. And that is the story I have promised to relate. I must promise
that we considered it—in those early and struggling days—a rise in

life when we took a small cottage at Hampstead, with woodbine
growing over the door, and resolved to eke out the very moderate
rent by the assistance of a lodger. It was a rise because we had previously occupied apartments, and one who has not experienced similar
feelings can hardly fancy with what joy we hailed the idea of dwelling
at last under a roof of our own.

We entered into possession of our cottage, and then came our
lodger, through the ready intervention of the *Times*, in the shape of a
lady, and a singular one. We took her to be about fifty years of age.
She was a tall fine woman, but distinguished unpleasantly by remarkable rigidity in her movements. Her step was slow, measured, and
dull, and as she trod her foot never seemed to leave the floor. There
was no rebound, no pliancy in her gait, which seemed rather that of a
statue on wheels than of a creature throbbing with the pulses of life.
Her hair was thick, but entirely grey; she arranged it simply and neatly,
without ornament and without a cap, but also with a total absence of
style. Her face was ashen pale and deeply lined. She came late at night
in a cab, and my one servant remarked to me how curious it was that
she, being evidently a lady, rode outside next the driver. I thought
it very extraordinary, but the fact soon glided out of my memory as
too trivial to retain a place in it. When I say 'glided out of my memory'
I am using an incorrect expression. It rather slid into some remote,
unused corner, to be furbished out again at any distant time, like the
present, when it might be wanted as one of the small coloured bits that
fit into the puzzle of my eccentric lodger's horrible story.

She came outside the cab, dressed in an old heathen gown, a black
cloak and bonnet, and an imperviously close gauze veil of the same
sombre hue, which she held about her face as if that were a secret enemy
everyone was curious to detect, and she terribly interested to conceal.
There was a large box upon the top of the cab. It was of very old-
fashioned make, and evidently originally designed as an addendum
to a travelling carriage. The exterior was covered with leather, bound
with iron, studded with nails, and secured with a big foreign lock,
supplemented by a clumsy hasp. It was not unlike its owner—old,
worn, and of a rusty black. The great handles clanked as the man lifted
it with difficulty and due assistance to the ground. It was not easy to
get it upstairs. Did it contain books, that it was so weighty? It evidently
held something very precious to the owner, for she watched its ascent
with strained eyes; and judging from the nervous interest she appeared
to take in it, I did not doubt she had ridden outside to be near her

treasure, and selected the time of night on purpose to do so. When the box was fairly upstairs, she sat down upon it and remained there. Within the cab we found only a small portmanteau.

She had given no name when answering our advertisement, but simply forwarded a stamped envelope addressed to 'Alpha, Post Office, Dover'. Kitty, the servant girl, asked if she would like some tea, and also by what name she should address her.

'I will take tea, thank you,' was the reply, in a half absent, slow, inward tone peculiar to her. 'My name is of no consequence. What am I to call you?'

'Kitty, if you please.'

'Very well then, Kitty, you will have occasion to address me in no other manner than as "madam" or, as you will pronounce it, "ma'am!"' And with that she gave Kitty a month's rent and asked for a receipt. 'Money is better than a name,' she added, in her listless, slow way, muttering to herself. 'What is my name to them? What *is* my name?'

As it appeared to vex her, and really did not matter to us, we asked the question no more, but spoke of her as 'the lady upstairs'. She was evidently eccentric. Sometimes she would walk round the garden in the twilight, covered with her gauze veil, and holding it in a tight, nervous grasp with a gloved hand, as she did the night when she came, her eyes apparently seeking the window of her room with a suspicious restlessness, which seemed to be a part of her eccentricity.

It appeared that the lady's portmanteau contained only a change of linen, originally fine and trimmed with costly lace, but now most elaborately yet neatly mended. But for this, a thimble, scissors, needle and thread, and the dress she came in, our lodger might have been destitute. Yet the large heavy box must contain something. Still, though the object of so much solicitude, we could never discover that she opened it. It was placed in such a position as to be visible from both rooms. During the day she always sat upon it. In the morning, when Kitty took in her can of hot water, the lady was ever awake, lying on her side, with her eyes fixed upon her precious box.

When first this quiet but eccentric inmate entered our house she had with her a roll of bank-notes and a case of valuable jewels. Although she barely allowed herself the necessaries of life, the former were changed away one by one, until at last, at her request, Harry procured a purchaser for her trinkets, at a fair price, through the intervention of a friend.

The budding months blossomed into years and fructified into the

seed that is sown in the eternity of the past, and we knew that the
means thus procured were exhausted. We felt deeply interested in our
tenant, in spite—perhaps because—of her strange habits, and fell into
a custom of conversing together about her as if she had been a friend.
If these jewels were her last possessions, what was to become of her?
What was a woman of her age to do?

Her age? That was a question. We felt some doubts about her age.
Kitty, who saw most of her, thought she had not passed so many years
in the world as we at first supposed. She appeared to have no friends
or acquaintances. No letters came, no visitors called, no post-bag was
troubled on her account.

Well! There was that mysterious chest. Our conjectures and
anxieties on her behalf always found a refuge and a consolation in that.
It must contain something. It was the hope, the *Ultima Thule* of our
fancies—the sword with which we cut the Gordian knot of our
perplexities.

'Depend upon it,' Harry remarked, 'the box holds plate—you
remember how heavy it was. Or perhaps it contains diamonds of
greater value and more in number than those I sold some time ago.'

Our speculations regarding the age of the lady were set at rest by
the arrival of the census. Armed with the formidable paper, I rapped
gently at the drawing-room door.

'Come in,' responded the low, dull, measured voice.

I entered and explained my errand. 'Shall I leave the paper with
you?' I suggested.

'My writing might be——' She commenced as if thinking aloud
and stopping suddenly upon remembering that she was no longer
alone. Turning on me her eyes—peculiar grey eyes, that looked as if
she never slept or wept—she added, 'Will you have the goodness to
add the particulars for me?'

'The name?' I inquired, dipping a pen in the ink.

'What is yours?' was the counter question.

'Mary Herbert.'

'Write Martha Herbert, then; that will do.'

I looked inquiringly. 'You know there is a penalty?'

'Yes; but the name is of little consequence—the name of a lone
woman. I have given you a name; will you not write it?'

I said no more, but inscribed the paper as directed. But the appella-
tion was evidently feigned.

'Your age?'

'Twenty-eight.'

The pen actually dropped from my hand as she said twenty-eight; and I looked up very quickly.

'Nay,' she replied, meeting my gaze, and without altering her monotonous tone, 'that is the simple truth. Are you very surprised? I suppose with my grey hair I look an old woman.'

'I can hardly believe, my dear madam, that you are not mistaken,' I ventured to remonstrate.

'I have given you reasons to doubt me, perhaps; but I have answered your query with regard to age truly. I am but eight-and-twenty— barely eight-and-twenty.'

Good heaven! thought I, what can have been the circumstances of your life that your hair is grey, your face thus lined, yourself all but turned from a being of flesh and blood to a thing of stone?—that you are thus self-immured and solitary, that you shun our society and have refused all our efforts at kindness? We had gathered even from her scanty denials of our offers of amusement that she was a linguist, a musician, an artist; and yet there she sat all day, on that chest, nursing her hands, or at most adding a darn to her worn linen.

The census further told me that she was born in the parish of St George, Hanover-square, and was a widow. Harry and I talked about her more than ever. We knew that she had spent all the money obtained for the jewels, even on her frugal wants. For two weeks she had paid no rent, ordered no food. We knew not what to do; whether or not to speak to her, or, if we spoke, what to propose.

It was Monday morning, and we were seated at breakfast when Kitty hurried in and told us that the lady upstairs was in a fit. I ran up, begging Harry himself to hasten for a doctor. The girl had spoken truly. The fit was not fatal; but the poor woman lay unconscious for days. When her reason returned, it was evident that she was rapidly sinking. The doctor informed us she had only a few hours to live. There were no friends to summon; and vain were my persuasions to induce her to see a clergyman, to confess any faith, or acknowledge connection with any church or sect. I sat by the bedside I had not quitted day or night since her illness. After lying quiet some time with her hand in mine, she at last said feebly, 'Open my portmanteau and take out the book.' I took the key she offered, and obeyed by bringing to her bedside a common clasped account-book, the only one I saw.

'You have shown me kindness. You have appeared interested in me. I have yearned to make you my friend. But my secrets are such as

during life could be confided to none. I have written them there for
you. Promise me not to open that book till I am dead.'

I gave my word, and, in obedience to her request, put the book into
my pocket.

'My grey hair, my wrinkled face, my twenty-eight years—you will
understand them; but will you feel pity?'

She was sinking rapidly, like the sun at eventide; and I pressed upon
her again my request to read from my Bible the words of One whose
mercy and forgiveness were more needed than mine.

She consented. I read for some time, and thought the words were
comforting, when she started up, her manner wild, her eyes startling,
'Look! look! look!' she cried, pointing with her forefinger and white-
draped arm to the iron-bound chest, 'look! look! look!' and with a
low cry the poor lady sank back on her couch dying. The struggle was
soon over, and all was quiet.

'Look! look! look!' What had she seen? What vision had fancy,
or conscience, or sudden delirium roused before her? I know not. I
saw only the large dark chest in the place where it had ever rested—
dull, shabby, and cumbrous.

We were worn out and tired, and glad to retire early to bed. I do
not know how long Harry and I had been asleep when we were
startled by a heavy noise in the room underneath. Harry sprang up
and seized the night-light. Surely it is the lid of the heavy chest suddenly slammed, and there are thieves in the house, thought I, as I ran
after my spouse, lest there might be danger for him alone, and just as
if a feeble woman in her night array, like myself, could be any protec-
tion. In moments of sudden fear we do not stay to reason, but act upon
impulse. In another moment we stood in the double chamber below.
It was untenanted, save by the dead. The great box stood as I had last
seen it. I tried the lock; it was quite secure. We called up Kitty, and
searched the house; bolts, bars, and locks were all intact. Then we
began to reason how absurd we had been to suppose that thieves would
slam a box-lid, or make a noise loud enough to wake the inmates of
the house, had they entered. We could not sleep any more that night,
but dressed ourselves and sat up watching; and Kitty lighted a fire,
prepared some tea, and shared our folly. The truth is, we had all been
fagged and distressed, and our nerves were unstrung. As for the noise,
it was one of those mysterious sounds never accounted for, but cast
amongst 'things not generally known' even to the inquiring mind of a
Timbs.

In the morning the doctor called in to see us, as he had promised to do, and with him and Kitty as witnesses we determined to open the chest or box, and relieve our minds of doubts as to what it contained. There might be property—in fact we had no doubt but what there was—and possibly traces of family connections, or friends with whom we ought to communicate.

The key was turned; the lid raised. The ticking of a bed, old, yellow, and discoloured, was folded over the contents. As we essayed to remove it, it fell to fragments in our hands, disclosing—good heavens!—such a sight as eyes have rarely rested upon. Kitty shrieked; I almost fainted, and Harry involuntarily caught me in his arms. Even the doctor blanched, and fell back a step or two. For there lay, under the fragments of the old ticking, the remains of a man. Little more than a skeleton, little more than a heap of rags, and more or less mouldy dust, hidden amongst which was a costly watch and chain, a set of studs, and a diamond ring of very great price—trinkets whose value would have kept the lady who lay dead in comfort for two or three years.

Who was this man? and what was the motive that led to this strange enclosure of his body? Were the remains those of a husband from whom, like Queen Jane, she could not part? or was it the body of a murdered man—a guilty lover—a jealous spouse, thrust from sight and concealed at the expense of a life-watch? This was the secret of the eccentricity of the woman who had kept ghastly companionship under our roof so long.

I remembered her book, and putting my hand into my pocket pulled it forth; for in the solemn hour of death, during the grief and fatigue that followed, and the subsequent foolish alarm of the night, I had forgotten it. Closing the lid over the ghastly spectacle, turning the key in the lock, and securing also the chamber-door, was the work of a short time; and afterwards we gathered in our little parlour together, to learn the terrible facts which Harry read us, and which I here copy from.

THE CONTENTS OF THE CLASPED VOLUME

I know not whether I am mad or sane. I know not whether I was mad when I did it. There is madness in our family. My mother died raving mad. The old earl, my grandfather, was methodically mad, and was kept under disguised restraint in his ancestral mansion, that the world might not know it. But it oozed out, as things concealed usually do, with exaggerations. If I am mad, I was not accountable for it, and cannot be judged for it. And if I am sane, I have expiated by a long life-watch of cruel and horrible self-torture. To live all my days in a house converted into a mausoleum; to be condemned to sit upon an unburied coffin; to be encumbered everywhere with a tenant who should be in the tomb; to live alone with death; to eat side by side with a skeleton; to taste food out of a blood-red hand, and have a blood-red sky ever before me—are parts of my punishment. I never see a blue sky or a grey distance. Everything has a sanguinary haze over it, as if I looked through spectacles of flame-colour. And yet I did not shed blood—ah, no, I did not do that.

I have formed a friendship for this woman, and I should like to talk to her; yet I cannot divulge my secret. She seems to love her husband; yet not as I loved mine. As I loved him? As I do love him—passionately, wildly, fearfully, madly, so that I can never take my gaze off his coffin; so that I rise in the darkness and silence of the night to kiss and embrace the cold wood; and I feel my passion and my remorse eating out my heart. I cannot weep. I never shed a tear now, as I never shed a tear then. My grief is cold and tearless, as my rage was cold and tearless and my happiness cold and tearless when he lived. Outwardly, only outwardly. Within I was and am a human volcano, and the fire is consuming my heart and brain, sense and being, slowly, slowly—heaven, how slowly! It is retribution.

In my girlhood I was beautiful, and gifted with extraordinary talents. Whatever I undertook I mastered. I studied astrology, and cast my nativity. I saw the doom then, but did not comprehend it. Could we literally know the future, of what use would it be? Should we be warned, advised, or guided? No! Doom is doom, and we should rush on blindly towards it.

In every accomplishment I excelled. And yet I was but fifteen years of age, living in retirement at a country seat with my governess, when I met my future husband. I was sketching the stump of a tree in a grove, he out with dog and gun. Our eyes met with a flash of light, and we loved each other. He was so handsome, a heathen might have thought him a deity descended from the clouds. His hair was fair, rich, and waving, over eyes blue as heaven, his complexion more delicate, if possible, than my own. His voice was soft, rich, and manly. He had travelled, and was as well read as myself. I did not discover all this at first. But we loved as our eyes met. Then we were impelled to speak.

We walked home and saw my chaperone—an interview which resulted in his seeking my father, whose parliamentary duties yet held him in London. No parent could object to such an unexceptionable suitor as Lionel; but an obstacle existed on his side, whose father, Lord—(I will betray no names, not even to her I fancy my friend; but for the credit of those so unwillingly related, suppress all nomenclature, and carry shame and crime alone to the grave)—Lord—refused to sanction his son's union with the daughter of a lunatic, the grandchild of an idiot.

But Lionel and I were mad for love. We met; we eloped; we married, and fled to the Continent to avoid the reproaches and interference of angry parents.

After I had consented to elope, I looked round our place for a receptacle wherein I might pack a few clothes I intended to take with me. In the coach-house I saw the old box or chest destined to play so awful a part in my wretched story. I contrived to deposit what I needed unobserved; and in the silence of the night, when all slept, I aroused the young groom, who slept over the stable, and offered him a handsome gift of gold, yellow and shining in the light of the lamp I held, if he would harness the horses and take me and that dingy box to where Lionel awaited us.

The coachman, an old family servant, might have refused to drive so young a mistress on so doubtful a journey. But Sam was of an age when such deeds raise sympathy in the breast; so he took his reward, and I, with my box, was hurried from my home.

Weary of travelling, we returned to England, and rented a small house—a mere cottage—not far from Broadstairs, where, as we thought, we ran little risk of being seen by anyone who knew us. My husband, being fond of bathing, sought the shore every morning, and I sat in the garden until he returned.

We had not been at Broadstairs very long when I fancied there was a change in his manner. I was certain some secret rested upon his mind, and I became aware also, that though he went to the shore, he ceased to bathe. Sitting alone with busy thoughts I grew jealous, and determined to watch him; so instead of remaining at home, one day I hurried along a by-road to a part of the esplanade that overlooked the sands. I cast my eyes downwards, and saw him walking with a young lady about my own age. After a time they left the sands and walked towards our home. They were too preoccupied to detect that they were followed, but sat down to talk by a quiet bank near a cornfield, where I hid myself amongst the wheat. I was not near enough to hear his words, to which she listened so earnestly, or hers, on which he seemed to hang with tender interest. I noticed him holding her hands fondly, twining her curls in his fingers; and I saw him kiss her before they parted. I watched this day after day, and yet I said nothing. She only passed a few minutes each time in his company, as if fearful of being missed by her friends. But was not that enough? was it not too much for a young loving wife to witness?

One morning I noticed a bouquet of flowers, just gathered, lying on the escritoire where he had been writing. Full of suspicion I diverted his glance to another part of the room, and with a hasty glance read the words scribbled upon a slip of paper: 'I will meet you at sunset on the sands, and, if your plans are ripe enough, we will leave Broadstairs tomorrow.' He returned to his desk, folded the note, and went out with it and the flowers. Could I not guess how the one would be concealed in the other, and for whom? Did I not know the golden-haired syren with the sweet baby-face that had bewitched him?

That morning I spent at home, a wretched prey to love, jealousy, and wrath. At all hazards the sunset meeting must be prevented. Should I charge him with perfidy, upbraid, entreat? Should I prevail? Should I risk failure? No; a thousand times no. As our dinner-hour drew near, a foolish, an evil, a vile idea entered my miserable mind. I was mad then; I know now that I was mad. I laughed when I remembered the laudanum in a tiny bottle on the mantelshelf of my dressing-room. I emptied it into the wine decanter. Lionel drank wine, but I did not. After dinner he slept. Coffee was brought, but still his slumber lasted. It was as I wished. I sat and watched him. The hours went on slowly. I sent the servants to bed, and the house was very quiet. It grew late, the wax lights—there was no gas—burned down low; he still slept very heavily. One, two, sounded—then three. It was broad daylight; and I drew up the blinds, for I was getting restless and alarmed. Daylight was let in, and it fell upon the arm-chair and upon the face of a dead man. I dropped at his feet; I tried to pray, but knelt there wordless and thoughtless. Then surely I was mad—carefully cunningly, strangely mad. As Heaven is my witness, I had only meant to cause a sleep to stop that meeting and to put off an explanation so bitterly humiliating, so stormy in the aspect of its gathering clouds.

I knelt before my dead husband and laughed. I had no part in the laughter; it was as if the voice of some strange spirit issued from my lips, and sounded curiously in my ear. I was aroused suddenly by hearing the servants come downstairs. I was alone with him; and they would say I had murdered him, and the fair girl with the golden hair and the baby's face would stand by and see me strangled out of life on a scaffold. How I found strength for the terrible task I cannot tell, but I took Lionel in my arms and carried him into our sleeping-chamber, which adjoined, threw open the windows that led from the dining-room into the garden, and then locked myself and my crime away together. I laid him on the floor by the great box, and knelt down.

Suddenly an idea came into my head. I opened the box, and taking out my clothing made it into a bundle. There was a closet in the room which I had once opened, and had seen amongst other domestic curiosities the old ticking of a bed. I took it out and covered it over Lionel, and with the same strange strength lifted him into the box. He was barely dead then, for his limbs were not stiff, and I folded them into the space. Then I locked up the box and dressed, and went in to breakfast. A note lay on the table. It was contained in a little pink envelope, directed in a girlish hand. As my eyes rested upon it my jealousy and anger rushed to life again. I felt glad Lionel was dead. I took up the note which she with the yellow hair and pink face must have sent, and tearing it open read, 'Dear Lionel'—dear Lionel! How the letters ran before my eyes! Did *she* dare to call him *her* dear Lionel! Ay, it was there, written upon the pink paper with perfumed ink.

Dear Lionel,

I have pleaded your cause with papa and mamma, but cannot move them; and because they think I must have seen you here, our governess is ordered to bring us all home by the first train tomorrow. But I do not despair; for if I can do nothing at present, I will yet reconcile them to you some day. I fear I shall not be allowed to write, but in silence and absence do not doubt that I am, and ever shall remain,

Your affectionate sister,
Edith.

His sister! Ah! was ever climax so terrible? This, then, must be his favourite sister Edith, of whom he had so often talked, but who was unknown to me. Alas! why had he kept their meeting secret? That, too, was obvious: could he expose me to the mortification of knowing that she was pleading for my recognition by his family, or that he was forced to meet a dearly-loved sister by stealth because he had chosen me to be his wife?

And Lionel was dead. I hardly comprehended that fact. Fear was upon me. I must fly, and I must conceal the deed. Twenty miles from my own home a lonely house stood in the midst of a wood. Report called it haunted, and no one of the simple country folk dared approach, far less inhabit it. In a feigned name, I wrote to the landlord, and requested he would let it to me, with permission to enter immediately, saying that I was anxious to secure a good house at the low rent I did not doubt he would be happy to accept. I would have given any price for the house, but I wished to give a likely reason, not the true one. My offer was accepted by return of post.

Meanwhile I had told my two servants that their master had left early in the morning for town, whither he wished me to follow him, as we found it necessary to take a long and unexpected journey. I had paid all debts when the landlord's letter came. Hurrying to London I there disposed of our valuable plate, and whatever I possessed, except a little linen, a few jewels, and the horrible sarcophagus, hereafter my life-watch. I was anxious to gain my new abode, as I knew the delays of a day or two would cause detection. But my route was purposely circuitous and broken to baffle any efforts that might be made to trace me, though under the family ban it was hardly likely.

The chest was placed in a large room—a sort of loft—at the top of the house; and after a few preparations had been made by three women who were induced to come to the haunted place whilst it was day, I was left alone. The fact of my having a large box put in the loft excited no suspicion. The conjecture was that it contained books.

There, without servants, without the companionship of a living soul, I dwelt alone for many years, until upon the death of the old landlord a new master of the soil desired to pull the house down. Then with my chest I travelled from place to place, a haunted, restless woman, asking of myself eternally, 'Am I sane or mad?'

I had written so much of my history, in this poor cottage at Hampstead, to give it some day to one who has been kind to me; but going over the details of my life has raised in my mind a horrible suspicion, more exquisitely agonising than all that has gone before—a suspicion the bare form of which, as it suddenly came before me, cast me into that frenzied fit which has closed the weary life of one who neither wants nor wishes to die—one who only desires to live her vague life on and on, gazing eternally at the sarcophagus. The idea, the certainty so terrible in its nature, is, that Lionel was not dead when I placed him in the chest. Lionel was under the influence of the narcotic, but living —Lionel my love, my husband, was put living into the tomb and stifled by his beautiful wife's mad hands; and his young wife of sixteen summers locked up his life and the secret of her crime and sat down heartlessly beside it to perform her cruel life-watch. Let her die.

The Haunted Chair

by

RICHARD MARSH

As with so many other Victorian writers, the reputation of Richard Marsh (1857–1915) rests nowadays on a single work, yet he was one of the era's more successful and prolific authors.

Educated at Eton and Oxford, Marsh started full-time writing at an early age and went on to publish over seventy books. He travelled widely, had many friends in the theatre and was a fanatical devotee of all sports, spending many days at Wimbledon and Lords. In fact, his entry in Who's Who, under 'Recreations', is simply 'loves them all'.

Richard Marsh specialised in three kinds of fiction, all successful: humorous stories (featuring among others solicitor's office boy, Sam Briggs); detective stories (in which he invented one of the first fictional women detectives, Judith Lee); and tales of terror and the supernatural. It is for his novel in the last category The Beetle *(1897) that he is now remembered, which is sad, for he wrote many other fine stories of the macabre. Two of his forgotten story collections contained several splendid ghost stories,* Marvels and Mysteries *(1900) and* Between the Dark and the Daylight *(1902), from which comes 'The Haunted Chair'.*

The time is certainly ripe for a revival of interest in Richard Marsh; his work has been neglected long enough. Someone else who shares this view is Marsh's grandson—the famous ghost story writer and anthologist, Robert Aickman.

I

'Well, that's the most staggering thing I've ever known!'

As Mr Philpotts entered the smoking-room, these were the words—with additions—which fell upon his, not unnaturally, startled ears. Since Mr Bloxham was the only person in the room, it seemed only too probable that the extraordinary language had been uttered by him—and, indeed, his demeanour went far to confirm the probability.

He was standing in front of his chair, staring about him in a manner which suggested considerable mental perturbation, apparently unconscious of the fact that his cigar had dropped either from his lips or his fingers and was smoking merrily away on the brand-new carpet which the committee had just laid down. He turned to Mr Philpotts in a state of what seemed really curious agitation.

'I say, Philpotts, did you see him?'

Mr Philpotts looked at him in silence for a moment, before he drily said, 'I heard you.'

But Mr Bloxham was in no mood to be put off in this manner. He seemed, for some cause, to have lost the air of serene indifference for which he was famed—he was in a state of excitement, which, for him, was quite phenomenal.

'No nonsense, Philpotts—did you see him?'

'See whom?' Mr Philpotts was selecting a paper from a side table. 'I see your cigar is burning a hole in the carpet.'

'Confound my cigar!' Mr Bloxham stamped on it with an angry tread. 'Did Geoff Fleming pass you as you came in?'

Mr Philpotts looked round with an air of evident surprise.

'Geoff Fleming!—Why, surely he's in Ceylon by now.'

'Not a bit of it. A minute ago he was in that chair talking to me.'

'Bloxham!' Mr Philpotts' air of surprise became distinctly more pronounced, a fact which Mr Bloxham apparently resented.

'What are you looking at me like that for pray? I tell you I was glancing through the *Field*, when I felt someone touch me on the shoulder. I looked round—there was Fleming standing just behind me. "Geoff." I cried, "I thought you were on the other side of the world—what are you doing here?" "I've come to have a peep at you," he said. He drew a chair up close to mine—this chair—and sat in it. I turned round to reach for a match on the table, it scarcely took me a second, but when I looked his way again hanged if he weren't gone.'

Mr Philpotts continued his selection of a paper—in a manner which was rather marked.

'Which way did he go?'

'Didn't you meet him as you came in?'

'I did not—I met no one. What's the matter now?'

The question was inspired by the fact that a fresh volley of expletives came from Mr Bloxham's lips. That gentleman was standing with his hands thrust deep into his trouser pockets, his legs wide open, and his eyes and mouth almost as wide open as his legs.

'Hang me,' he exclaimed, when, as it appeared, he had temporarily come to the end of his stock of adjectives, 'if I don't believe he's boned my purse.'

'Boned your purse!' Mr Philpotts laid a not altogether flattering emphasis upon the 'boned!' 'Bloxham! What do you mean?'

Mr Bloxham did not immediately explain. He dropped into the chair behind him. His hands were still in his trouser pockets, his legs were stretched out in front of him, and on his face there was not only an expression of amazement, but also of the most unequivocal bewilderment. He was staring at the vacant air as if he were trying his hardest to read some riddle.

'This is a queer start, upon my word, Philpotts,' he spoke in what, for him, were tones of unwonted earnestness. 'When I was reaching for the matches on the table, what made me turn round so suddenly was because I thought I felt someone tugging at my purse—it was in the pocket next to Fleming. As I told you, when I did turn round Fleming was gone—and, by Jove, it looks as though my purse went with him.'

'Have you lost your purse?—is that what you mean?'

'I'll swear that it was in my pocket five minutes ago, and that it's not there now; that's what I mean.'

Mr Philpotts looked at Mr Bloxham as if, although he was too polite to say so, he could not make him out at all. He resumed his selection of a paper.

'One is liable to make mistakes about one's purse; perhaps you'll find it when you get home.'

Mr Bloxham sat in silence for some moments. Then, rising, he shook himself as a dog does when he quits the water.

'I say, Philpotts, don't ladle out this yarn of mine to the other fellows, there's a good chap. As you say, one is apt to get into a muddle about one's purse, and I dare say I shall come across it when I get home. And perhaps I'm not very well this afternoon; I am feeling out of sorts, and that's a fact. I think I'll just toddle home and take a seidlitz, or a pill, or something. Ta ta!'

When Mr Philpotts was left alone he smiled to himself, that superior smile which we are apt to smile when conscious that a man has been making a conspicuous ass of himself on lines which may be his, but which, we thank Providence, are emphatically not ours. With not one, but half a dozen papers in his hand, he seated himself in the chair which Mr Bloxham had recently relinquished. Retaining a single paper, he placed the rest on the small round table on his left—the table on which were the matches for which Mr Bloxham declared he had reached. Taking out his case, he selected a cigar almost with the same care which he had shewn in selecting his literature, smiling to himself all the time that superior smile. Lighting the cigar he had chosen with a match from the table, he settled himself at his ease to read.

Scarcely had he done so than he was conscious of a hand laid gently on his shoulder from behind.

'What! back again?'

'Hullo, Phil!'

He had taken it for granted, without troubling to look round, that Mr Bloxham had returned, and that it was he who touched him on the shoulder. But the voice which replied to him, so far from being Mr Bloxham's was one the mere sound of which caused him not only to lose his bearing of indifference but to spring from his seat with the agility almost of a jack-in-the-box. When he saw who it was had touched him on the shoulder, he stared.

'Fleming! Then Bloxham was right, after all. May I ask what brings you here?'

The man at whom he was looking was tall and well-built, in age about five and thirty. There were black cavities beneath his eyes; the man's whole face was redolent, to a trained perception, of something which was, at least, slightly unsavoury. He was dressed from head to foot in white duck—a somewhat singular costume for Pall Mall, even on a summer afternoon.

Before Mr Philpotts' gaze, his own eyes sank. Murmuring something which was almost inaudible, he moved to the chair next to the one which Mr Philpotts had been occupying, the chair of which Mr Bloxham had spoken.

As he seated himself, Mr Philpotts eyed him in a fashion which was certainly not too friendly.

'What did you mean by disappearing just now in that extraordinary manner, frightening Bloxham half out of his wits? Where did you get to?'

The newcomer was stroking his heavy moustache with a hand which, for a man of his size and build, was unusually small and white. He spoke in a lazy, almost inaudible, drawl.

'I just popped outside.'

'Just popped outside! I must have been coming in just when you went out. I saw nothing of you; you've put Bloxham into a pretty state of mind.'

Re-seating himself, Mr Philpotts turned to put the paper he was holding on to the little table. 'I don't want to make myself a brute, but it strikes me that your presence here at all requires explanation. When several fellows club together to give another fellow a fresh start on the other side of the world——'

Mr Philpotts stopped short. Having settled the paper on the table to his perfect satisfaction, he turned round again towards the man he was addressing—and as he did so he ceased to address him, and that for the sufficiently simple reason that he was not there to address—the man had gone! The chair at Mr Philpotts' side was empty; without a sign or a sound its occupant had vanished, it would almost seem, into space.

II

Under the really remarkable circumstances of the case, Mr Philpotts preserved his composure to a singular degree. He looked round the room; there was no one there. He again fixedly regarded the chair at his side; there could be no doubt that it was empty. To make quite sure, he passed his hand two or three times over the seat; it met with not the slightest opposition. Where could the man have got to? Mr Philpotts had not, consciously, heard the slightest sound; there had not been time for him to have reached the door. Mr Philpotts knocked the ash off his cigar. He stood up. He paced leisurely two or three times up and down the room.

'If Bloxham is ill, I am not. I was never better in my life. And the man who tells me that I have been the victim of an optical delusion is talking of what he knows nothing. I am prepared to swear that it was Geoffrey Fleming who touched me on the shoulder; that he spoke to me; and that he seated himself upon that chair. Where he came from, or where he has gone to, are other questions entirely.' He critically examined his finger nails.

'If those Psychical Research people have an address in town, I think I'll have a talk with them. I suppose it's three or four minutes since the man vanished. What's the time now? Whatever has become of my watch?'

He might well ask—it had gone, both watch and chain—vanished, with Mr Fleming, into air. Mr Philpotts stared at his waistcoat, too astonished for speech. Then he gave a little gasp.

'This comes of playing Didymus! The brute has stolen it! I must apologise to Bloxham. As he himself said, this is a queer start, upon my honour! Now, if you like, I do feel a little out of sorts; this sort of thing is enough to make one. Before I go, I think I'll have a drop of brandy.'

As he was hesitating, the smoking-room door opened to admit Frank Osborne. Mr Osborne nodded to Mr Philpotts as he crossed the room.

'You're not looking quite yourself, Philpotts.'

Mr Philpotts seemed to regard the observation almost in the light of an impertinence.

'Am I not? I was not aware that there was anything in my appearance to call for remark.' Smiling, Mr Osborne seated himself in the chair which the other had not long ago vacated. Mr Philpotts regarded him attentively. 'You're not looking quite yourself, either.'

'I'm not feeling myself!—I'm not! I'm worried about Geoff Fleming.'

Mr Philpotts slightly started.

'About Geoff Fleming?—what about Fleming?'

'I'm afraid—well, Phil, the truth is that I'm afraid that Geoff's a hopeless case.'

Mr Philpotts was once more busying himself with the papers which were on the side table.

'What do you mean?'

'As you know, he and I have been very thick in our time, and when he came a cropper it was I who suggested that we who were at school with him might have a whip round among ourselves to get the old chap a fresh start elsewhere. You all of you behaved like bricks, and when I told him what you had done, poor Geoff was quite knocked over. He promised voluntarily that he would never touch a card again, or make another bet, until he had paid you fellows off with thumping interest. Well, he doesn't seem to have kept his promise long.'

'How do you know he hasn't?'

'I've heard from Deecie.'

'From Deecie?—where's Fleming?'

'In Ceylon—they'd both got there before Deecie's letter left.'

'In Ceylon!' exclaimed Mr Philpotts excitedly, staring hard at Mr Osborne. 'You are sure he isn't back in town?'

In his turn, Mr Osborne was staring at Mr Philpotts.

'Not unless he came back by the same boat which brought Deecie's letter. What made you ask?

'I only wondered.'

'Mr Philpotts turned again to the paper. The other went on.

'It seems that a lot of Australian sporting men were on the boat on which they went out. Fleming got in with them. They played—he played too. Deecie remonstrated—but he says that it only seemed to make bad worse. At first Geoff won—you know the usual sort of thing; he wound up by losing all he had, and about four hundred pounds beside. He had the cheek to ask Deecie for the money.' Mr Osborne paused. Mr Philpotts uttered a sound which might have been indicative of contempt—or anything. 'Deecie says that when the winners found out that he couldn't pay, there was a regular row. Geoff swore, in that wild way of his, that if he couldn't pay them before he died, he would rise from the dead to get the money.'

Mr Philpotts looked round with a show of added interest.

'What was that he said?'

'Oh, it was only his wild way of speaking—you know that way of his. If they don't get their money before he dies, and I fancy that it's rather more than even betting that they won't, I don't think that there's much chance of his rising from his grave to get it for them. He'll break that promise, as he has broken so many more. Poor Geoff! It seems that we might as well have kept our money in our pockets; it doesn't seem to have done him much good. His prospects don't look very rosy—without money, and with a bad name to start with.'

'As I fancy you have more than once suspected, Frank, I never have had a high opinion of Mr Geoffrey Fleming. I am not in the least surprised at what you tell me, any more than I was surprised when he came his cropper. I have always felt that, at a pinch, he would do anything to save his own skin.' Mr Osborne said nothing, but he shook his head. 'Did you see anything of Bloxham when you came in?'

'I saw him going along the street in a cab.'

'I want to speak to him! I think I'll just go and see if I can find him in his rooms.'

III

Mr Frank Osborne scarcely seemed to be enjoying his own society when Mr Philpotts had left him. As all the world knows, he is a man of sentiment—of the true sort, not the false. He has had one great passion in his life—Geoffrey Fleming. They began when they were at

Chilchester together, when he was big, and Fleming still little. He did his work for him, fought for him, took his scrapes upon himself, believed in him, almost worshipped him. The thing continued when Fleming joined him at the University. Perhaps the fact that they both were orphans had something to do with it; neither of them had kith nor kin. The odd part of the business was that Osborne was not only a clear-sighted, he was a hard-headed man. It could not have been long before it dawned upon him that the man with whom he fraternised was a naturally bad egg. Fleming was continually coming to grief; he would have come to eternal grief at the very commencement of his career if it had not been for Osborne at his back. He went through his own money; he went through as much of his friend's as his friend would let him. Then came the final smash. There were features about the thing which made it clear, even to Frank Osborne, that in England, at least, for some years to come, Geoffrey Fleming had run his course right out. He strained all his already strained resources in his efforts to extricate the man from the mire. When he found that he himself was insufficient, going to his old schoolfellows, he begged them, for his sake—if not for Fleming's—to join hands with him in giving the scapegrace still another start. As a result, interest was made for him in a Ceylon plantation, and Mr Fleming with, under the circumstances, well-lined pockets, was despatched over the seas to turn over a new leaf in a sunnier clime.

How he had vowed that he would turn over a new leaf, actually with tears upon his knees! And this was how he had done it; before he had reached his journey's end, he had gambled away the money which was not his, and was in debt besides. Frank Osborne must have been fashioned something like the dog which loves its master the more, the more he illtreats it. His heart went out in pity to the scamp across the seas. He had no delusions; he had long been conscious that the man was hopeless. And yet he knew very well that if he could have had his way he would have gone at once to comfort him. Poor Geoff! What an all-round mess he seemed to have made of things—and he had had the ball at his feet when he started—poor, dear old Geoff! With his knuckles Mr Osborne wiped a suspicious moisture from his eyes. Geoff was all right—if he had only been able to prevent money from slipping from between his fingers, had been gifted with a sense of *meum et tuum*—not a nicer fellow in the world!

Mr Osborne sat trying to persuade himself into the belief that the man was an injured paragon though he knew very well that he was an irredeemable scamp. He endeavoured to see only his good qualities, which was a task of exceeding difficulty—they were hidden in such a cloud of blackness. At least, whatever might he said against Geoff— and Mr Osborne admitted to himself that there might be something —it was certain that Geoff loved him almost as much as he loved Geoff. Mr Osborne declared to himself—putting pressure on himself to prevent his making a single mental reservation—that Geoff Fleming, in spite of all his faults, was the only person in the wide, wide world who did love him. And he was a stranger in a strange land, and in trouble again—poor dear old Geoff! Once more Mr Osborne's knuckles went up to wipe that suspicious moisture from his eyes.

While he was engaged in doing this, a hand was laid gently on his shoulder from behind. It was, perhaps, because he was unwilling to be detected in such an act that, at the touch, he rose from his seat with a start—which became so to speak, a start of petrified amazement when he perceived who it was who had touched him. It was the man of whom he had been thinking, the friend of his boyhood—Geoffrey Fleming.

'Geoff!' he gasped. 'Dear old Geoff!' He paused, seemingly in doubt whether to laugh or cry. 'I thought you were in Ceylon!'

Mr Fleming did exactly what he had done when he came so unexpectedly on Mr Philpotts—he moved to the chair at Mr Osborne's side. His manner was in contrast to his friend's—it was emphatically not emotional.

'I've just dropped in,' he drawled.

'My dear old boy!' Mr Osborne, as he surveyed his friend, seemed to become more and more torn by conflicting emotions. 'Of course I'm very glad to see you Geoff, but how did you get in here? I thought that they had taken your name off the books of the club.' He was perfectly aware that Mr Fleming's name had been taken off the books of the club, and in a manner the reverse of complimentary. Mr Fleming offered no remark. He sat looking down at the carpet stroking his moustache. Mr Osborne went stammeringly on—

'As I say, Geoff—and as, of course you know—I am very glad to see you, anywhere; but—we don't want any unpleasantness, do we? If some of the fellows came in and found you here, they might make themselves nasty. Come round to my rooms; we shall be a lot more comfortable there, old man.'

Mr Fleming raised his eyes. He looked his friend full in the face. As he met his glance, Mr Osborne was conscious of a curious sort of shiver. It was not only because the man's glance was, to say the least, less friendly than it might have been—it was because of something else, something which Mr Osborne could scarcely have defined.

'I want some money.'

Mr Osborne smiled, rather fatuously.

'Ah, Geoff, the same old tale! Deecie has told me all about it. I won't reproach you; you know, if I had some, you should have it; but I'm not sure that it isn't just as well for both ourselves that I haven't, Geoff.'

'You have some money in your pocket now.'

Mr Osborne's amazement grew apace—his friend's manner was so very strange.

'What a nose you always have for money; however did you find that out? But it isn't mine. You know Jim Baker left me guardian to that boy of his, and I've been drawing the youngster's dividends—it's only seventy pounds, Geoff.'

Mr Fleming stretched out his hand—his reply was brief and to the point.

'Give it to me!'

'Give it to you!—Geoff!—young Baker's money!'

Mr Fleming reiterated his demand.

'Give it to me!'

His manner was not only distinctly threatening, it had a peculiar effect upon his friend. Although Mr Osborne had never before shown fear of any living man, and had, in that respect, proved his superiority over Fleming many a time, there was something at that moment in the speaker's voice, or words, or bearing, or in all three together, which set him shivering, as if with fear, from head to foot.

'Geoff!—you are mad! I'll see what I can find for you, but I can't give you young Baker's dividends.'

Mr Osborne was not quite clear as to exactly what it was that happened. He only knew that the friend of his boyhood—the man for whom he had done so much—the only person in the world who loved him—rose and took him by the throat, and, forcing him backwards, began to rifle the pocket which contained the seventy pounds. He was so taken by surprise, so overwhelmed by a feeling of utter horror, against which he was unable even to struggle, that it was only when he felt the money being actually withdrawn from his pocket that he made an attempt at self-defence. Then, when he made a frantic clutch at his assailant's felonious arm, all he succeeded in grasping was the empty air. The pressure was removed from his throat. He was able to look about him. Mr Fleming was gone. He thrust a trembling hand into his pocket—the seventy pounds had vanished too.

'Geoff! Geoff!' he cried, the tears streaming from his eyes. 'Don't play tricks with me! Give me back young Baker's dividends!'

When no one answered and there seemed no one to hear, he began searching round and round the room with his eyes, as if he suspected Mr Fleming of concealing himself behind some article of furniture.

'Geoff! Geoff!' he continued crying. 'Dear old boy!—give me back young Baker's dividends!'

'Hullo!' exclaimed a voice—which certainly was not Mr Fleming's. Mr Osborne turned. Colonel Lanyon was standing with the handle of the open door in his hand. 'Frank, are you rehearsing for a five-act tragedy?'

Mr Osborne replied to the Colonel's question with another.

'Lanyon, did Geoffrey Fleming pass you as you came in?'

'Geoffrey Fleming!' The Colonel wheeled round on his heels like a teetotum. He glanced behind him. 'What the deuce do you mean, Frank? If I catch that thief under the roof which covers me, I'll make a case for the police of him.'

Then Mr Osborne remembered what, in his agitation, he had momentarily forgotten, that Geoffrey Fleming had had no bitterer, more out-spoken, and, it may be added, more well-merited an opponent than Colonel Lanyon in the Climax Club. The Colonel advanced towards Mr Osborne.

'Do you know that that's the blackguard's chair you're standing by?'

'His chair!'

Mr Osborne was leaning with one hand on the chair on which Mr Fleming had, not long ago, been sitting.

'That's what he used to call it himself—with his usual impudence. He used to sit in it whenever he took a hand. The men would give it up to him—you know how you gave everything up to him, all the lot of you. If he couldn't get it he'd turn nasty—wouldn't play. It seems that he had the cheek to cut his initials on the chair—I only heard of it the other day, or there'd have been a clearance of him long ago. Look here—what do you think of that for a piece of rowdiness?'

The Colonel turned the chair upside down. Sure enough in the woodwork underneath the seat were the letters, cut in good-sized characters—'G.F.'

'You know that rubbishing way in which he used to talk. When men questioned his exclusive right to the chair, I've heard him say he'd prove his right by coming and sitting in it after he was dead and buried—he swore he'd haunt the chair. Idiot!—What is the matter with you, Frank? You look as if you'd been in a rough and tumble—your necktie's all anyhow.'

'I think I must have dropped asleep, and dreamed—yes, I fancy I've been dreaming.'

Mr Osborne staggered, rather than walked, to the door, keeping one hand in the inside pocket of his coat. The Colonel followed him with his eyes.

'Frank's ageing fast,' was his mental comment as Mr Osborne disappeared. 'He'll be an old man yet before I am.'

He seated himself in Geoffrey Fleming's chair.

It was, perhaps, ten minutes afterwards that Edward Jackson went into the smoking-room—'Scientific' Jackson, as they call him, because of the sort of catch phrase he is always using—'Give me science!' He had scarcely been in the room a minute before he came rushing to the door shouting—

'Help, help!'

Men came hurrying from all parts of the building. Mr Griffin came from the billiard-room, where he is always to be found. He had a cue in one hand, and a piece of chalk in the other. He was the first to address the vociferous gentleman standing at the smoking-room door.

'Jackson!—What's the matter?'

Mr Jackson was in such a condition of fluster and excitement that it was a little difficult to make out, from his own statement, what was the matter.

'Lanyon's dead! Have any of you seen Geoff Fleming? Stop him if you do—he's stolen my pocket-book!' He began mopping his brow with his bandanna handkerchief, 'God bless my soul! an awful thing! —I've been robbed—and old Lanyon's dead!'

One thing was quickly made clear—as they saw for themselves when they went crowding into the smoking-room—Lanyon was dead. He was kneeling in front of Geoffrey Fleming's chair, clutching at either side of it with a tenacity which suggested some sort of convulsion. His head was thrown back, his eyes were still staring wide open, his face was distorted by a something which was half fear, half horror— as if, as those who saw him afterwards agreed, he had seen sudden, certain death approaching him, in a form which even he, a seasoned soldier, had found too horrible for contemplation.

Mr Jackson's story, in one sense, was plain enough, though it was odd enough in another. He told it to an audience which evinced unmistakable interest in every word uttered.

'I often come in for a smoke about this time, because generally the place is empty, so that you get it all to yourself.'

He cast a somewhat aggressive look upon his hearers—a look which could hardly be said to convey a flattering suggestion.

'When I first came in I thought that the room was empty. It was only when I was half-way across that something caused me to look round. I saw that someone was kneeling on the floor. I looked to see who it was. It was Lanyon. "Lanyon!" I cried. "Whatever are you doing there?" He didn't answer. Wondering what was up with him and why he didn't speak, I went closer to where he was. When I got there I didn't like the look of him at all. I thought he was in some sort of a fit. I was hesitating whether to pick him up, or at once to summon assistance, when——'

Mr Jackson paused. He looked about him with an obvious shivver.

'By George! when I think of it now, it makes me go quite creepy. Cathcart, would you mind ringing for another drop of brandy?'

The brandy was rung for. Mr Jackson went on.

'All of a sudden, as I was stooping over Lanyon, someone touched me on the shoulder. You know, there hadn't been a sound—I hadn't heard the door open, not a thing which could suggest that anyone was approaching. Finding Lanyon like that had made me go quite queer, and when I felt that touch on my shoulder it so startled me that I fairly screeched. I jumped up to see who it was. And when I saw'—Mr Jackson's bandanna came into play—'who it was, I thought my eyes would have started out of my head. It was Geoff Fleming.'

'Who?' came in chorus from his auditors.

'It was Geoffrey Fleming. "Good God!—Fleming!" I cried. "Where did you come from? I never heard you. Anyhow, you're just in the nick of time. Lanyon's come to grief—lend me a hand with him." I bent down, to take hold of one side of poor old Lanyon, meaning Fleming to take hold of the other. Before I had a chance of touching Lanyon, Fleming, catching me by the shoulder, whirled me round— I had had no idea the fellow was so strong, he gripped me like a vice. I was just going to ask what the dickens he meant by handling me like that, when, before I could say Jack Robinson, or even had time to get my mouth open, Fleming, darting his hand into my coat pocket, snatched my pocket-book clean out of it.'

He stopped, apparently to gasp for breath. 'And pray, what were you doing while Mr Fleming behaved in this exceedingly peculiar way—even for Mr Fleming?' inquired Mr Cathcart.

'Doing!' Mr Jackson was indignant. 'Don't I tell you I was doing nothing? There was no time to do anything—it all happened in a flash. I had just come from my bankers—there were a hundred and thirty pounds in that pocket-book. When I realised that the fellow had taken it, I made a grab at him. And'—again Mr Jackson looked furtively about him, and once more the bandanna came into active play—'directly I did so, I don't know where he went to, but it seemed to me that he vanished into air—he was gone, like a flash of lightning. I told myself I was mad—stark mad! but when I felt for my pocket-book, and found that that was also gone, I ran yelling to the door.'

IV

It was, as the old-time novelists used to phrase it, about three weeks after the events transpired which we have recorded in the previous chapter. Evening—after dinner. There was a goodly company assembled in the smoking-room at the Climax Club. Conversation was general. They were talking of some of the curious circumstances which had attended the death of Colonel Lanyon. The medical evidence at the inquest had gone to show that the Colonel had died of one of the numerous, and, almost innumerable, varieties of heart disease. The finding had been in accordance with the medical evidence. It seemed to be felt, by some of the speakers, that such a finding scarcely met the case.

'It's all very well,' observed Mr Cathcart, who seemed disposed to side with the coroner's jury, 'for you fellows to talk, but in such a case, you must bring in some sort of verdict—and what other verdict could they bring? There was not a trace of any mark of violence to be found upon the man.

'It's my belief that he saw Fleming, and that Fleming frightened him to death.'

It was Mr Jackson who said this. Mr Cathcart smiled a rather provoking smile.

'So far as I observed, you did not drop any hint of your belief when you were before the coroner.'

'No, because I didn't want to be treated as a laughing-stock by a lot of idiots.'

'Quite so; I can understand your natural objection to that, but still I don't see your line of argument. I should not have cared to question Lanyon's courage to Lanyon's face while he was living. Why should you suppose that such a man as Geoffrey Fleming was capable of such a thing as, as you put it, actually frightening him to death? I should say it was rather the other way about. I have seen Fleming turn green, with what looked very much like funk, at the sight of Lanyon.'

Mr Jackson for some moments smoked in silence.

'If you had seen Geoffrey Fleming under the circumstances in which I did, you would understand better what it is I mean.'

'But, my dear Jackson, if you will forgive my saying so, it seems to me that you don't show to great advantage in your own story. Have you communicated the fact of your having been robbed to the police?'

'I have.'

'And have you furnished them with the numbers of the notes which were taken?'

'I have.'

'Then, in that case, I shouldn't be surprised if Mr Fleming were brought to book any hour of any day. You'll find he has been lying close in London all the time—he soon had enough of Ceylon.'

A newcomer joined the group of talkers—Frank Osborne. They noticed, as he seated himself, how much he seemed to have aged of late and how particularly shabby he seemed just then. The first remark which he made took them all aback.

'Geoff Fleming's dead.'

'Dead!' cried Mr Philpotts, who was sitting next to Mr Osborne.

'Yes—dead. I've heard from Deecie. He died three weeks ago.'

'Three weeks ago!'

'On the day on which Lanyon died.'

Mr Cathcart turned to Mr Jackson, with a smile.

'Then that knocks on the head your theory about his having frightened Lanyon to death; and how about your interview with him—eh Jackson?'

Mr Jackson did not answer. He suddenly went white. An intervention came from an unexpected quarter—from Mr Philpotts.

'It seems to me that you are rather taking things for granted, Cathcart. I take leave to inform you that I saw Geoffrey Fleming, perhaps less than half-an-hour before Jackson did.'

Mr Cathcart stared.

'You saw him!—Philpotts!'

Then Mr Bloxham arose and spoke.

'Yes, and I saw him, too—didn't I, Philpotts?'

Any tendency on the part of the auditors to smile was checked by the tone of exceeding bitterness in which Frank Osborne was also moved to testify.

'And I—I saw him, too!—Geoff!—dear old boy!'

'Deecie says that there were two strange things about Geoff's death. He was struck by a fit of apoplexy. He was dead within the hour. Soon after he died, the servant came running to say that the bed was empty on which the body had been lying. Deecie went to see. He says that, when he got into the room, Geoff was back, again upon the bed, but it was plain enough that he had moved. His clothes and hair were in disorder, his fists were clenched, and there was a look upon his face which had not been there at the moment of his death, and which, Deecie says, seemed a look partly of rage and partly of triumph.

'I have been calculating the difference between Cingalese and Greenwich time. It must have been between three and four o'clock when the servant went running to say that Geoff's body was not upon the bed—it was about that time that Lanyon died.'

He paused—and then continued—

'The other strange thing that happened was this. Deecie says that the day after Geoff died a telegram came for him, which, of course, he opened. It was an Australian wire, and purported to come from the Melbourne sporting man of whom I told you.' He turned to Mr Philpotts. 'It ran, "Remittance to hand. It comes in rather a miscellaneous form. Thanks all the same." Deecie can only suppose that Geoff had managed, in some way, to procure the four hundred pounds which he had lost and couldn't pay, and had also managed, in some way, to send it on to Melbourne.'

There was silence when Frank Osborne ceased to speak—silence which was broken in a somewhat startling fashion.

'Who's that touched me?' suddenly exclaimed Mr Cathcart, springing from his seat.

They stared.

'Touched you!' said someone. 'No one's within half a mile of you. You're dreaming, my dear fellow.'

Considering the provocation was so slight, Mr Cathcart seemed strangely moved.

'Don't tell me that I'm dreaming—someone touched me on the shoulder!—What's that?'

'That' was the sound of laughter proceeding from the, apparently, vacant seat. As if inspired by a common impulse, the listeners simultaneously moved back.

'That's Fleming's chair,' said Mr Philpotts, beneath his breath.

Coolies

by

W. CARLTON DAWE

As the British Empire spread across nearly one-fifth of the entire globe, so new fields opened up for writers of novels and short stories. Africa provided H. Rider Haggard with the source material for his string of successful novels, as it did to a lesser degree with other writers such as Bertram Mitford and F. A. M. Webster. India gave Rudyard Kipling the background for many of his tales, while authors such as Somerset Maugham, Joseph Conrad and H. de Vere Stacpoole weaved stories from their experiences in the Far East and the South Seas.

As well as these more famous names, many other writers who had obviously travelled the world produced works of fiction based on their experiences. One of them was W. Carlton Dawe, who apparently knew the Far East well, and wrote a now forgotten book of short stories called Yellow and White *(1895). Dawe was obviously intrigued with the shifting relationship between white man and the Oriental races, as were others of his contemporaries like B. L. Putnam Weale and Lafcadio Hearn. In 'Coolies' he spins a nautical tale of terror around the voyage of a boatload of coolies and the ever present 'Yellow Peril'.*

Cheong-Wo did not bear a very good name even among his un-principled compatriots, though I doubt if we could justly blame him for what happened during the voyage. I have since heard that several of our passengers were very badly 'wanted' by the police, and that Cheong-Wo was well paid to ship them out of the colony; but that is what any yellow man would do, or white one either, if he thought he wouldn't get found out. Both are 'on the make'; honestly on it if possible, if not, one must seize every trifling advantage. The aggregate mounts up rapidly. In China one must either 'squeeze' or be 'squeezed', and as the former is the more pleasant sensation, its cultivation is obvious. Might is always right; but cunning is the supreme test of intelligence.

We were chartered this time to carry coolies from Hong Kong to Singapore and Penang, returning through the Straits to Bangkok, where we were to load with rice. On this particular occasion the afore-mentioned Cheong-Wo was the important person who had chartered us, and I can't say that he was neglectful of his own interest, for he not alone presented each of us officers with a box of good cigars, but the night before we sailed he had as many of us ashore as could come, and gave us the best dinner we had had for a long time. You may be sure that the 'old man', which is the familiar way sailors speak of their captain—behind his back—also came in for something substantial. It was not likely that Cheong, who had propitiated the juniors, would forget that all-powerful one.

So, early one Thursday morning away we went with eighteen hundred of the ugliest, dirtiest wretches on board that it had ever been my lot to see—filthier, I believe, than the cargo of pilgrims we took to Jeddah last year. Pilgrims, I admit, are universally given the palm for filth; it is a part of their sanctity: they are human sewers, and worse; but I think that even the most devout pilgrim that ever jour-neyed to the sacred shrine at Mecca could not give many points to several of the wretches we had aboard. At least, for the sake of the poor devils who have to carry them, I hope not. I was never on such a floating midden in my life, and I pray to heaven, apart from what happened, that I may never be again. To poke your nose down a hatchway, to get to leeward of a ventilator, or to pass 'tween decks, was to inhale the concentrated essence of eighteen hundred unpre-cedented stinks. To describe the scene is impossible, the details would be too revolting; but perhaps it is not altogether impossible to imagine eighteen hundred filthy creatures all huddled together for four or five days, afraid to leave their belongings for a moment.

All went well with us till we had passed the dangerous Paracels, a cluster of rocks lying in the track of steamers bound from Hong Kong to Singapore, upon which many a good ship had rushed to her doom. Even the thoughtless coolie breathes freer when he knows that he has passed that treacherous spot; while captain and officers, though not dreading it, heave an inward sigh of satisfaction as they think of it far astern.

But, as I was saying, everything went well with us till we had passed this place. Our passengers seemed an innocent, well-behaved lot, albeit not over-cleanly. There were few disturbances among them, and little prowling in forbidden quarters, though once or twice we caught two or three ugly fellows in places where they had no right to be; but as one stands on no ceremony with coolies, they were somewhat unceremoniously hustled back to their own quarters. Yet when we were well on our voyage, and the Paracels passed, this prowling about increased to an alarming extent. No matter at what time of day or night you happened to be about the ship, you would find one of these fellows sneaking around somewhere, and not infrequently when you expostulated with him, he would show his teeth. At night they spread themselves across the decks in such a way that you could scarcely move without walking on them; and though you might tread on the faces of eleven men with impunity, the twelfth might uprise and hamstring you, or, with a friend or two, toss you over the side, and who but themselves would be the wiser? When you have eighteen hundred of the lowest class Chinamen aboard, you must not be surprised at anything.

As we drew nearer Singapore this prowling about grew more general, till we were pestered out of our lives. Our worthy passengers did not alone frequent the after-deck, which they knew they had no right to do, but they even took to peeping into the saloon and cabins. This was more than we could bear. Though only a 'tramp', we had our dignity, and could not tolerate this setting our authority at defiance. One afternoon the captain, as he passed down the companion, caught a coolie, a thick, one-eyed, villainous-looking fellow, making his way into the saloon. Without more ado the old man seized him by the pigtail, and gave him sundry sledge-hammer cuffs alongside of the ear, and then sent him spinning backwards with a kick. There were some horrid screams and oaths, and for a moment the fellow looked like fighting; but thinking better of it, he picked himself up and, growling beneath his breath, slunk off.

That was the beginning of the bother. The next move was one which for brazen impudence fairly staggered me.

I was keeping the first dog-watch at the time. We were making good headway in a smooth sea, with every prospect of reaching Singapore before another forty-eight hours had passed. The sky was clear, the glass set fair. On the starboard bow the sun, a great golden chrysanthemum, was sloping down to the west. I never knew a brighter day bring in a blacker night.

Presently the captain joined me on the bridge, and, after making a few of the usual inquiries, perched himself up in the port corner, and took a good look round, I, in the meantime, continuing my walk between the starboard corner and the binnacle. After a while he beckoned me to him.

'I don't like the look of those damned coolies,' he said. 'Have you noticed anything?'

'Nothing really suspicious, sir. They are always a bad lot, of course; but I think they know how far they can go.'

He laughed. 'I've taught one of them a lesson anyway.' And he told me what he had done.

I knew the man well enough, an ugly one-eyed pig. He had been prowling about the ship ever since we had left Hong Kong.

'But the best of the joke,' continued the old man seriously, as though not quite sure of the humour of the thing, 'is that that one-eyed cuckoo actually came up to me just now and inquired if we were really going to Singapore. What do you think he meant?'

'I am glad we have not three or four hundred like him,' I answered evasively. 'We should want a detachment of soldiers to guard them.'

The old man began to laugh, then stopped midway, looking quickly over my shoulder. I saw his eyes start as though they would jump from his head. Then he bounded past me. Turning round, I saw that three of our passengers had mounted the bridge by the starboard ladder, and that the leader of the trio was the squat, one-eyed blackguard whom the captain had thrashed that afternoon.

'Well,' yelled the skipper, who, when his authority was disputed, was a fiend incarnate, 'what do you want?' Only he embellished this simple question with a whole gallery of beautiful adjectives.

The chow grinned servilely, showing a row of dirty yellow teeth.

'Me likee speakee you, cap'n.'

'You infernal——' began the old man. But no. Since I cannot give the captain's impressive language in full, it would be folly to attempt any other. When the gods are angry the heavens thunder and the world quakes. Our captain was a god in his way, and when he spoke in anger, his rage coloured the atmosphere. He, however, gave the impudent Chinaman to understand that the bridge was the Olympus of the gods, and that neither mortals nor inferior deities had any right there. The one-eyed yellow man bowed and smiled. A Chinaman always smiles, though the smile is not always pretty.

'Wing solly, welly solly,' he said, 'but all 'ee same he come top side speak along of cap'n.'

'Well,' said the old man, unbending like a god, 'what the dooce do you want?'

'Me no wantee go Singlaplore.'

'Eh?' roared the captain, as though he doubted his hearing.

'Wing no wantee go Singlaplore side. Sabbee?'

'Oh,' said the old man sarcastically, 'wouldn't like to go to Singapore, eh? Now, where would you like me to take you? Please give it a name.'

This delicate irony was lost upon Wing.

'Tonking way,' he said seriously: 'Flenchyman's China. Plenty better than Singlaplore.'

'Sorry to disappoint you,' said the old man suavely, 'but this ship's going to Singapore. Now clear, damn you, clear, or I'll break your damned neck.' And, his suavity gone, he strode savagely forward. The man, however, did not budge, though his two companions flew down the ladder, where, on the deck below, half a dozen more ugly wretches awaited them.

'Are you going?' roared the captain, pointing down to the deck.

'All li, all li.'

But his movements were so slow that the old man's boot had to waken him up a bit.

'Pretty cool, Anderson?' said he, turning to me.

'Very, sir. I think I should put that one-eyed chap in irons.'

'Oh, I guess he's had enough for one day,' was the laughing reply. 'You won't forget to call me if you see anything?'

'No, sir.'

And so away he went, an awful bully of a man, but one in whom there was a lot of good run wild. I know I liked him with all his faults; and though at times I could have punched his head, at others I would have done anything for him.

Early the next morning the mate came to my berth and roughly awakened me.

'Hallo, Joe, what the devil are you doing?'

I sprang up, rubbing my eyes.

'For God's sake come on deck!' he whispered hoarsely. 'The old man's missing.'

'Missing?'

'Yes. Come as soon as you can.' And he was gone.

In two minutes I joined him on the bridge, and in the early morning light I thought his face looked ghastly.

'What is it, old chap?' I asked.

'My God!' he whined, 'this is a nice business and no mistake. The old man's missing. I went below to call him half an hour ago and he wasn't in his room. I have searched everywhere, but there's not a trace of him to be seen.'

'But he must be about somewhere. He couldn't fall overboard.'

'No,' said the mate in a scared voice, 'he couldn't very well *fall* overboard; but suppose he was *chucked*?'

I started. Visions of the one-eyed Wing and his villainous companions flashed before me.

'They wouldn't dare,' I stammered.

'Ah, wouldn't they. I tell you what it is, Anderson, we've got the choicest crowd of blackguards aboard this boat that you'll find between here and Shanghai. My God!' he groaned, 'we may thank our stars if we don't get our damned throats cut between this and Singapore.'

'Nonsense!' I answered, disgusted at the cowardice of the man. 'Let us go down and fish out our revolvers, and put the engineers on guard. We ought to be in Singapore to-night.'

'O my God!' he moaned, 'I don't think we shall ever see Singapore again.'

'Not if you let them see you in that state. I'll go and warn the third and the engineers. You keep a sharp look-out.'

'Wait a minute, Anderson. I—I think you'd better not risk it.'

Knowing why he wished me to stay, I laughingly pooh-poohed all idea of danger.

'Then let us have a look at the chart first.'

We went into the chart-room, which was a house built on a level with the bridge, the door of which was set in the back, or afterpart of it. Here, spread out on the top of the locker, which answered the purpose of a table, lay the chart, and the mate and I at once began to study it. Along the chart the captain had drawn our course, marking off the length of each day's run, and putting the date opposite it. There was the addition he had made at noon yesterday; the last, I was afraid, he would ever make.

'Well, Anderson,' said the mate, 'what do you make of it?'

I respected his feelings. He was not a quick or skilful navigator.

'We should be abreast the lighthouse between nine and ten to-night.'

'Are you sure?'

'Work it out yourself.'

The mate did not take the hint.

'Well, let us hope you're right, Anderson. But seventeen hours! My God, what an eternity!'

I was turning away from him in disgust when I heard a scuffle outside by the binnacle. The next moment the quartermaster who was steering, shouted loudly, 'Look out, sir!' I had only time to spring forward, unhitch the door, and slam it to when the foremost ruffian threw himself upon it.

'The window. Quick, quick!' I yelled to the mate.

In the front of the chart-room, looking out over the bridge, and so out across the bows of the ship, was a window, the glass of which slid in and out like a screen. There was also a sliding shutter of wood outside the glass again. This, luckily, the mate had seized in his fright. It came to with a bang, and we were safe for a while.

Save for a pale gleam of light which played about the end of the window, we were in utter darkness, and I could hear the mate moaning as he clutched the ring of the shutter to keep it in its place.

'My God!' he whined, 'we're in for it now.'

Though believing he was right, I would not gratify him by admitting as much. I struck a match and lit the lamp which was always kept in the chart-room—which, in fact, the mate had only put out an hour before.

'Let's see what's here,' I said, as I began to search the lockers. 'Perhaps we shall find something we want.'

'No dashed fear,' whined the mate. 'You never find a thing when you want it.' And he began to feebly curse his star, the mother who bore him, and all things beneath the sun. The way he blasphemed in his terror might have been amusing were it not for its extreme pathos.

And yet on opening the second small drawer I discovered a revolver —the captain's I knew it to be—which I held delightedly before my companion's eyes.

'There,' I cried, 'what do you think of this?'

For a moment a ray of hope brightened his dull eyes. Then a gloomy look leapt into them.

'It would just be my dashed luck if it wasn't loaded.'

An icy wind swept across my heart.

'It's not,' I said, after examining it.

'I thought as much,' he added consolingly.

But there might be cartridges somewhere in the locker! I searched high and low but without success. Two of the big drawers were filled with charts, the other one with nautical odds and ends, among which I noticed a battered compass, a coil of india-rubber tubing, an old sextant, and one barrel of a pair of glasses. But not a cartridge: not even the shell of one.

The mate looked at me despairingly: a look of blank, unutterable terror.

'My God! we're done for,' he wailed. 'These devils will rip us up, Anderson, and then chuck us overboard.'

'They may do what they like with me when I am dead,' I answered; 'but I'm not dead yet.'

'No, but you soon will be. I know them, Anderson. They're devils, fiends incarnate. They'll torture us, I tell you—torture us, by God. They'll cut us into strips and grill them before our eyes.'

'Damn you, shut up!' I shouted, as a wild sensation of frizzling ran down my backbone. 'It's bad enough to know those devils are prowling about unchecked, without being plagued with your confounded croaking. If you can't suggest a way out of this, you had better hold your row.'

Remembering his dignity, that he was my superior officer, he tried to look offended; but the time and place forbade any outburst. Indeed, the rap which came upon the shutter at that moment knocked all the dignity out of him.

'Wha-at's that?' he gasped.

'Our friends want to come in.'

'Don't budge, Anderson; my God! don't budge.'

'But, my dear sir, we can't stay here all day. Let us see what they want.'

He implored, he entreated; but quietly shoving him aside, I flung back the shutter. Wing, the one-eyed coolie, who seemed to be the ringleader, and three others immediately sprang forward; but in an instant they drew up sharp, for I had covered them with my empty revolver.

'Well,' I said, 'what is all this about? Do you know that this means hanging when we get to Singapore?'

The one-eyed rascal grinned in his oily, unpleasant fashion, and I knew by the way he was hitching his trousers behind that he was hiding a knife. But I caught no glimpse of a revolver, for which I was devoutly thankful. My own harmless weapon had an evident effect upon them.

'Me plenty sabbee,' he grinned, 'but me no go Singlaplore. Singlaplore too muchee no good. Me wantee speakee mate. He all the same belong cap'n now.'

'They want to speak to you,' I said. 'Come, don't let them think you're frightened.'

'My God!' he whispered, 'I'm not frightened.' But it was a wretched, craven face he turned to the pirates.

The one-eyed scoundrel bowed.

'Good mornin', cap'n,' he said. 'You all the same belong cap'n now. Udder cap'n, he say he wantee go Singlaplore. This ship no go Singlaplore. Udder cap'n, he say he will go Singlaplore, so he jumpee overboard to swimee-swimee. Sabbee? Suppose new cap'n, he wantee go Singlaplore, he also have to swimee-swimee. Sabbee?'

The mate's face grew livid with terror.

'What do you want?' he groaned.

'No wantee this ship go Singlaplore. Singlaplore too muchee dam swingee-swingee,' and he encircled his ugly neck with an imaginary noose. 'Me wantee go Flenchyman's China. New cap'n, he find nice spot, takee ship there, Wing let him go flee,—new cap'n, he no takee ship there, Wing slit him thloat.'

'My God, Anderson!' groaned the mate, 'what shall we do? These devils have got possession of the ship. They'll slit our damned throats as sure as eggs.'

'Let them slit and be damned,' I answered angrily. 'Of one thing you may be sure, they're not to be trusted. It's only a ruse to get us out of this. You may go if you like. I don't. That villain, Wing as he calls himself, knows well enough how to steer to pick up the coast of Cochin China. Look here,' and I unhitched the little compass that hung at my watch-chain, 'we're steering west by north now.'

My companion looked thunderstruck.

'We're fast getting out of the track of ships,' he said. 'Anderson, we're lost.'

'Not yet. Tell them you will think over their proposal. I have an idea.'

The mate did as he was bidden, and I pulled the shutter to.

That the engines should be running freely all this time betokened one of two things: that either the engineers were unconscious of what had happened above deck, or that they had all been overpowered and the engines were running unattended. If the latter were the case, I knew we should not go long without a dreadful breakdown; if the former, there was still some hope, for those three sturdy Scotsmen in the engine-room were worth half a dozen men.

In the left-hand corner of the chart-room was a metal speaking-tube which led down into the engine-room, but which I had never seen anyone use. In fact, I did not know if it was in working order, for there was not even a whistle in the orifice. However, there was the faint hope that there might be one in the other end. As I leant over it I could distinctly hear the clank, clank of the engines. But there was, unfortunately, no whistle for me to sound the alarm upon. I halloed, I roared, I whistled down it, but in vain. Nothing but the monotonous clank, clank of the engines greeted my ear.

In the meantime the rascals outside were growing impatient. They tapped at the shutter, rapped loudly on the door, even tried to burst it in; but like all ships' doors it opened outwards, so that the task they set themselves was not an easy one. Still, I knew that we could not hold the place for long, and I felt a queer shudder run down my back as I thought of the squat, one-eyed villain, the master of my fate. I turned despairingly to the speaking-tube. Our only chance of salvation was through those sturdy Scotsmen. If they failed us, or were prisoners, we were as good as lost.

As I placed my ear to the tube I heard the voice of our second engineer, Duncan Macpherson, cry out, 'Hallo, there! What the de'il's the matter wi' them? Goodness, goodness, goodness!' And then he began to shriek and whistle like a madman.

'Duncan, Duncan,' I cried, as soon as he had stopped his noise.

'Ay, man, it's me,' came up the answer. 'So ye're there? I've been tryin' to speak to ye for the last half-hour. What's the matter?'

'The ship is in the hands of the coolies. The captain has been killed, the mate and I are in the chart-room, prisoners. Have you any one with you?'

'Only the third, and the third officer. The chief went up an hour ago, and I'm afraid they've nabbed him. Can't ye get out of the house and make a rush for it?'

'We have no arms of any description. The pirates swarm the bridge. They are even now trying to force the door.'

'Dear, dear! and it's almost as bad wi' us. They tried to rush us here, but we managed to shut them out. Every time I look up I see a dirty face peerin' down through the gratin'.'

A pause followed, during which the monotonous clank, clank of the engines was mixed with the scratchings and scrapings on the wood outside. Presently the voice came again.

'Are ye there, Anderson?'

'Yes.'

'I've been thinkin' that if ye could only use this speakin'-tube in some way or other, I could send ye up a beautiful jet of hot water that would peel the skin off any blasted pirate between hell and Hong Kong.'

'It can't be done,' I added despairingly. 'The pipe only rises a foot above the locker. It would be no use. We should scald ourselves.'

'Ah, now, if ye only had a nice length of tubin' ye might do somethin'.'

My heart gave a quick throb. I remembered the piece in the locker. When I told him of it he said, 'Verra weel. When ye have fixed it on, just ye whistle down and let me know.'

In a moment I had the tubing out of the locker, and to my delight found that it was in splendid preservation, and some nine or ten feet in length. To unscrew the wooden cup and fix the tube over the pipe was done with a rapidity which must have astonished the mate, who, pale and speechless, stood clinging to the ring of the shutter. In the drawer, which was full of odds and ends, I found plenty of good stout lashing, and with this I securely bound the tubing to the pipe.

I do not think the whole business could have taken more than half a minute; yet short as it was the blows upon the chart-house redoubled, as though our assailants were trying to beat in the door with hammers or axes. There was no time to be lost. I whistled down the tube and told the engineer I was ready.

'Verra weel,' he answered. 'Just look out that ye dinna scald yoursel.'

I held the nozzle of the tube towards the door.

'Now,' I said to the mate, 'when I say the word, you fling open the window. I think we have a very pretty surprise in store for them.'

'If it comes off,' he answered. 'But you know, there is many a slip 'twixt cup and lip.'

I felt like pointing the hose at him and giving him the first dose, but at that moment my attention was arrested by a curious smoky smell which came in from under the door.

'Look, look,' shrieked the mate, 'they're going to burn us out!' and he fairly jumped with terror.

'Not at all,' I answered, enjoying the joke in a deadly sort of way, 'they're going to smoke us out.'

'And that Ning-po varnish burns like hell.' He was referring to the new coat of varnish we had but lately given the deckhouses. 'Oh, my God, my God!' he moaned, 'why did I ever come to sea?'

I wondered why, though I had scant time for wonder. With almost incredible swiftness the smoke grew in volume, a thick, pungent smoke which proclaimed the use of tar. Presently the crackling of wood was heard. I knew it would not be long before the house was ablaze. And still no message from below! Had anything happened? Had the engineer's calculations in any way proved faulty? The mate groaned and moaned, mixing his supplications to heaven with strings of the most abandoned oaths. It was horrible to hear him, even more horrible to see him as he shrank back closer and closer in the corner, his face ghastly, his eyes vacant with terror. A little more of it and I knew he would be a raving madman. Well, poor devil, so much the better for him. Before this day was over I might have cause to envy him such a merciful stroke of Providence.

My eyes stung with the smoke: I knew that I was inhaling it in great mouthfuls. I developed a sudden coughing and sneezing. The mate, I believed, was already half-unconscious. What with the smoke and my streaming eyes I could scarcely see him. The situation was becoming intolerable. And still no sign from the engineer! Had he failed in his attempt?

At the thought the cold perspiration oozed out of me, and for a moment or two my faculties were numbed. Pulling myself together with a great effort I turned to the mate to tell him to open the window— for it was better to die by the knives of the pirates than be choked in this fashion—when I felt the hose in my hand tremble. A moment's acute suspense; then followed a sudden hissing of wind, and out spluttered a torrent of steam and boiling water.

'Open, open!' I cried excitedly.

With a last effort, and like a man in a dream, the mate swung back the shutter, and then fell senseless to the floor.

In an instant a dozen hideous, grinning wretches, bared knives in their hands, rushed to the aperture, the one-eyed scoundrel, Wing, to the fore. The next moment he threw himself back with a horrible shriek, for I had turned the hose fair in his face, and the steam and boiling water had blinded and scalded him. The others stopped, surprised, awestruck; but before they had time to realise the situation, I served three or four others in a similar manner. These set up a horrible screaming, struggling fiercely to get away; but before the bridge was cleared of them a dozen at least were howling with pain.

Once the bridge was clear I opened the door of the chart-room and extinguished the flames, which were rapidly getting a good hold of the woodwork. This I did by means of the invaluable hose. Then, looking away aft, a curious sight met my gaze. The fellows whom I had scalded had all fled to the after-part of the ship, where they were joined by about twenty or thirty others, the whole lot, by the way they shrieked and gesticulated, evidently being in a state of great excitement. Then suddenly out of the engine-room skylight I saw the head and shoulders of the second engineer rise. In one hand he held the big brass nozzle of our fire hose. The next moment it spouted out a perfect torrent of steam and boiling water. The engineer clambered out on to the deck and coolly walked towards the mutineers. About twenty yards off he stood and directed the scalding flood upon them. Some ran this way and that way, others dashed madly past him with fearful shrieks, but I doubt if a single one escaped a horrible scalding.

After that we had no more trouble with our passengers. The ring-leaders were all ironed and handed over to the authorities at Singapore, which port we reached in the early hours of the following day. About a month afterwards six of them, including the one-eyed Wing, who had been nearly scalded to death, 'suffered the extreme penalty of the law'.

Our mate, thanks to the energetic manner in which he had suppressed the outbreak, was at once given command of the ship.

The Three Souls

by

ERCKMANN-CHATRIAN

Literary collaborations have always been few and far between, certainly where tales of terror are concerned, and successful partnerships rare indeed. Two Continental authors who managed to write so well together that the critic Edward Wright described their work as 'reading like the production of a single mind' were the Alsatian friends Emile Erckmann (1822–1899) and Alexandre Chatrian (1826–1890).

Erckmann met Chatrian in Phalsbourg, his home town, in 1847, where Chatrian was an usher in the college at which Erckmann was studying law. Their decision to start writing together was followed by the publication of their first book, Contes Fantastiques, *that same year. For nearly forty years they collaborated on novels, short stories, poems and plays, until a quarrel and lawsuit over alleged slander broke up their friendship and partnership. The death of Chatrian a year after the legal case was quite probably hastened by the bitter end of their long relationship.*

Specialising in military history and tales of their native Alsace, Erckmann–Chatrian also produced many successful plays, of which the most well known today is probably The Polish Jew, *produced here by Sir Henry Irving under the title* The Bells. *As well as these and other literary works, they were fond of producing the occasional tale of terror. Precious few have survived to this day—readers interested in seeing more can find three of their stories in other books I have edited— though they were among the most original and entertaining tales of their kind on the Continent in those days. Apart from one or two books of their longer stories, such as* The Man Wolf *(1876) and* The Wild Huntsman *(1877), few of their weird stories have appeared here at all. 'The Three Souls', a tale from their first volume, does not seem to have been published in Britain in English since it was written. I think that this translation, by Eithne Fearnley-Whittingstall, will bring to a wider audience the talents of two of Europe's finest and least regarded writers*

*of tales of terror. In this rare tale, they deal in chilling fashion with an
exceedingly original piece of metaphysics. In the days it was written,
all things were possible . . .*

In 1815 I was doing my sixth year of transcendental philosophy in
Heidelberg. University life is the life of a lord: you get up at midday:
you smoke your pipe: you empty one or two small glasses of schnapps:
and then you button your overcoat up to your chin, put on your hat
in the Prussian manner over the left ear and you go quietly to listen,
for half an hour, to the well known Professor Hâsenkopf. Everyone is
free to yawn or even to go to sleep if that suits him.

When the lecture is over, you go to the inn, stretch your legs under
the table; the pretty serving girls rush about with dishes of sausages,
slices of ham and tankards of strong beer. You hum a tune, you drink,
you eat. One whistles for the inn's dog Hector, the other grabs Char-
lotte or Gretel by the waist. . . . At times fighting breaks out, cudgel
blows shower down, tankards totter and beer mugs fall. The watch
comes and he arrests you and you go and spend the night in jail.

And thus, the days, the months and the years pass! One meets, in
Heidelberg, future princes, dukes and barons; one also meets the sons
of cobblers, schoolmasters and respectable business men. The young
lordlings keep to their own clique, but the rest mingle in brotherly
fashion.

I was thirty-two then, my beard was beginning to turn grey; the
tankard, pipe and sauerkraut were going down in my estimation. I
felt in need of a change. Such was my melancholy state of mind,
when towards the end of the spring of this year, 1815, a horrible event
occurred which taught me that I didn't know everything, and that the
philosophical career is not always strewn with roses.

Among my friends was a certain Wolfgang Scharf, the most unbending logician that I have ever met. Imagine a small gaunt man, with
sunken eyes, white lashes, red hair cut short, hollow cheeks adorned
by a bushy beard and broad shoulders covered in magnificent rags.
To see him creeping along the walls, a cob of bread under his arm,
his eyes ablaze, his spine arched, you would have thought he was an
old tom cat looking for his queen. But Wolfgang thought only of
metaphysics. For the past five years he had been living on bread and
water in a garret in the old part of the town. Never had a bottle of
foaming beer or Rhine wine cooled his ardour for knowledge, never
had a slice of ham weighted down the course of his sublime medita-

tions. As a consequence the poor devil was frightening to look at. I say frightening because, in spite of his apparent state of marasmus, there was in his bony frame a terrifying cohesive force. The muscles of his jaws and hands stood out like cords of steel; moreover, his shady look averted pity.

For some reason, this strange being, in the midst of his voluntary isolation, seemed to have time for me. He would come and see me and, seated in my armchair, his fingers shaking convulsively, he would share with me his metaphysical lucubrations. One day he touched on a subject which found me lacking a suitable answer.

'Kasper,' he said to me in a sharp voice, and, proceeding through interrogation in the manner of Socrates, 'Kasper, what is the soul?'

'According to Thales it is a sort of magnet. According to Plato, a substance which moves of its own accord. According to Asclepius, an arousal of the senses. Anaximander says that it is a compound of earth and water, Empodocles the blood, Hippocrates a spirit spread through the body. Zeno, the quintessence of the four elements. Xenocrates . . .'

'Good! good! But what do you think is the substance of the soul?'

'Me, Wolfgang? I say, with Lactantius, that I know nothing about it. I am an Epicurean by nature. Now according to the Epicureans, all judgement comes from the senses; as the soul does not fall under my senses, I am unable to judge.'

'However, Kasper, remark that a crowd of animals such as fishes or insects live deprived of one or more senses. Who knows if we possess all the senses? If there don't exist some which we've never even thought of?'

'It's possible, but in doubt I refrain from passing judgement.'

'Do you think, Kasper, that one can know something without having learnt it?'

'No. All knowledge proceeds from experience or study.'

'But then, my friend, how does it come about that the hen's chicks, as they come out of the egg, start to run about, to take their food by themselves? How does it happen that they recognise the sparrow-hawk in the middle of the clouds, that they hide under their mother's wings? Have they learnt to know their enemy in the egg?'

'It's instinct, Wolfgang. All animals obey instinct.'

'And so it appears that instinct consists of knowing what one has never learnt?'

'Ha!' I exclaimed. 'You are asking too much of me. What can I say?'

He smiled disdainfully, flung the flap of his ragged coat over his shoulder and went out without saying another word.

I considered him a madman, but a madman of the harmless sort. Who would have thought that a passion for metaphysics could be dangerous?

Things really started to happen when the old cake-seller, Catherine Wogel, suddenly disappeared. This good woman, her tray hanging by a pink ribbon from her stork-like neck, usually presented herself at the inn at about eleven o'clock. The students joked readily with her, reminding her of some childhood escapades, of which she made no secret and laughed fit to split her sides.

'Ha! why yes!' she would say, 'I haven't always been fifty! I've had some good times! Well! afterwards . . . do I regret it? Ah! if only it could all begin again!'

She would breathe a sigh and everyone would laugh.

Her disappearance was noticed on the third day. 'What the devil has become of Catherine?' 'Could she be ill?' 'That's odd, she looked so well the last time we saw her.'

It was learnt that the police were looking for her. As for me, I didn't doubt that the poor old woman, a little too affected by kirsch, had stumbled into the river.

The following morning as I left Hâsenkopf's lecture, I met Wolfgang, skirting the pavements of the cathedral. He had hardly noticed me when he came up to me with his eyes agleam. He said, 'I am looking for you Kasper . . . I am looking for you. The hour of triumph has come . . . you are going to follow me.'

His look, his gesture, his pallor, betrayed extreme agitation. As he seized me by the arm, dragging me towards the square of the Tanners, I could not help an indefinable feeling of fear, without having the courage to resist. The side street which we hurriedly followed plunged behind the cathedral, into a block of houses as old as Heidelberg. The roofs leaning at right angles; the wooden balconies where fluttered the washing of the lower classes; the exterior stairs with their worm-eaten handrails; the hundreds of ragged figures, leaning out of the attic windows and looking eagerly at the strangers who were penetrating their lair; the long poles, going from one roof to the other, laden with bloody hides; then the thick smoke escaping from zigzag pipes at every floor; all this blended together and passed before my eyes like a resurrection of the Middle Ages. The sky was fine, its azure angles scalloped by the old gables, and its luminous rays stretching out now and then over the tumble-down walls, added to my emotion by the strangeness of the contrast.

It was one of those moments when man loses all presence of mind. I didn't even think of asking Wolfgang where we were going.

After the populous neighbourhood where poverty swarms, we reached the deserted square where Wolfgang lived. Suddenly Wolfgang, whose dry, cold hand seemed riveted to my wrist, led me into a hovel with broken windows, between an old shed, abandoned long since, and the stall of the abattoir.

'You first,' he said.

I followed a high wall of dry earth, at the end of which was a spiral staircase with broken steps. We climbed across the débris and, although my friend didn't stop repeating to me in an impatient voice 'higher . . . higher . . .' I stopped at times, gripped by terror, on the pretext of getting my breath and examining the recesses of the gloomy dwelling, but really to deliberate whether it wasn't in fact time to flee.

At last we reached the foot of a ladder whose steps disappeared through a loft in the midst of the darkness. I still ask myself to-day how I had the rashness to climb this ladder without demanding the slightest explanation from my friend Wolfgang. It appears that madness is contagious.

And so there I was climbing, with him behind me. I got right to the top, I put my foot on the dusty floor, I looked around; it was a huge attic, the roof pierced by three skylights, the grey wall of the gable climbing up on the left to the rafters. There was a small table laden with books and papers in the middle, the beams crossing one another over our heads in the darkness. Impossible to look out, for the skylights were ten or twelve feet above the floor.

I noticed, as my eyes became accustomed to the gloom, a large door with a vent, chest-high, cut in the wall of the gable.

Wolfgang, without a word, made me sit down on a crate which served him as an armchair, and taking up a crock of water in the darkness, drank for a long time, while I looked at him quite bemused.

'We are in the attic of the old abattoir,' he said with a strange smile, putting down his earthenware crock. 'The council has voted funds to build another one outside the town. I have been here for five years without paying any rent. Not a soul has come here to disturb my studies.'

He sat down on some logs piled up in a corner.

'Now then,' he resumed, 'let's get to the point. Are you quite sure, Kasper, that we have a soul?'

'Look here, Wolfgang,' I angrily answered him. 'If you have brought me here to discuss metaphysics, you have made a great mistake. I was just leaving Hâsenkopf's lecture and I was going to the inn to have lunch when you intercepted me. I have had my daily dose of abstraction. It is enough for me. Therefore, explain yourself clearly or let me get back on the track of food.'

'You then, only live for food,' he said in a sharp tone. 'Do you realise that I have spent days without touching food for the love of science?'

'To each his taste; you live on syllogisms or horned arguments; me, I like sausages and beer.'

He had become quite pale, his lips were trembling, but he mastered his anger.

'Kasper,' he said, 'since you don't wish to answer me, at least listen to my explanations. Man needs admirers and I want you to admire me. I want you to be in some way overwhelmed by the sublime discovery I have just made. It's not asking too much, I think, one hour's attention for ten years of conscientious studies?'

'So be it. I am listening to you, but hurry up!'

A new quivering agitated his face and gave me food for horrifying thought. I was repenting of having climbed the ladder, and I assumed a serious look so as not to infuriate the maniac further. My meditative physiognomy appeared to calm him a little, because, after a few moments of silence, he resumed.

'You are hungry, well here's my bread and here's my crock. Eat, drink, but listen.'

'You need not trouble, Wolfgang, I shall listen anyway to you without that.'

He smiled bitterly and continued:

'Not only do we have a soul, a thing accepted since the beginning of history, but from plant to man, all beings live. They are animated, therefore they have a soul. You don't need six years of study under Hâsenkopf to agree with me that all organised beings have one soul at least. But the more their organisation perfects itself, the more complicated it gets, and the more the souls multiply. This is what distinguishes animate beings from each other. The plant has only one soul. the vegetable soul. Its function is simple, unique—merely nutrition, by the air, by means of the leaves, and by the earth through the roots. The animal has two souls. First of all the vegetable soul, whose functions are the same as those of the plant—nutrition by the lungs and intestines, which are true plants; and the animal soul, so called, which has as its function feeling and whose organ is the heart. Finally man, who is up to the present the height of earthly creation, has three souls —the vegetable soul, the animal soul whose functions are exercised as in the beast, and the human soul which has its object, reason and intelligence, and its organ is the brain. The more the animal nears man in the perfection of its cerebral organisation, the more it shares in this third soul, such as the dog, the horse, the elephant. But alone the man of genius possesses it in all its fullness.'

At this point Wolfgang stopped and fixed his eyes on me.

'Well,' he said, 'what have you got to say?'

'Well, it's a theory like any other. There is only the proof missing.'

A sort of frenzied exultation took hold of Wolfgang at this reply. He leapt up, hands in the air, and exclaimed: 'Yes! Yes! The proof is missing. That is what has been tormenting my soul for ten years. That's what was the cause of so many late nights, of so much moral suffering, so many privations! Because it was on myself, Kasper, that I wanted to experiment first of all. Fasting impressed more and more this sublime conviction on my mind, without its being possible for me to establish any proof of it. But, at last, I have found it. You are going to hear the three souls show themselves, declare themselves . . . you will hear them.'

After this explosion of enthusiasm which gave me the shudders, so much energy did it indicate, so much fanaticism, he suddenly became cold again and, sitting down with his elbows on the table, he resumed, pointing out the lofty wall of the gable.

'The proof is there, behind this wall. I shall show it to you presently. But above all you must follow the progressive step of my ideas. You know the opinions of the classic philosophers on the nature of souls. They accepted four of them, united in man. Caro, the flesh, a mixture of earth and water which death dissolves; Manes, the spirit, which wanders around tombs—its name comes from manere, to remain, to stay; Umbra, the shade, more immaterial than Manes, it disappears after visiting its relatives; finally Spiritus, the spirit, the immaterial substance which climbs up to the gods. This classification appeared right to me; it was a question of breaking down the human being so as to establish the distinct existence of the three souls, an abstraction made from the flesh. Reason told me that each man, before reaching his highest development, must have passed through the state of plant or animal; in other words that Pythagoras had caught sight of the reality, without being able to provide proof of it. Well, as for myself, I wanted to solve this problem. It was necessary to successively extinguish the three souls in myself, then revive them. I had recourse to rigorous fasting. Unfortunately, the human soul, in order to let the animal soul act freely, had to succumb first. Hunger made me lose the faculty of observing myself in the animal state. By exhausting myself I was putting myself in the position of not being able to judge. After a host of fruitless attempts on my own organism I remained convinced that there was only one way of attaining my goal; that was to act on a third person. But who would want to be a party to this type of observation?'

Wolfgang paused, his lips contracted and brusquely he added:

'I needed a subject at any cost. I decided to experiment on a worthless being.'

At this point I shuddered. This man then was capable of anything.

'Have you understood?' he said.

'Very well; you needed a victim.'

'To study,' he added, coldly.

'And you have found one?'

'Yes! I promised to let you hear the three souls. It will perhaps be difficult now: but yesterday you would have heard them in turn howl, roar, implore, grind their teeth!'

An icy shiver ran through me. Wolfgang, impassive, lit a small lamp which he usually used for his work and went over to the low door on the left.

'Look!' he said, putting his hand forward into the darkness. 'Come near and look, then listen.'

In spite of the most funereal presentiments, in spite of the inward shudder which shook me, lured by the attraction of the mystery, I looked through the vent. Behind the door, extending some three yards back, was a dark pit about ten feet deep. The only door, in or out, was the one through which I was peering. I realised that it was one of those storage spaces built into the ceiling of the abattoir, where butchers piled up the hides from the slaughterhouse so as to let them turn green, before delivering them to the tanners. It was empty and for a few seconds I saw only this hole full of shadows.

'Have a good look,' said Wolfgang in a low voice. 'Don't you see a bundle of clothes gathered together in a corner? It's old Catherine Wogel, the cake-seller, who . . .'

He didn't have time to finish, because a wild piercing cry, similar to that of an enraged cat, made itself heard in the pit. A frightened and frightening shape leapt up, seeming to want to claw its way up the wall. More dead than alive, my brow covered with a cold sweat, I darted backwards, exclaiming:

'It's horrible!'

'Did you hear it?' said Wolfgang, his face lit up by an infernal joy. 'Isn't that the cry of the cat? Ha ha! The old woman, before reaching the human state was formerly a cat or a panther. Now the beast wakes again. Oh! Hunger, hunger and especially thirst works miracles!'

He wasn't looking at me, he was revelling. A loathsome satisfaction lit up his countenance, his attitude, his smile.

The mewings of the poor old woman had stopped. The madman, having placed his lamp on the table, began to gloat over his 'experiment'.

'She has been fasting for four days. I lured her here under the pretext of selling her a small cask of kirsch. I pushed her into the pit and shut her in. Drunkenness has been the ruin of her. She is now atoning for her excessive thirst. The first two days the human soul was revealed in all its strength. She beseeched me, she implored me, she proclaimed her innocence, saying that she had done nothing to me, that I had no right to do this to her. Then madness took possession of her. She overwhelmed me with reproaches, called me a monster, an inhuman wretch and so forth. On the third day, which was yesterday, the human soul disappeared completely. The cat brought out its claws. It was hungry; its teeth became long; it started to miaow, to roar. Fortunately we are in a secluded place. Last night the people in the square of the Tanners must have thought there was a real cat fight: there were shrieks that would make one shudder! Now, when the beast is exhausted do you know, Kasper, what will result? The vegetable soul will have its turn. It dies the last. You know, of course, that the hair and nails of corpses still grow under the earth; there even forms in the interstices of the skull a sort of human lichen which is called moss. It is thought to be a mould engendered by the juices of the brain. Finally the vegetable soul itself withdraws. Then, Kasper, the proof of the three souls will be complete.'

These words struck my ears as the reasoning of delirium in the most horrible nightmare. The screeching of Catherine Wogel went through me to the very marrow of my bones. I didn't know myself any more, I was losing my head.

I stood up and grabbed the maniac by the throat, dragging him towards the ladder.

'You wretch!' I said to him. 'Who has given you permission to lay hands on your fellow man? on the creature of God? To satisfy your infamous curiosity? I shall hand you over to justice!'

He was so surprised by my aggression that at first he made no resistance, and let himself be dragged towards the ladder without replying. But suddenly, turning round with the suppleness of a wild animal, he in turn seized me by the neck. His hand, as powerful as a steel spring, raised me off the ground and held me against the wall while with the other he drew the bolt of the door to the pit. Realising his intentions, I made a terrible effort to get free. I set my back athwart the door. But he was endowed with superhuman strength. After a quick and desperate struggle I felt myself lifted up for the second time and hurled into space, while above me echoed these strange words:

'Thus perish rebellious flesh! Thus triumph the immortal soul!'

I had hardly touched the bottom of the pit, bruised and aching all over, when the heavy door closed ten feet above me, shutting off from my eyes the greyish light of the attic.

II

I was caught like a rat in a trap. My consternation was such that I rose to my feet without a moan.

'Kasper,' I said to myself, leaning up against the wall with a strange calmness, 'it is now a matter of devouring the old woman, or being devoured by her . . . Choose! As for wanting to get out of this pit, it's a waste of time. Wolfgang has you in his clutches, he will not let you go. The walls are made of stone and the floor of thick oak planks. No one has seen you cross the square of the Tanners and no one knows you in this district. No one will think of looking for you here. It's all over, Kasper, it's all over. Your last resource is this poor Catherine Wogel, or rather, you are each other's last resource.'

All this passed through my mind like a flash of lightning. When, at that very moment, the pale head of Wolfgang, with his little lamp appeared at the vent, and when, my hands clasped together through terror, I wanted to beseech him, I realised that I was stammering dreadfully. Not a word came from my trembling lips. He, seeing me like this, began to smile, and I heard him whispering in the silence.

'The coward . . . he beseeches me.'

This finished me. I fell to the ground, and I would have remained in a faint had not the fear of being attacked by the old woman made me come to my senses. However, she still did not move. Wolfgang's head disappeared . . . I heard the maniac crossing his garret, move back the table, cough a little. My ear was so attuned that the slightest noise reached me. I heard the old woman yawning, and, as I turned round, I noticed for the first time her eyes glittering in the dark. At the same time I heard Wolfgang go down the ladder and I counted the steps one by one until the sound died away in the distance. Where had the scoundrel gone to? I did not know, but during all that day and the following night he did not reappear. It was only the following day at about eight o'clock in the evening, just as the old woman and I were howling enough to bring the walls down, that he returned.

I hadn't closed my eyes. I no longer felt fear or rage. I was hungry . . . devouringly hungry. And I knew that the hunger would get even worse.

However, hardly had a faint noise made itself heard in the attic than I became silent and looked up. The vent was lit up. Wolfgang had lit his lamp. Undoubtedly he was going to come and see me. With this expectation, I prepared a touching prayer, but the lamp went out. No one came.

It was perhaps the most frightful moment of my torture. I realised that Wolfgang, knowing that I was not yet exhausted, would not bother to even give me a glance. In his eyes I was only an interesting subject, only ripe for science in two or three days' time—between life and death. I seemed to feel my hair slowly turn to grey on my head. Finally my terror became such that I lost all feeling.

At about midnight, I was wakened by something touching me. I leapt up in disgust. The old woman, attracted by hunger, had drawn near. Her hands were fastened onto my clothes. At the same time the screeching of a cat filled the pit and froze me with terror.

I expected a terrible battle to fight her; but the poor wretch was very weak; after all, she was in her fifth day of captivity.

Then Wolfgang's words came back into my mind: 'Once the animal soul is dead the vegetable soul will have the upper hand . . . the hair and nails grow in the grave . . . and the green moss . . . the mould takes root in the interstices of the skull.' I pictured for myself the old woman reduced to this state, her skull covered with mouldy lichen, and myself, lying next to her, our souls spinning their moist vegetation beside each other, in the silence.

This image took such a hold of my mind that I no longer felt the pangs of hunger. Stretched out against the wall, my eyes wide open, I looked in front of me without seeing anything.

And as I was like this, more dead than alive, a vague light shone above in the darkness. I looked up. The pale face of Wolfgang was leaning through the ventilator. He wasn't laughing. He appeared to feel neither joy, satisfaction or remorse: he was observing me!

Oh! how this face frightened me! Had he laughed, had he enjoyed his vengeance, I would have hoped to bend him ... but he just observed!

We remained thus, our eyes fixed on each other, one terror stricken, the other cold, calm, attentive, as if facing an inert object. The insect pierced by a needle, which one observes under a microscope, if it thinks, if it understands the eye of man, must have these sort of visions.

I had to die to satisfy the curiosity of a monster. I understood that entreaty would be useless, so I said nothing.

After having looked at me for long enough, the maniac, obviously pleased by his observations, turned his head to look at the old woman. I mechanically followed the direction of his gaze. What I saw haunts me to this day. A haggard head, emaciated, the limbs shrivelled up and so sharp that they seemed to have pierced the rags which covered them. Something mis-shapen, hideous. A dead person's head, the hair scattered around the skull like tall withered grass and, in the midst of all that, shining eyes kindled by fever ... and two long yellow teeth.

Even more dreadful, I saw two snails already crawling over the skeletal figure. When I had seen all that beneath the wan beam of the lamp, falling like a thread in the midst of the darkness, I closed my eyes with a convulsive shudder, and said to myself: ' That's how I shall be in five days' time.'

When I re-opened my eyes the lamp had been withdrawn.

'Wolfgang!' I exclaimed. 'God's above us ... God sees us ... Wolfgang ... Woe to monsters!'

The rest of the night was spent in terror.

After having dreamed again, in the delirium of the fever, of the chances which were left to me of escaping, and not finding any, suddenly I resolved to die. This determination gave me some moments

of calm. I went over in my mind the arguments of Hâsenkopf relating
to the immortality of the soul, and, for the first time, I found in them
an invincible force.

'Yes,' I exclaimed, 'man's passage through this world is only a time
of testing. Injustice, greed, the most deadly passions dominate the
heart of man. The weak are crushed by the strong. The poor by the
rich. Virtue is but a word on earth. But everything returns to order
after death. God sees the injustice of which I am a victim, he will take
into account the sufferings that I endure. He will pardon me my
immoderate appetites, my excessive love of good living. Before
admitting me into his breast he wanted to purify me by rigorous
fasting. I offer my sufferings to the Lord.'

However, I must admit to you that in spite of my profound con-
trition, the longing for the inn and my merry friends, for this good
existence which flowed out in the midst of the singing and the excellent wine, made me utter many sighs. I could hear the bubbling of the
bottles, the clinking of the glasses and my stomach would groan like a
living person. It formed as it were an extra being inside of me, which
protested against the philosophical arguments of Hâsenkopf.

The worst of my sufferings was thirst. It was unbearable at this
point; so much so that I sucked the saltpetre on the wall to refresh
myself.

When daylight appeared in the vent, vague, uncertain, I suddenly
had an extraordinary fit of rage.

'The rogue is there,' I said to myself. 'He has bread, a jug of water,
he is drinking . . . !'

Then I imagined him raising to his lips his large jug. I seemed to see
torrents of water trickling down his throat. It was a delicious river
flowing, flowing endlessly. I could see the wretch's throat swell up
with pleasure, rise up, descend voluptuously, his stomach fill up. Anger,
despair, indignation took possession of me and I started to stammer,
running around the pit. 'Water . . . water . . . water . . .' And the old
woman, coming to life again, repeated behind me like a mad thing,
'Water . . . water . . . water . . .' She followed me, crawling about, her
rags flapping. Hell has nothing more terrible.

In the middle of this scene the pale face of Wolfgang appeared for
the third time at the vent. It was about eight o'clock. Stopping, I said
to him:

'Wolfgang! Listen, let me drink just a mouthful from your jug
and I shall allow you to let me die of hunger! I shan't reproach you!'

And I cried. 'What you are doing to me,' I resumed, 'is too barbarous. Your immortal soul will answer before God for it. Still, for this old woman, as you so disconcertingly said, it is experimentation on a worthless being. But me, I have studied, and I find your system very good. I am worthy of understanding you. I admire you. Let me just have water. What does it matter to you? One has never come across a conception as sublime as yours. It is certain that the three souls exist! Yes! I want to make it known. I shall be your strongest supporter. Won't you let me have just one mouthful of water?'

Without a reply he withdrew.

My exasperation then knew no limits. I threw myself against the wall hard enough to break my bones. I cursed the wretch in the harshest terms.

In the midst of this fury I suddenly noticed that the old woman had collapsed, and I conceived the idea of drinking her blood. Extreme necessity carries man to excesses that would make one shudder. It is then that the wild beast is aroused in us and all sentiment of justice, of good-will fades before the instinct of self-preservation.

'What need does she have of blood?' I asked myself. 'Will she not die soon? If I delay all her blood will be dried up!'

A red mist passed before my eyes. Fortunately as I was stooping toward the old woman, my strength left me and I fell beside her, my face in her rags, in a faint.

How long did this absence of feeling last. I do not know, but I was drawn from it by an odd incident, the memory of which will always remain imprinted on my mind. I was drawn from it by the plaintive howling of a dog. This howling, so weak, so piteous, so poignant; cries more moving even than the crying of a man, and which one cannot hear without suffering. I got up, my face bathed in tears, not knowing from where came these cries, so consistent with my own suffering. I listened. Judge my amazement when I realised that it was me who was howling like this.

From then on all sorts of memory fades from my mind. What is certain is that I stayed another two days in the pit, under the maniac's eye, whose enthusiasm on seeing his theory proved was such that he didn't hesitate to summon several of our philosophers to delight in their admiration.

Six weeks later I awoke in a small room in the Rue Plat d'Etain, surrounded by my friends, who congratulated me on having escaped from this lesson in transcendental philosophy.

It was a pathetic moment when Ludwig Bremer brought me the mirror, and, when seeing myself more emaciated than Lazarus as he came out of the tomb, I could not help shedding tears.

Poor Catherine Wogel had given up the ghost.

I cannot even say that justice dealt with this scoundrel Wolfgang. Instead of hanging him, according to his just deserts, after proceedings of six months it was established that this abominable being fell into the category of mystic madman, the most dangerous of all. Consequently he was consigned to a cell in a lunatic asylum where visitors can still hear him hold forth in a curt peremptory voice on the three souls.

He accuses humanity of ingratitude and claims that it should, in all fairness, erect statues to him for his magnificent discovery.

A Strange Goldfield

by

GUY BOOTHBY

Australia is a very rare source of Victorian tales of terror, both in location and author nationality. There were one or two writers who achieved fame with their Australian tales, among them Rolf Boldrewood, J. A. Barry and Andrew Robertson, but probably the most famous (and he had to come to England to achieve that fame) was Guy Boothby (1867–1905).

Boothby was born in Adelaide, and at one time before he came to Britain in 1894, he was private secretary to the mayor of that city. Boothby's main claim to literary fame was his sinister creation Dr Nikola, who chased the secret of eternal life through five enthralling novels. Nikola was Boothby's finest work and, despite many other novels equally full of incident and excitement, such as The Curse of The Snake *(1902), it is for Nikola that Boothby is now remembered.*

But Guy Boothby also wrote several books of short stories, among them Bushigrams *(1897),* Uncle Joe's Legacy *(1902) and* The Lady Of The Island *(1904). 'A Strange Goldfield' comes from the last-named work and, although it didn't appear in print until after the Victorian era, I have included it in this Victorian volume as it was obviously written at that time. In this one story at least, Boothby returns to his native Australia to tell one of the few ghost stories set in that continent that appeared in the Victorian era. And it's not a bad one, either.*

Of course nine out of every ten intelligent persons will refuse to believe that there could be a grain of truth in the story I am now going to tell you. The tenth may have some small faith in my veracity, but what I think of his intelligence I am going to keep to myself.

In a certain portion of a certain Australian Colony two miners, when out prospecting in what was then, as now, one of the dreariest parts of the Island Continent, chanced upon a rich find. They applied to Government for the usual reward, and in less than a month three thousand people were settled on the Field. What privations they had to go through to get there, and the miseries they had to endure when the *did* reach their journey's end, have only a remote bearing on this story, but they would make a big book.

I should explain that between Railhead and the Field was a stretch of country some three hundred miles in extent. It was badly watered, vilely grassed, and execrably timbered. What was even worse, a considerable portion of it was made up of red sand, and everybody who has been compelled to travel over that knows what it means. Yet these enthusiastic seekers after wealth pushed on, some on horseback, some in bullock waggons, but the majority travelled on foot; the graves, and the skeletons of cattle belonging to those who had preceded them punctuating the route, and telling them what they might expect as they advanced.

That the Field did not prove a success is now a matter of history, but that same history, if you read between the lines, gives one some notion of what the life must have been like while it lasted. The water supply was entirely insufficient, provisions were bad and ruinously expensive; the men themselves were, as a rule, the roughest of the rough, while the less said about the majority of the women the better. Then typhoid stepped in and stalked like the Destroying Angel through the camp. Its inhabitants went down like sheep in a drought, and for the most part rose no more. Where there had been a lust of gold there was now panic, terror—every man feared that he might be the next to be attacked, and it was only the knowledge of those terrible three hundred miles that separated them from civilisation that kept many of them on the Field. The most thickly populated part was now the cemetery. Drink was the only solace, and under its influence such scenes were enacted as I dare not describe. As they heard of fresh deaths, men shook their fists at Heaven, and cursed the day when they first saw pick or shovel. Some, bolder than the rest, cleared out just as they stood; a few eventually reached civilisation, others perished in the desert. At last the Field was declared abandoned, and the dead were left to take their last long sleep, undisturbed by the clank of windlass or the blow of pick.

It would take too long to tell all the different reasons that combined to draw me out into that 'most distressful country'. Let it suffice that our party consisted of a young Englishman named Spicer, a wily old Australian bushman named Matthews, and myself. We were better off than the unfortunate miners, inasmuch as we were travelling with camels, and our outfits were as perfect as money and experience could make them. The man who travels in any other fashion in that country is neither more nor less than a madman. For a month past we had been having a fairly rough time of it, and were then on our way south, where we had reason to believe rain had fallen, and, in consequence, grass was plentiful. It was towards evening when we came out of a gully in the ranges and had our first view of the deserted camp. We had no idea of its existence, and for this reason we pulled up our animals and stared at it in complete surprise. Then we pushed on again, wondering what on earth place we had chanced upon.

'This is all right,' said Spicer, with a chuckle. 'We're in luck. Grog shanties and stores, a bath, and perhaps girls.'

I shook my head.

'I can't make it out,' I said. 'What's it doing out here?'

Matthews was looking at it under his hand, and, as I knew that he had been out in this direction on a previous occasion, I asked his opinion.

'It beats me,' he replied; 'but if you ask me what I think I should say it's Gurunya, the Field that was deserted some four or five years back.'

'Look here,' cried Spicer, who was riding a bit on our left, 'what are all these things—graves, as I'm a living man. Here, let's get out of this. There are hundreds of them and before I know where I am old Polyphemus here will be on his nose.'

What he said was correct—the ground over which we were riding was literally bestrewn with graves, some of which had rough, tumble-down head boards, others being destitute of all adornment. We turned away and moved on over safer ground in the direction of the Field itself. Such a pitiful sight I never want to see again. The tents and huts, in numerous cases, were still standing, while the claims gaped at us on every side like new-made graves. A bullock dray, weather-worn but still in excellent condition, stood in the main street outside a grog shanty whose sign-board, strange incongruity, bore the name of 'The Killarney Hotel'. Nothing would suit Spicer but that he must dismount and go in to explore. He was not long away, and when he returned it was with a face as white as a sheet of paper.

'You never saw such a place,' he almost whispered. 'All I want to do is to get out of it. There's a skeleton on the floor in the back room with an empty rum bottle alongside it.'

He mounted, and, when his beast was on its feet once more, we

went on our way. Not one of us was sorry when we had left the last
claim behind us.

Half a mile or so from the Field the country begins to rise again.
There is also a curious cliff away to the left, and, as it looked like being
a likely place to find water, we resolved to camp there. We were
within a hundred yards or so of this cliff when an exclamation from
Spicer attracted my attention.

'Look!' he cried. 'What's that?'

I followed the direction in which he was pointing, and, to my surprise, saw the figure of a man running as if for his life among the rocks.
I have said the figure of a man, but, as a matter of fact, had there been
baboons in the Australian bush, I should have been inclined to have
taken him for one.

'This is a day of surprises,' I said. 'Who can the fellow be? And what
makes him act like that?'

We still continued to watch him as he proceeded on his erratic
course along the base of the cliff—then he suddenly disappeared.

'Let's get on to camp,' I said, 'and then we'll go after him and
endeavour to settle matters a bit.'

Having selected a place we offsaddled and prepared our camp. By
this time it was nearly dark, and it was very evident that, if we wanted
to discover the man we had seen, it would be wise not to postpone the
search too long. We accordingly strolled off in the direction he had
taken, keeping a sharp look-out for any sign of him. Our search,
however, was not successful. The fellow had disappeared without
leaving a trace of his whereabouts behind him, and yet we were all
certain that we had seen him. At length we returned to our camp for
supper, completely mystified. As we ate our meal we discussed the
problem and vowed that, on the morrow, we would renew the search.
Then the full moon rose over the cliff, and the plain immediately
became well-nigh as bright as day. I had lit my pipe and was stretching
myself out upon my blankets when something induced me to look
across at a big rock, some half-dozen paces from the fire. Peering round
it, and evidently taking an absorbing interest in our doings, was the
most extraordinary figure I have ever beheld. Shouting something to
my companions, I sprang to my feet and dashed across at him. He saw
me and fled. Old as he apparently was, he could run like a jack-rabbit,
and, though I have the reputation of being fairly quick on my feet,
I found that I had all my work cut out to catch him. Indeed, I am
rather doubtful as to whether I should have done so at all had he not

tripped and measured his length on the ground. Before he could get up I was on him.

'I've got you at last, my friend,' I said. 'Now you just come along back to the camp, and let us have a look at you.'

In reply he snarled like a dog and I believe would have bitten me had I not held him off. My word, he was a creature, more animal than man, and the reek of him was worse than that of our camels. From what I could tell he must have been about sixty years of age—was below the middle height, had white eyebrows, white hair and a white beard. He was dressed partly in rags and partly in skins, and went barefooted like a black fellow. While I was overhauling him the others came up—whereupon we escorted him back to the camp.

'What wouldn't Barnum give for him?' said Spicer. 'You're a beauty, my friend, and no mistake. What's your name?'

The fellow only grunted in reply—then, seeing the pipes in our mouths, a curious change came over him, and he muttered something that resembled 'Give me.'

'Wants a smoke,' interrupted Matthews. 'Poor beggar's been without for a long time, I reckon. Well, I've got an old pipe, so he can have a draw.'

He procured one from his pack saddle, filled it and handed it to the man, who snatched it greedily and began to puff away at it.

'How long have you been out here?' I asked, when he had squatted himself down alongside the fire.

'Don't know,' he answered, this time plainly enough.

'Can't you get back?' continued Matthews, who knew the nature of the country on the other side.

'Don't want to,' was the other's laconic reply. 'Stay here.'

I heard Spicer mutter, 'Mad—mad as a March hare.'

We then tried to get out of him where he hailed from, but he had either forgotten or did not understand. Next we inquired how he managed to live. To this he answered readily enough, 'Carnies.'

Now the carny is a lizard of the iguana type, and eaten raw would be by no means an appetizing dish. Then came the question that gives me my reason for telling this story. It was Spicer who put it.

'You must have a lonely time of it out here,' said the latter. 'How do you manage for company?'

'There is the Field,' he said, 'as sociable a Field as you'd find.'

'But the Field's deserted, man,' I put in. 'And has been for years.'

The old fellow shook his head.

'As sociable a Field as ever you saw,' he repeated. 'There's Sailor Dick and 'Frisco, Dick Johnson, Cockney Jim, and half a hundred of thom. Thoy'ro taking it out poworful rioh on tho Goldon South, co I heard when I was down at "The Killarney", a while back.'

It was plain to us all that the old man was, as Spicer had said, as mad as a hatter. For some minutes he rambled on about the Field, talking rationally enough, I must confess—that is to say, it would have seemed rational enough if we hadn't known the true facts of the case. At last he got on to his feet, saying, 'Well, I must be going—they'll be expecting me. It's my shift on with Cockney Jim.'

'But you don't work at night,' growled Matthews, from the other side of the fire.

'We work always,' the other replied. 'If you don't believe me, come and see for yourselves.'

'I wouldn't go back to that place for anything,' said Spicer.

But I must confess that my curiosity had been aroused, and I determined to go, if only to see what this strange creature did when he got there. Matthews decided to accompany me, and, not wishing to be left alone, Spicer at length agreed to do the same. Without looking round, the old fellow led the way across the plain towards the Field. Of all the nocturnal excursions I have made in my life, that was certainly the most uncanny. Not once did our guide turn his head, but pushed on at a pace that gave us some trouble to keep up with him. It was only when we came to the first claim that he paused.

'Listen,' he said, 'and you can hear the camp at work. Then you'll bdicvc mc.'

We *did* listen, and as I live we could distinctly hear the rattling of sluice-boxes and cradles, the groaning of windlasses—in fact, the noise you hear on a goldfield at the busiest hour of the day. We moved a little closer, and, believe me or not, I swear to you I could see, or thought I could see, the shadowy forms of men moving about in that ghostly moonlight. Meanwhile the wind sighed across the plain, flapping what remained of the old tents and giving an additional touch of horror to the general desolation. I could hear Spicer's teeth chattering behind me, and, for my own part, I felt as if my blood were turning to ice.

'That's the claim, the Golden South, away to the right there,' said the old man, 'and if you will come along with me, I'll introduce you to my mates.'

But this was an honour we declined, and without hesitation. I wouldn't have gone any further among those tents for the wealth of all the Indies.

'I've had enough of this,' said Spicer, and I can tell you I hardly recognised his voice. 'Let's get back to camp.'

By this time our guide had left us, and was making his way in the direction he had indicated. We could plainly hear him addressing imaginary people as he marched along. As for ourselves, we turned about and hurried back to our camp as fast as we could go.

Once there, the grog bottle was produced, and never did three men stand more in need of stimulants. Then we set to work to find some explanation of what we had seen, or had fancied we saw. But it was impossible. The wind might have rattled the old windlasses, but it could not be held accountable for those shadowy grey forms that had moved about among the claims.

'I give it up,' said Spicer, at last. 'I know that I never want to see it again. What's more, I vote that we clear out of here to-morrow morning.'

We all agreed, and then retired to our blankets, but for my part I do not mind confessing I scarcely slept a wink all night. The thought that that hideous old man might be hanging about the camp would alone be sufficient for that.

Next morning, as soon as it was light, we breakfasted, but, before we broke camp, Matthews and I set off along the cliff in an attempt to discover our acquaintance of the previous evening. Though, however, we searched high and low for upwards of an hour, no success rewarded us. By mutual consent we resolved not to look for him on the Field. When we returned to Spicer we placed such tobacco and stores as we could spare under the shadow of the big rock, where the Mystery would be likely to see them, then mounted our camels and resumed our journey, heartily glad to be on our way once more.

Gurunya Goldfield is a place I never desire to visit again. I don't like its population.

An Alpine Divorce

by

ROBERT BARR

Now for a story years ahead of its time, from a book far in advance of its contemporary works. Revenge! *by Robert Barr (1850–1912) was a unique volume for the time it was written, being short stories dealing uncompromisingly with passion and greed, all using the motif of revenge.*

Robert Barr, one of the most popular and prolific contributors to magazines and journals of the late 1800s, was born in Glasgow and emigrated to Canada as a young man. Strangely, his early career was in the field of education, as the headmaster of a public school, and he began his journalistic work when he moved to Detroit. He returned to England in 1881, where he eventually went into partnership with Jerome K. Jerome on the popular journal The Idler. *Most of Barr's journalism was published under the pen-name of Luke Sharp and he reserved his own name for his highly successful fiction career.*

Barr is now mainly remembered for his detective stories, but he also wrote romances and occasional tales of terror. Revenge! *contains his best work in this field and 'An Alpine Divorce' is one of the finest tales he ever wrote. The fact that it utilises a plot device since flogged to death by less skilled writers contributing to mystery magazines and the like does not detract from it in the slightest, in my opinion. Just remember when reading it that Barr was probably the first to use this idea and, certainly in his day, he was unique in not being afraid to tackle such a sardonic plot.*

In some natures there are no half-tones; nothing but raw primary colours. John Bodman was a man who was always at one extreme or the other. This probably would have mattered little had he not married a wife whose nature was an exact duplicate of his own.

Doubtless there exists in this world precisely the right woman for any given man to marry, and vice versa; but when you consider that a human being has the opportunity of being acquainted with only a few hundred people, and out of the few hundred that there are but a dozen or less whom he knows intimately, and out of the dozen, one or two friends at most, it will easily be seen, when we remember the number of millions who inhabit this world, that probably, since the earth was created, the right man has never yet met the right woman. The mathematical chances are all against such a meeting, and this is the reason that divorce courts exist. Marriage at best is but a compromise, and if two people happen to be united who are of an uncompromising nature there is trouble.

In the lives of these two young people there was no middle distance. The result was bound to be either love or hate, and in the case of Mr and Mrs Bodman it was hate of the most bitter and arrogant kind.

In some parts of the world incompatibility of temper is considered a just case for obtaining a divorce, but in England no such subtle distinction is made, and so, until the wife became criminal, or the man became both criminal and cruel, these two were linked together by a bond that only death could sever. Nothing can be worse than this state of things, and the matter was only made the more hopeless by the fact that Mrs Bodman lived a blameless life, and her husband was no worse, but rather better, than the majority of men. Perhaps, however, that statement held only up to a certain point, for John Bodman had reached a state of mind in which he resolved to get rid of his wife at all hazards. If he had been a poor man he would probably have deserted her, but he was rich, and a man cannot freely leave a prospering business because his domestic life happens not to be happy.

When a man's mind dwells too much on any one subject, no one can tell just how far he will go. The mind is a delicate instrument, and even the law recognises that it is easily thrown from its balance. Bodman's friends—for he had friends—claim that his mind was unhinged; but neither his friends nor his enemies suspected the truth of the episode, which turned out to be the most important, as it was the most ominous, event in his life.

Whether John Bodman was sane or insane at the time he made up his mind to murder his wife, will never be known, but there was certainly craftiness in the method he devised to make the crime appear the result of an accident. Nevertheless, cunning is often a quality in a mind that has gone wrong.

Mrs Bodman well knew how much her presence afflicted her husband, but her nature was as relentless as his, and her hatred of him was, if possible, more bitter than his hatred of her. Wherever he went she accompanied him, and perhaps the idea of murder would never have occurred to him if she had not been so persistent in forcing her presence upon him at all times and on all occasions. So, when he announced to her that he intended to spend the month of July in Switzerland, she said nothing, but made her preparations for the journey. On this occasion he did not protest, as was usual with him, and so to Switzerland this silent couple departed.

There is an hotel near the mountain-tops which stands on a ledge over one of the great glaciers. It is a mile and a half above the level of the sea, and it stands alone, reached by a toilsome road that zigzags up the mountain for six miles. There is a wonderful view of snow-peaks and glaciers from the verandahs of this hotel, and in the neighbourhood are many picturesque walks to points more or less dangerous.

John Bodman knew the hotel well, and in happier days he had been intimately acquainted with the vicinity. Now that the thought of murder arose in his mind, a certain spot two miles distant from this inn continually haunted him. It was a point of view overlooking everything, and its extremity was protected by a low and crumbling wall. He arose one morning at four o'clock, slipped unnoticed out of the hotel, and went to this point, which was locally named the Hanging Outlook. His memory had served him well. It was exactly the spot, he said to himself. The mountain which rose up behind it was wild and precipitous. There were no inhabitants near to overlook the place. The distant hotel was hidden by a shoulder of rock. The mountains on the other side of the valley were too far away to make it possible for any casual tourist or native to see what was going on on the Hanging Outlook. Far down in the valley the only town in view seemed like a collection of little toy houses.

One glance over the crumbling wall at the edge was generally sufficient for a visitor of even the strongest nerves. There was a sheer drop of more than a mile straight down, and at the distant bottom were jagged rocks and stunted trees that looked, in the blue haze, like shrubbery.

'This is the spot,' said the man to himself, 'and to-morrow morning is the time.'

John Bodman had planned his crime as grimly and relentlessly, and as coolly, as ever he had concocted a deal on the Stock Exchange. There was no thought in his mind of mercy for his unconscious victim. His hatred had carried him far.

The next morning after breakfast, he said to his wife: 'I intend to take a walk in the mountains. Do you wish to come with me?'

'Yes,' she answered briefly.

'Very well, then,' he said; 'I shall be ready at nine o'clock.'

'I shall be ready at nine o'clock,' she repeated after him.

At that hour they left the hotel together, to which he was shortly to return alone. They spoke no word to each other on their way to the Hanging Outlook. The path was practically level, skirting the mountains, for the Hanging Outlook was not much higher above the sea than the hotel.

John Bodman had formed no fixed plan for his procedure when the place was reached. He resolved to be guided by circumstances. Now and then a strange fear arose in his mind that she might cling to him and possibly drag him over the precipice with her. He found himself wondering whether she had any premonition of her fate, and one of his reasons for not speaking was the fear that a tremor in his voice might possibly arouse her suspicions. He resolved that his action should be sharp and sudden, that she might have no chance either to help herself, or to drag him with her. Of her screams in that desolate region he had no fear. No one could reach the spot except from the hotel, and no one that morning had left the house, even for an expedition to the glacier—one of the easiest and most popular trips from the place.

Curiously enough, when they came within sight of the Hanging Outlook, Mrs Bodman stopped and shuddered. Bodman looked at her through the narrow slits of his veiled eyes, and wondered again if she had any suspicion. No one can tell, when two people walk closely together, what unconscious communication one mind may have with another.

'What is the matter?' he asked gruffly. 'Are you tired?'

'John,' she cried with a gasp in her voice, calling him by his Christian name for the first time in years, 'don't you think that if you had been kinder to me at first, things might have been different?'

'It seems to me,' he answered, not looking at her, 'that it is rather late in the day for discussing that question.'

'I have much to regret,' she said quaveringly. 'Have you nothing?'

'No,' he answered.

'Very well,' replied his wife, with the usual hardness returning to her voice. 'I was merely giving you a chance. Remember that.'

Her husband looked at her suspiciously.

'What do you mean?' he asked, 'giving me a chance? I want no chance nor anything else from you. A man accepts nothing from one he hates. My feeling towards you is, I imagine, no secret to you. We are tied together, and you have done your best to make the bondage insupportable.'

'Yes,' she answered, with her eyes on the ground, 'we are tied together—we are tied together!'

She repeated these words under her breath as they walked the few remaining steps to the Outlook. Bodman sat down upon the crumbling wall. The woman dropped her alpenstock on the rock, and walked nervously to and fro, clasping and unclasping her hands. Her husband caught his breath as the terrible moment drew near.

'Why do you walk about like a wild animal?' he cried. 'Come here and sit down beside me, and be still.'

She faced him with a light he had never before seen in her eyes—a light of insanity and of hatred.

'I walk like a wild animal,' she said, 'because I am one. You spoke a moment ago of your hatred of me; but you are a man, and your hatred is nothing to mine. Bad as you are, much as you wish to break the bond which ties us together, there are still things which I know you would not stoop to. I know there is no thought of murder in your heart, but there is in mine. I will show you, John Bodman, how much I hate you.'

The man nervously clutched the stone beside him, and gave a guilty start as she mentioned murder.

'Yes,' she continued, 'I have told all my friends in England that I believed you intended to murder me in Switzerland.'

'Good God!' he cried. 'How could you say such a thing?'

'I say it to show how much I hate you—how much I am prepared to give for revenge. I have warned the people at the hotel, and when we left two men followed us. The proprietor tried to persuade me not to accompany you. In a few moments those two men will come in sight of the Outlook. Tell them, if you think they will believe you, that it was an accident.'

The mad woman tore from the front of her dress shreds of lace and scattered them around.

Bodman started up to his feet, crying, 'What are you about?' But before he could move towards her she precipitated herself over the wall, and went shrieking and whirling down the awful abyss.

The next moment two men came hurriedly round the edge of the rock, and found the man standing alone. Even in his bewilderment he realised that if he told the truth he would not be believed.

The Story of Baelbrow

by

E. and H. HERON

Victorian London can be summed up in so many popular images—foggy streets, horses' hooves and hansom cabs, gaslight, the music hall, Jack the Ripper—but probably the most popular image of all is that of a certain gentleman who lived at 221b Baker Street and had a partner named Doctor Watson. That even this famous man was not alone in his chosen profession has been admirably illustrated in the anthology series The Rivals of Sherlock Holmes. *But Holmes and his friends dealt in the natural; there were others who dealt in the supernatural, and for want of a better name, might be termed the psychic detectives.*

Probably the most famous was William Hope Hodgson's Carnacki, who has even influenced Dennis Wheatley's Duc de Richelieu. Among the other noted ghost hunters were Algernon Blackwood's John Silence, Mrs L. T. Meade's Mr Bell, M. P. Shiel's Prince Zaleski, and E. and H. Heron's Flaxman Low.

Flaxman Low's adventures were originally recorded in Pearson's Magazine *and collected into a brief volume* Ghost Stories *(1916). E. and H. Heron was the pen-name of the mother and son writing pair, Kate and Hesketh Prichard, and Flaxman Low was reputed to be a thinly-disguised portrait of one of the leading scientists of the Victorian era. The Prichards were rather proud of Mr Low, for, as they said, 'he is the first student in this field of inquiry who has had the boldness and originality to break free from old and conventional methods and to approach the elucidation of so-called supernatural problems on the lines of natural law.' Flaxman Low was most definitely a scientist, and rightly so: in Victorian times science had not acquired the bad name which it has today. At Baelbrow, however, Flaxman Low encounters a creature from the days before science was even thought of, and a very nasty one at that.*

It is a matter for regret that so many of Mr Flaxman Low's reminiscences should deal with the darker episodes of his experiences. Yet this is almost unavoidable, as the more purely scientific and less strongly marked cases would not, perhaps, contain the same elements of interest for the general public, however valuable and instructive they might be to the expert student. It has also been considered better to choose the completer cases, those that ended in something like satisfactory proof, rather than the many instances where the thread broke off abruptly amongst surmisings, which it was never possible to subject to convincing tests.

North of a low-lying strip of country on the East Anglian coast, the promontory of Bael Ness thrusts out a blunt nose into the sea. On the Ness, backed by pinewoods, stands a square, comfortable stone mansion, known to the countryside as Baelbrow. It has faced the east winds for close upon three hundred years, and during the whole period has been the home of the Swaffam family, who were never in anywise put out of conceit of their ancestral dwelling by the fact that it had always been haunted. Indeed, the Swaffams were proud of the Baelbrow Ghost, which enjoyed a wide notoriety, and no one dreamt of complaining of its behaviour until Professor Van der Voort of Louvain laid information against it, and sent an urgent appeal for help to Mr Flaxman Low.

The Professor, who was well acquainted with Mr Low, detailed the circumstances of his tenancy of Baelbrow, and the unpleasant events that had followed thereupon.

It appeared that Mr Swaffam, senior, who spent a large portion of his time abroad, had offered to lend his house to the Professor for the summer season. When the Van der Voorts arrived at Baelbrow, they were charmed with the place. The prospect, though not very varied, was at least extensive, and the air exhilarating. Also the Professor's daughter enjoyed frequent visits from her betrothed—Harold Swaffam —and the Professor was delightfully employed in overhauling the Swaffam library.

The Van der Voorts had been duly told of the ghost, which lent distinction to the old house, but never in any way interfered with the comfort of the inmates. For some time they found this description to be strictly true, but with the beginning of October came a change. Up to this time and as far back as the Swaffam annals reached, the ghost had been a shadow, a rustle, a passing sigh—nothing definite or troublesome. But early in October strange things began to occur, and the terror culminated when a housemaid was found dead in a corridor three weeks later. Upon this the Professor felt that it was time to send for Flaxman Low.

Mr Low arrived upon a chilly evening when the house was already beginning to blur in the purple twilight, and the resinous scent of the pines came sweetly on the land breeze. Van der Voort welcomed him in the spacious, fire-lit hall. He was a stout man with a quantity of white hair, round eyes emphasised by spectacles, and a kindly, dreamy face. His life-study was philology, and his two relaxations chess and the smoking of a big bowled meerschaum.

'Now, Professor,' said Mr Low when they had settled themselves in the smoking-room, 'how did it all begin?'

'I will tell you,' replied Van der Voort, thrusting out his chin, and tapping his broad chest, and speaking as if an unwarrantable liberty had been taken with him. 'First of all, it has shown itself to me!'

Mr Flaxman Low smiled and assured him that nothing could be more satisfactory.

'But not at all satisfactory!' exclaimed the Professor. 'I was sitting here alone, it might have been midnight—when I hear something come creeping like a little dog with its nails, tick-tick, upon the oak flooring of the hall. I whistle, for I think it is the little "Rags" of my daughter, and afterwards opened the door, and I saw'—he hesitated and looked hard at Low through his spectacles, 'something that was just disappearing into the passage which connects the two wings of the house. It was a figure, not unlike the human figure, but narrow and straight. I fancied I saw a bunch of black hair, and a flutter of something detached, which may have been a handkerchief. I was overcome by a feeling of repulsion. I heard a few clicking steps, then it stopped, as I thought, at the museum door. Come, I will show you the spot.'

The Professor conducted Mr Low into the hall. The main staircase, dark and massive, yawned above them, and directly behind it ran the passage referred to by the Professor. It was over twenty feet long, and about midway led past a deep arch containing a door reached by two steps. Van der Voort explained that this door formed the entrance to a large room called the Museum, in which Mr Swaffam, senior, who was something of a dilettante, stored the various curios he picked up during his excursions abroad. The Professor went on to say that he immediately followed the figure, which he believed had gone into the museum, but he found nothing there except the cases containing Swaffam's treasures.

'I mentioned my experience to no one. I concluded that I had seen the ghost. But two days after, one of the female servants coming through the passage, in the dark, declared that a man leapt out at her from the embrasure of the Museum door, but she released herself and ran screaming into the servants' hall. We at once made a search but found nothing to substantiate her story.

'I took no notice of this, though it coincided pretty well with my own experience. The week after, my daughter Lena came down late one night for a book. As she was about to cross the hall, something leapt upon her from behind. Women are of little use in serious investigations—she fainted! Since then she has been ill and the doctor says "Run down".' Here the Professor spread out his hands. 'So she leaves for a change to-morrow. Since then other members of the household have been attacked in much the same manner, with always the same result, they faint and are weak and useless when they recover.

'But, last Wednesday, the affair became a tragedy. By that time the servants had refused to come through the passage except in a crowd of three or four—most of them preferring to go round by the terrace to reach this part of the house. But one maid, named Eliza Freeman, said she was not afraid of the Baelbrow Ghost, and undertook to put out the lights in the hall one night. When she had done so, and was returning through the passage past the Museum door, she appears to have been attacked, or at any rate frightened. In the grey of the morning they found her lying beside the steps dead. There was a little blood upon her sleeve but no mark upon her body except a small raised pustule under the ear. The doctor said the girl was extraordinarily anæmic, and that she probably died from fright, her heart being weak. I was surprised at this, for she had always seemed to be a particularly strong and active young woman.'

'Can I see Miss Van der Voort to-morrow before she goes?' asked Low, as the Professor signified he had nothing more to tell.

The Professor was rather unwilling that his daughter should be questioned, but he at last gave his permission, and next morning Low had a short talk with the girl before she left the house. He found her a very pretty girl, though listless and startlingly pale, and with a frightened stare in her light brown eyes. Mr Low asked if she could describe her assailant.

'No,' she answered. 'I could not see him for he was behind me. I only saw a dark, bony hand, with shining nails, and a bandaged arm pass just under my eyes before I fainted.'

'Bandaged arm? I have heard nothing of this.'

'Tut—tut, mere fancy!' put in the Professor impatiently.

'I saw the bandages on the arm,' repeated the girl, turning her head wearily away, 'and I smelt the antiseptics it was dressed with.'

'You have hurt your neck,' remarked Mr Low, who noticed a small circular patch of pink under her ear.

She flushed and paled, raising her hand to her neck with a nervous jerk, as she said in a low voice:

'It has almost killed me. Before he touched me, I knew he was there! I felt it!'

When they left her the Professor apologised for the unreliability of her evidence, and pointed out the discrepancy between her statement and his own.

'She says she sees nothing but an arm, yet I tell you it had no arms! Preposterous! Conceive a wounded man entering this house to frighten the young women! I do not know what to make of it! Is it a man, or is it the Baelbrow Ghost?'

During the afternoon when Mr Low and the Professor returned from a stroll on the shore, they found a dark-browed young man with a bull neck, and strongly marked features, standing sullenly before the hall fire. The Professor presented him to Mr Low as Harold Swaffam.

Swaffam seemed to be about thirty, but was already known as a far-seeing and successful member of the Stock Exchange.

'I am pleased to meet you, Mr Low,' he began, with a keen glance, 'though you don't look sufficiently high-strung for one of your profession.'

Mr Low merely bowed.

'Come, you don't defend your craft against my insinuations?' went on Swaffam. 'And so you have come to rout out our poor old ghost from Baelbrow? You forget that he is an heirloom, a family possession! What's this about his having turned rabid, eh, Professor?' he ended, wheeling round upon Van der Voort in his brusque way.

The Professor told the story over again. It was plain that he stood rather in awe of his prospective son-in-law.

'I heard much the same from Lena, whom I met at the station,' said Swaffam. 'It is my opinion that the women in this house are suffering from an epidemic of hysteria. You agree with me, Mr Low?'

'Possibly. Though hysteria could hardly account for Freeman's death.'

'I can't say as to that until I have looked further into the particulars.

I have not been idle since I arrived. I have examined the Museum. No one has entered it from the outside, and there is no other way of entrance except through the passage. The flooring is laid, I happen to know, on a thick layer of concrete. And there the case for the ghost stands at present.' After a few moments of dogged reflection, he swung round on Mr Low, in a manner that seemed peculiar to him when about to address any person. 'What do you say to this plan, Mr Low? I propose to drive the Professor over to Ferryvale, to stop there for a day or two at the hotel, and I will also dispose of the servants who still remain in the house for say, forty-eight hours. Meanwhile you and I can try to go further into the secret of the ghost's new pranks?'

Flaxman Low replied that this scheme exactly met his views, but the Professor protested against being sent away. Harold Swaffam, however, was a man who liked to arrange things in his own fashion, and within forty-five minutes he and Van der Voort departed in the dogcart.

The evening was lowering, and Baelbrow, like all houses built in exposed situations, was extremely susceptible to the changes of the weather. Therefore, before many hours were over, the place was full of creaking noises as the screaming gale battered at the shuttered windows, and the tree-branches tapped and groaned against the walls.

Harold Swaffam on his way back, was caught in the storm and drenched to the skin. It was, therefore, settled that after he had changed his clothes he should have a couple of hours' rest on the smoking-room sofa, while Mr Low kept watch in the hall.

The early part of the night passed over uneventfully. A light burned faintly in the great wainscotted hall, but the passage was dark. There was nothing to be heard but the wild moan and whistle of the wind coming in from the sea, and the squalls of rain dashing against the windows. As the hours advanced, Mr Low lit a lantern that lay at hand, and, carrying it along the passage tried the Museum door. It yielded, and the wind came muttering through to meet him. He looked round at the shutters and behind the big cases which held Mr Swaffam's treasures, to make sure that the room contained no living occupant but himself.

Suddenly he fancied he heard a scraping noise behind him, and turned round, but discovered nothing to account for it. Finally, he laid the lantern on a bench so that its light should fall through the door into the passage, and returned again to the hall, where he put out the lamp, and then once more took up his station by the closed door of the smoking-room.

A long hour passed, during which the wind continued to roar down the wide hall chimney, and the old boards creaked as if furtive footsteps were gathering from every corner of the house. But Flaxman Low heeded none of these; he was awaiting for a certain sound.

After a while, he heard it—the cautious scraping of wood on wood. He leant forward to watch the Museum door. Click, click, came the curious dog-like tread upon the tiled floor of the Museum, till the thing, whatever it was, paused and listened behind the open door. The wind lulled at the moment, and Low listened also, but no further sound was to be heard, only slowly across the broad ray of light falling through the door grew a stealthy shadow.

Again the wind rose, and blew in heavy gusts about the house, till even the flame in the lantern flickered; but when it steadied once more, Flaxman Low saw that the silent form had passed through the door, and was now on the steps outside. He could just make out a dim shadow in the dark angle of the embrasure.

Presently, from the shapeless shadow came a sound Mr Low was not prepared to hear. The thing sniffed the air with the strong, audible inspiration of a bear, or some large animal. At the same moment, carried on the draughts of the hall, a faint, unfamiliar odour reached his nostrils. Lena Van der Voort's words flashed back upon him—this, then, was the creature with the bandaged arm!

Again, as the storm shrieked and shook the windows, a darkness passed across the light. The thing had sprung out from the angle of the door, and Flaxman Low knew that it was making its way towards him through the illusive blackness of the hall. He hesitated for a second; then he opened the smoking-room door.

Harold Swaffam sat up on the sofa, dazed with sleep.

'What has happened? Has it come?'

Low told him what he had just seen. Swaffam listened half-smilingly.

'What do you make of it now?' he said.

'I must ask you to defer that question for a little,' replied Low.

'Then you mean me to suppose that you have a theory to fit all these incongruous items?'

'I have a theory, which may be modified by further knowledge,' said Low. 'Meantime, am I right in concluding from the name of this house that it was built on a barrow or burying-place?'

'You are right, though that has nothing to do with the latest freaks of our ghost,' returned Swaffam decidedly.

'I also gather that Mr Swaffam has lately sent home one of the many cases now lying in the Museum?' went on Mr Low.

'He sent one, certainly, last September.'

'And you have opened it,' asserted Low.

'Yes; though I flattered myself I had left no trace of my handiwork.'

'I have not examined the cases,' said Low. 'I inferred that you had done so from other facts.'

'Now, one thing more,' went on Swaffam, still smiling. 'Do you imagine there is any danger—I mean to men like ourselves? Hysterical women cannot be taken into serious account.'

'Certainly; the gravest danger to any person who moves about this part of the house alone after dark,' replied Low.

Harold Swaffam leant back and crossed his legs.

'To go back to the beginning of our conversation, Mr Low, may I remind you of the various conflicting particulars you will have to reconcile before you can present any decent theory to the world?'

'I am quite aware of that.'

'First of all, our original ghost was a mere misty presence, rather guessed at from vague sounds and shadows—now we have a something that is tangible, and that can, as we have proof, kill with fright. Next Van der Voort declares the thing was a narrow, long and distinctly armless object, while Miss Van der Voort has not only seen the arm and hand of a human being, but saw them clearly enough to tell us that the nails were gleaming and the arm bandaged. She also felt its strength. Van der Voort, on the other hand, maintained that it clicked along like a dog—you bear out this description with the additional information that it sniffs like a wild beast. Now what can this thing be? It is capable of being seen, smelt, and felt, yet it hides itself, successfully in a room where there is no cavity or space sufficient to afford covert to a cat! You still tell me that you believe that you can explain?'

'Most certainly,' replied Flaxman Low with conviction.

'I have not the slightest intention or desire to be rude, but as a mere matter of common sense, I must express my opinion plainly. I believe the whole thing to be the result of excited imaginations, and I am about to prove it. Do you think there is any further danger to-night?'

'Very great danger to-night,' replied Low.

'Very well; as I said, I am going to prove it. I will ask you to allow me to lock you up in one of the distant rooms, where I can get no help from you, and I will pass the remainder of the night walking about the passage and hall in the dark. That should give proof one way or the other.'

'You can do so if you wish, but I must at least beg to be allowed to look on. I will leave the house and watch what goes on from the window in the passage, which I saw opposite the Museum door. You cannot, in any fairness, refuse to let me be a witness.'

'I cannot, of course,' returned Swaffam.

'Still, the night is too bad to turn a dog out into, and I warn you that I shall lock you out.'

'That will not matter. Lend me a macintosh, and leave the lantern lit in the Museum, where I placed it.'

Swaffam agreed to this. Mr Low gives a graphic account of what followed. He left the house and was duly locked out, and, after groping his way round the house, found himself at length outside the window of the passage, which was almost opposite to the door of the Museum. The door was still ajar and a thin band of light cut out into the gloom. Further down the hall gaped black and void. Low, sheltering himself as well as he could from the rain, waited for Swaffam's appearance. Was the terrible yellow watcher balancing itself upon its lean legs in the dim corner opposite, ready to spring out with its deadly strength upon the passer-by?

Presently Low heard a door bang inside the house, and the next moment Swaffam appeared with a candle in his hand, an isolated spread of weak rays against the vast darkness behind. He advanced steadily down the passage, his dark face grim and set, and as he came Mr Low experienced that tingling sensation, which is so often the forerunner of some strange experience. Swaffam passed on towards the other end of the passage. There was a quick vibration of the Museum door as a lean shape with a shrunken head leapt out into the passage after him. Then all together came a hoarse shout, the noise of a fall and utter darkness.

In an instant, Mr Low had broken the glass, opened the window, and swung himself into the passage. There he lit a match and as it flared he saw by its dim light a picture painted for a second upon the obscurity beyond.

Swaffam's big figure lay with outstretched arms, face downwards and as Low looked a crouching shape extricated itself from the fallen man, raising a narrow vicious head from his shoulder.

The match spluttered feebly and went out, and Low heard a flying step click on the boards, before he could find the candle Swaffam had dropped. Lighting it, he stooped over Swaffam and turned him on his back. The man's strong colour had gone, and the wax-white face looked whiter still against the blackness of hair and brows, and upon his neck under the ear was a little raised pustule, from which a thin line of blood was streaked up to the angle of his cheek-bone.

Some instinctive feeling prompted Low to glance up at this moment. Half extended from the Museum doorway were a face and bony neck —a high-nosed, dull-eyed, malignant face, the eye-sockets hollow, and the darkened teeth showing. Low plunged his hand into his pocket, and a shot rang out in the echoing passage-way and hall. The wind sighed through the broken panes, a ribbon of stuff fluttered along the polished flooring, and that was all, as Flaxman Low half dragged, half carried Swaffam into the smoking-room.

It was some time before Swaffam recovered consciousness. He listened to Low's story of how he had found him with a red angry gleam in his sombre eyes.

'The ghost has scored off me,' he said, with an odd, sullen laugh, 'but now I fancy it's my turn! But before we adjourn to the Museum to examine the place, I will ask you to let me hear your notion of things. You have been right in saying there was real danger. For myself I can only tell you that I felt something spring upon me, and I knew no more. Had this not happened I am afraid I should never have asked you a second time what your idea of the matter might be,' he added with a sort of sulky frankness.

'There are two main indications,' replied Low. 'This strip of yellow bandage, which I have just now picked up from the passage floor, and the mark on your neck.'

'What's that you say? Swaffam rose quickly and examined his neck in a small glass beside the mantelshelf.

'Connect those two, and I think I can leave you to work it out for yourself,' said Low.

'Pray let us have your theory in full,' requested Swaffam shortly.

'Very well,' answered Low good-humouredly—he thought Swaffam's annoyance natural in the circumstances—'The long, narrow figure which seemed to the Professor to be armless is developed on the next occasion. For Miss Van der Voort sees a bandaged arm and a dark hand with gleaming—which means, of course, gilded—nails. The clicking sound of the footsteps coincides with these particulars, for we know that sandals made of strips of leather are not uncommon in company with gilt nails and bandages. Old and dry leather would naturally click upon your polished floor.'

'Bravo, Mr Low! So you mean to say that this house is haunted by a mummy!'

'That is my idea, and all I have seen confirms me in my opinion.'

'To do you justice, you held this theory before to-night—before, in fact, you had seen anything for yourself. You gathered that my father had sent home a mummy, and you went on to conclude that I had opened the case?'

'Yes. I imagine you took off most of, or rather all, the outer bandages, thus leaving the limbs free, wrapped only in the inner bandages which were swathed round each separate limb. I fancy this mummy was preserved on the Theban method with aromatic spices, which left the skin olive-coloured, dry and flexible, like tanned leather, the features remaining distinct, and the hair, teeth, and eyebrows perfect.'

'So far, good,' said Swaffam. 'But now, how about the intermittent vitality? The pustule on the neck of those whom it attacks? And where is our old Baelbrow ghost to come in?'

Swaffam tried to speak in a rallying tone, but his excitement and lowering temper were visible enough, in spite of the attempts he made to suppress them.

'To begin at the beginning,' said Flaxman Low, 'everybody who, in a rational and honest manner, investigates the phenomena of spiritism will, sooner or later, meet in them some perplexing element, which is not to be explained by any of the ordinary theories. For reasons into which I need not now enter, this present case appears to me to be one of these. I am led to believe that the ghost which has for so many years given dim and vague manifestations of its existence in this house is a vampire.'

Swaffam threw back his head with an incredulous gesture.

'We no longer live in the middle ages, Mr Low! And besides, how could a vampire come here?' he said scoffingly.

'It is held by some authorities on these subjects that under certain conditions a vampire may be self-created. You tell me that this house is built upon an ancient barrow, in fact, on a spot where we might naturally expect to find such an elemental psychic germ. In those dead human systems were contained all the seeds for good and evil. The power which causes these psychic seeds or germs to grow is thought, and from being long dwelt on and indulged, a thought might finally gain a mysterious vitality, which could go on increasing more and more by attracting to itself suitable and appropriate elements from its environment. For a long period this germ remained a helpless intelligence, awaiting the opportunity to assume some material form, by means of which to carry out its desires. The invisible is the real; the material only subserves its manifestation. The impalpable, reality already existed, when you provided for it a physical medium for action by unwrapping the mummy's form. Now, we can only judge of the nature of the germ by its manifestation through matter. Here we have every indication of a vampire intelligence touching into life and energy the dead human frame. Hence the mark on the neck of its victims, and their bloodless and anæmic condition. For a vampire, as you know, sucks blood.'

Swaffam rose, and took up the lamp.

'Now, for proof,' he said bluntly. 'Wait a second, Mr Low. You say you fired at this appearance?' And he took up the pistol which Low had laid down on the table.

'Yes, I aimed at a small portion of its foot which I saw on the step.'

Without more words, and with the pistol still in his hand, Swaffam led the way to the Museum.

The wind howled round the house, and the darkness, which precedes the dawn, lay upon the world, when the two men looked upon one of the strangest sights it has ever been given to men to shudder at.

Half in and half out of an oblong wooden box in a corner of the great room, lay a lean shape in its rotten yellow bandages, the scraggy neck surmounted by a mop of frizzled hair. The toe strap of a sandal and a portion of the right foot had been shot away.

Swaffam, with a working face, gazed down at it, then seizing it by its tearing bandages, he flung it into the box, where it fell into a life-like posture, its wide, moist-lipped mouth gaping up at them.

For a moment Swaffam stood over the thing; then with a curse he raised the revolver and shot into the grinning face again and again with a deliberate vindictiveness. Finally he rammed the thing down into the box, and, clubbing the weapon, smashed the head into fragments with a vicious energy that coloured the whole horrible scene with a suggestion of murder done.

Then, turning to Low, he said:

'Help me to fasten the cover on it.'

'Are you going to bury it?'

'No, we must rid the earth of it,' he answered savagely. 'I'll put it into the old canoe and burn it.'

The rain had ceased when in the daybreak they carried the old canoe down to the shore. In it they placed the mummy case with its ghastly occupant, and piled faggots about it. The sail was raised and the pile lighted, and Low and Swaffam watched it creep out on the ebb-tide, at first a twinkling spark, then a flare and waving fire, until far out to sea the history of that dead thing ended 3000 years after the priests of Armen had laid it to rest in its appointed pyramid.